"I'm goin' to be just like him. Right, Dad?"

Em's spine went rigid. One day away from her and her son had fixated on this man. Or had Roger... "Did you tell him to call you that?"

Roger shrugged. "It's something I thought—"

"We've got to talk." She moved back to Sammy and kissed him on the forehead. "I'll be here all night, and I'll take you home tomorrow."

"Can't I go home with Dad and my brothers?"

Em seethed, but she kept her features calm. "We'll talk about it tomorrow."

She grabbed hold of Roger's elbow and spun him around. The moment they were safely past the nurses' station she lit into him. "How could you? He called you Dad, and you didn't blink an eye."

Roger placed a finger over his lips as he glanced around. "I told him to."

Appalled, Em stood motionless. "You told him? How can you play with my child's emotions that way?"

"Em, listen," Roger said as he grasped her arms above her elbows. "He knows it's just for today."

"You have no idea what you've started."

Dear Reader,

Thank you for choosing *Just Like Em*. Do you remember having a crush on a boy much older than you? Em cringes with that memory when she again meets Roger. Fifteen years ago, back when she was fourteen and he was a senior in college, she tried every means she could think of to make him notice her. And he did—with total loathing. When he meets this attractive woman at Metro, he can't believe she's the same woman who tried to destroy his love life. If he'd managed to get his hands on her during their last encounter, he'd still be serving a jail sentence.

Em and Roger have a second chance. She's divorced, having left a man who didn't love her and used her for a free ride. Roger lost the love of his life two years before. Now, if he could just put the memory of his dead wife behind him, he might see what a wonderful life he could have with Em. I tried my best to make them see how perfect they were for each other. Hope I succeeded.

I was displaced, and many of my experiences are detailed through Em and the help she provides Roger. Also, I have asthma, an affliction not as severe as Em's son, but something that keeps me on top of the subject. Although I've never been a smoker, I've witnessed how difficult it is to give up the addiction in my friends and family, and I admire how Em eventually gives it up.

And oh, yes, the heat in Phoenix can be a challenge, something we adjust to eventually. We enjoy our 300 plus days of sun, and appreciate not having to shovel any snow.

I hope you've had a few laughs as well as poignant moments and maybe shared some similar experiences. Reach me through www.heartwarmingauthors.blogspot.com. I'd love to hear from you.

Marion Eckholm

HARLEQUIN HEARTWARMING

Marion Ekholm

Just Like Em

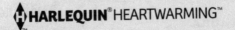
HARLEQUIN® HEARTWARMING™

Recycling programs
for this product may
not exist in your area.

ISBN-13: 978-0-373-36665-1

JUST LIKE EM

Copyright © 2014 by Marion Ekholm

Printed in U.S.A.

www.Harlequin.com

MARION EKHOLM

Back in fifth grade in Plainville, Connecticut, I was writing stories and reading them to my friends. I always wanted to be either a writer or an artist. Neither one seemed like a possibility in my day, when most women became either teachers or secretaries. But I had determination on my side and a mother willing to help me with my dreams. I earned my BFA at Rhode Island School of Design and became a lace designer in New York City, met my husband and moved to New Jersey. Years later, I took stock of my life. I had a career, two children, a beautiful home and opportunities to travel extensively–but I'd never written anything other than letters. I began writing for real and eventually became an editor of a newspaper and sold numerous short stories and magazine articles. Thanks to Harlequin Heartwarming, I'm now a novelist. The horizon is endless.

This book is dedicated to my mother, Pearl Suess, who I've missed nearly every day since her death in 1970. She totally encouraged me, trusted me and backed me in everything I did—except my decision to go to college. Our one argument—even now I choke up thinking of it—was about the lack of money. The argument lasted a week of crying and door slamming on both sides. And then she held me in her arms and said, "You're going to college." She worked cleaning houses and eventually a cafeteria position that she kept until all my college loans were paid off. Thank you, Mom. You're responsible for all the good things in my life.

Acknowledgments

I've been so fortunate over the years to have my critique partners. Not only do they help me with the written word, but also with my life. Special thanks to Shelley Mosley and Sandra Lagesse. I love you guys. Also, Carol Webb, Kim Watters and Deborah Mazoyer.

Laurie Schnebly Cambell, who volunteered her time as mentor at Desert Rose RWA in Phoenix, read my book and provided positive feedback. You're an angel.

More thanks to the wonderful people I've met through Romance Writers of America, including Jane Toombs, Mildred Lubke, Vicki Lewis Thompson and Roz Denny Fox, who helped me on my journey.

And kudos to Gail Centola, aka Angela Adams, who I met at a conference so many years ago. Thanks to her constant prodding and encouragement during some low points in my life, I've kept on writing.

Additional thanks to Harlequin and their editors, who I've been fortunate to meet at so many conferences, especially Paula Eykelhof and Victoria Curran. I really appreciate all your help and encouragement.

And special thanks to my son, David, my daughter, Sandy, and my granddaughters, Rebecca and Michelle. You've been a wonderful blessing.

CHAPTER ONE

IF THIS WASN'T the worst day of his life, it sure came close. Roger Holden adjusted his sunglasses against the brilliant summer Arizona sun and dashed across the parking lot to his air-conditioned office building. Already, waves of heat radiated from the blacktop, enveloping him.

Just before reaching the entrance to Metro Industries, he stopped. His gut twisted when he recognized a longtime friend dabbing her eyes. He offered the gray-haired woman his handkerchief and placed an arm around her shoulders.

"Come on, Hilda. Let's get out of this heat." She let him guide her inside.

"I know you're not to blame for all the problems," she said as they entered the cool foyer.

Roger gave her arm a gentle squeeze. At least one person out there knew the layoffs weren't his fault.

"Just the same, the situation is frustrating." She sighed and folded his handkerchief before returning it to him. "Fifteen years. Who would have guessed?" A sob caught in her throat. "I decided to take the company's offer and retire." She sighed again and looked away. "It won't be so bad. I'll be able to spend more time with my grandchildren."

"Would you like me to come with you? Help you pack your desk?"

She patted his arm. "Thanks, but you have work to do, and I need to say goodbye to my friends. I'll get one of the guards to help." Hilda started toward the security gate, stopped and turned to offer a weak smile. "You take care, now, and let me know where you end up."

Roger stayed in the foyer while Hilda waited at the bank of elevators with one of the uniformed guards. She needed some private time to compose herself. So did he, for that matter.

Although he wasn't to blame for people losing their jobs, every problem relating to them had become his responsibility. Hilda, like so many of the older employees, had agreed to early retirement. At least her future was determined. Most of the other people in the customer-relation department of the Metro-Mintro credit card company, including Roger, had no idea what they'd be doing six months from now. He hoped most of the employees affected by the department being transferred to Seattle would stay to the end. He really needed people who knew their jobs, not temporary help who would have to be trained.

Movement by the exit caught his attention. During these hard times, when so many people felt alienated, he made it a point to acknowledge everyone. Although the woman looked familiar, his brain refused to identify her. He searched for the required official badge with the employee's photo and name.

"Hi," he said, when his search proved fruitless.

"Hello, Roger."

He might have dropped the conversation there except for the familiarity. She'd called him by his first name, not the usual "Mr. Holden" he got from people he didn't know well. Why couldn't he place her?

He removed his sunglasses and approached her, aware almost immediately of the defiance in her eyes. Or was it fear? He saw those emotions often lately, and he couldn't leave her without offering some encouragement.

"How've you been?" he asked.

"Fine, and you?"

Up close and personal, she didn't look fine. In fact, she appeared totally rattled. He had avoided discussing the dreadful reorganizations with employees, but if it would help her to talk…

"Did the downsizing affect you?"

Her eyebrow raised. "No. I was…" She gestured toward the door then dropped her hand. "What about you?"

"Once I get my department transferred I'm…" He jerked his thumb at the door to show how swiftly he'd be out of Metro.

"Oh, I'm sorry to hear that." She placed a hand on his forearm. Her touch felt like a cool balm against his sun-warmed skin and refreshed him. Too soon, she pulled away, flipped her wrist and glanced at a gold watch.

"I've got to rush. Sorry about your job." Just before reaching the door, she added, "Say hello to Jodie for me."

Jodie? Roger nodded to acknowledge his sister's name, but the fact that this woman knew his sister offered no further information. *Who is she?* he wondered all the way up to his office.

EMMY LOU TURNER tried concentrating on the traffic, but the memory of seeing Roger still filled her mind. More than half her lifetime had passed since she'd had that childish crush on him, but he still tantalized. Dark hair falling over his forehead. Shoulders straining the seams of his dress shirt. Why hadn't he lost his hair and grown a potbelly like most men his age?

When she'd seen him approach the building, her knees had succumbed to some long-forgotten signal and turned to mush. Then, her last encounter with Roger flashed through her mind, and she cringed. For one moment she'd actually considered jumping the turnstile in an attempt to hide, but the guard would have prevented her. She'd prayed Roger would miss her completely. And he would have, too, if he had continued with that older woman to the elevators.

But Em's fears about Roger remembering proved groundless. He no longer looked at her with the same murderous contempt. Thank heavens. If he had...

No, she wasn't going to think about the past. They'd acted like adults this time around, although she doubted he had the slightest idea who she was. But she'd definitely appealed to him. She saw it in his eyes, in his effort to hold her attention.

Em laughed outright as she recalled his expression when she mentioned his sister. The man didn't have a clue. With a glance at herself in the rearview mirror, she continued to chuckle. "If I had stayed there a minute longer, he'd have asked who I was. Wouldn't that have been a hoot?"

Immediately, she sobered. "Right. And once

he knew..." Shuddering, Em banished the memory of their last encounter from her mind.

She really needed to call Jodie. They'd lost touch over the years, but now that Em had returned to Phoenix, she hoped to reestablish their friendship.

Em pulled into a chain store's parking lot and stopped in the area reserved for employees. After checking herself in the mirror and repositioning a few hairs in her French twist, she stepped out of the air-conditioned car.

"Oh, this heat," she mumbled. She slipped out of her pink silk jacket and wished she could remove the rest of her clothing. Would she ever readjust to these high temperatures? She had to for Sammy's sake. Her son suffered from asthma, and his doctor said the dry air in Phoenix would improve his condition.

Unfortunately, the temporary jobs she'd taken since arriving in Arizona didn't have medical benefits. A job at Metro would have provided excellent medical coverage for her and her son, so she wouldn't have to hound her ex-husband for help every time Sammy had an asthma attack.

Just stay healthy, Sammy, she thought, as she headed for her office. Unlike Roger, at least she had a job.

ALL THE WAY up to his office, Roger focused on the woman in the lobby. She knew Jodie. Maybe if he called his sister, she could enlighten him.

He plopped down in his desk chair and reached for the phone. *Probably met her at one of those parties.* Jodie and Harve had get-togethers all the time, but Roger had stopped socializing when his wife had become sick. He started to pick up the phone then paused, concentrating on the couples he'd met.

Maybe, though, the woman wasn't part of a couple. Jodie had been trying to fix him up with dozens of her friends over the past two years since Karen's death. No matter how much he insisted no one could replace Karen, it didn't keep his sister from interfering in his life. Until he knew exactly who the mystery lady was, he had no intention of fueling Jodie's matchmaking.

Spinning his chair away from his desk, he focused on the downsizing. The buzz had been ongoing for months. Five days ago the rumors became official. Metro Industries planned to move an entire division from Phoenix to Seattle over the next six months. At least the jobs had stayed in the United States and hadn't been outsourced to another country.

Roger had an enormous task ahead of him,

organizing the transfer and placating the workers so that most of them stayed until the work was completed. He tried to focus on the steps required to make the transition smooth, but his effort was wasted.

Had the woman worn a ring? Except for a watch and earrings, he didn't recall any other jewelry.

"You idiot," he said under his breath. He glanced at the picture of Karen and their children on his desk. "I know, I know. I've got more important things to do than wonder about a strange woman." He was probably obsessing over her just to avoid his present problems.

But maybe he could settle this once and for all. He decided to check with Human Resources. Anyone coming off the streets looking for employment would have to enter HR and fill out paperwork. "Hi, Linda. Roger Holden here." He tapped a pencil on a note pad and tried to sound casual. "Do you still get people off the street looking for jobs?"

"Sure."

"Did someone come in today?" Roger asked. "Pink suit. Tall. Blonde. Hair pulled back in one of those severe—you know—things?" He flipped his finger around the back of his head in an attempt to find the word.

"Yes. But the newest company policy states

we can't have any new hires. You'll have to pick an administrative assistant from the displaced group or settle for a temp."

"I don't want to hire her. I just want to know her name." He held the pencil poised. The pause that followed was long enough that he realized he should have prefaced his request with further explanations.

"Even a VP has to follow policy, Roger."

He chuckled as he pictured Linda in full HR regalia. "The woman knew my name," he said, "and I can't place her. I thought you could help me out."

Another pause. "I know who you mean. She comes once a week to see if anything's available. Wasn't too happy to hear about the downsizing."

"Who is?" Roger muttered.

"Here it is. Emmy Lou Turner. Ring any bells?"

Emmy Lou Turner. Roger scribbled the name across the pad and repeated it under his breath. "Turner, Turner." He didn't know anyone with that name. "Nope. Nothing."

"Her maiden name was Masters."

Masters, he wrote and drew several lines under it. That sounded more familiar, but he still couldn't place the name.

"No." He sighed with genuine disappointment. "I haven't the slightest idea who she is, but I appreciate your help. Thanks, Linda."

Roger hung up, annoyed with himself for letting such a nonsensical issue take up so much of his time. Who was Emmy Lou Masters Turner, and why couldn't he place her? In a fit of exasperation, he tossed the pencil across his desk. It came to a halt in front of Karen's picture.

"Do *you* remember an Emmy Lou Turner?" He sat up in his chair. "Right. Forget her and get back to work."

LATER, AFTER A HEARTY supper of enchiladas, courtesy of Sophia Sanchez, their housekeeper and nanny, the Holden family relaxed in the pool to cool off. An enthusiastic game of catch followed between Roger and his six-year-old twin sons. His daughter preferred to continue doing laps in the pool.

Roger unobtrusively watched Samantha. At thirteen, she no longer cared to be part of the family group. Come August she'd start her freshman year in high school. Already he saw physical changes that she attempted to hide under baggy shirts, not to mention all her mood swings. One minute she was giggling like his little girl, the next she was wearing makeup and behaving like a young woman he hardly recognized.

He had tried broaching the subjects a mother would normally handle. Boys, dating, bras, menstrual periods—subjects he himself hardly understood. At least she had Sophia and Jodie to help her in those areas. He could deal with the physical changes. After all, they were to be expected at her age. But the mood swings and flippant attitude had him climbing the wall. Now that Samantha refused to involve him in her personal life, he couldn't even talk to her anymore.

The ball whizzed by his ear and Roger made a hasty catch before flinging it to one of the twins.

"Hey, Dad. We gonna have to move?" Chip asked as he caught the ball. Both boys had most of their dark hair cut off for the summer. Another toss in Roger's general direction sent him dashing for the softball so it wouldn't land in the pool.

"No, sport." He threw it to Chaz, the other twin. "Why do you ask?"

"My friend Tommy's dad lost his job. He had to move."

"Yeah, Dad," both boys chorused. "We don't wanna move."

"Hey, didn't I tell you there was nothing to

worry about?" He tried to sound upbeat, as though losing a job held no consequences. Yet the distress he faced daily was becoming more difficult to disguise in lighthearted chatter.

LATER, WHEN HIS children were in bed, Roger continued to brood over the downsizing. He had begun to second-guess every decision he made, and his heart ached as he searched for answers. Would he be able to find another position in Phoenix? Assuming he did, would it pay enough to keep their home and present lifestyle? If only he had someone to talk to, confide in. At times like these, the need for his wife became unbearable.

Roger entered the living room, with its white walls and turquoise rug, and settled on the dark turquoise recliner that faced the painted portrait of his wife. "What am I going to do, sweetheart?" he whispered. "What on earth am I going to do?"

The portrait had been a gift from his in-laws to celebrate Karen's thirtieth birthday. It had been painted only months before she discovered the lump in her breast. The artist had captured the softness in her dark brown curls. And that dress…

In the painting she looked so vibrant and full of life, as though at any moment she could join him on the chair and encircle him with her warmth. Why did she have to leave them when everyone needed her so?

Roger looked away from the painting as his thoughts returned to the present. Downsizing, damn! He'd been at Metro since college graduation, and had climbed steadily in a company that had provided his family with security. Or so he'd thought. Now he was going to be tossed out with several hundred other employees.

Movement caught his eye. When he glanced over, he saw Sophia in the doorway, wringing her hands.

Her usually neat coif looked mussed. She had been with him since the twins were born, had nursed Karen through her cancer. He wouldn't know what to do without Sophia. Would he be able to afford her once his job disappeared? He had to.

"I hope you're not worried about this downsizing business. Your job is always secure here."

Pushing several strands of her white-streaked black hair back, Sophia eased onto the white leather couch. "It's not that," she said in a thick Spanish accent, wrapping her arms around one of the pink-and-turquoise pillows. "I have my own bad news. I'm getting married in a month."

Roger moved to the edge of his chair. "That's wonderful news. You and José finally set the date?" José was their weekly gardener, and he and Sophia planned to move into Sophia's small suite once they finally wed.

"Labor Day weekend."

With a quick slap to his knee, Roger stood. "Well, that's not much time, but we still can have the reception in the backyard...."

Sophia shook her head. "We're getting married in Tucson. José wants to move back there and take care of his mother. She's very sick."

Roger fell back into his chair and grasped the arms for support. "You're leaving us?"

Sophia wiped away a tear. "I don't want to, but my José..."

Although his insides had twisted into knots, Roger controlled his emotions so he wouldn't upset her even more. He waved his hand and said, "No, no, Sophia. We wish you the best. We'll manage. A month, you say?"

Sophia nodded.

After she left for her suite, Roger sat numbly, staring at Karen's picture. "You hear that? Life can't get worse. How can I ever replace Sophia?"

The telephone rang.

"I'll get it," Samantha shouted from her upstairs bedroom. She pounded down the steps with enough noise to wake the whole house. Why wasn't she asleep? But then, she considered herself above her brothers and usually read until her eyes drooped shut.

"No, I'll get it. It's probably for me anyway," he said, rising from the chair. Maybe it was Hilda needing another chance to vent or a manager wanting to consult with him before Monday's major meeting.

He arrived at the staircase in time to hear Samantha say, "Yeah, he's here. What'cha want?"

When he reached for the receiver, she maneuvered away from him and held it close to her ear. Soft brown curls, still damp from her swim, complemented a delicate long neck. She looked more and more like Karen every day.

Roger put his hands on his hips and waited, not too patiently, for his call. How come he could handle a whole boardroom of people and never feel out of control? His boys didn't give him trouble, either. Yet in his own household he felt powerless, his authority usurped by this teenager who flaunted hers.

"Who is it?" He tapped a bare foot on the cool tile that ran through the hall.

"Aunt Jodie." Several high-pitched giggles followed.

"What'd she say?"

Instead of answering him, his daughter

turned her back and stuck a finger in her ear.
Another giggle.

Roger started to walk away, then Samantha
said, "It's for you." She held the phone out to
him, then dropped it onto the straight-backed
chair in the hallway. He grabbed it just before
it skittered to the floor.

"Get to bed," he said, his hand covering the
mouthpiece. She turned and looked down her
nose in haughty annoyance, a quality inherited
from her mother's side of the family.

"What's Sam doing up at this hour?" Jodie
asked, after Roger greeted her.

"She was in bed when you phoned. And
don't call her Sam. She hates that name."

"Just a minute." A long pause followed while
Jodie talked in muffled tones to her husband.
Roger yawned. He'd keep the conversation
short and try to catch up on some much-needed
sleep.

With the phone against his ear, he walked
into the kitchen. The aroma of enchiladas hung
in the air, making his mouth water. He'd miss
Sophia's cooking. He clutched the door handle of the refrigerator and momentarily closed
his eyes. He'd miss more than the food. Opening the door, he searched the cool interior for
a snack.

"Remember Emmy Lou Masters?" Jodie asked when she came back on the line.

Roger jolted and smacked his forehead against the refrigerator light switch, causing it to flicker. He moved away from the fridge, massaging his sore forehead. Was his sister psychic? How could she know who had shown up at his work? "Why?"

"The operative word is either a yes or a no."

He took in a deep breath and let it out slowly. "Yes, I recognize the name. No, I don't remember her. Why are you asking?" Roger ran his free hand through his hair and scratched the back of his neck. After circling the barstools by the sink, he settled on a padded kitchen chair.

"She called today. Said she bumped into you at Metro."

"Not literally. Kind of embarrassing, actually. I couldn't place her. Did I meet her at one of your parties?"

Jodie chuckled. "Not recently."

What did that mean? "Is she a friend of yours or not?"

"Of course she is."

He heard the taunt in her voice, the same one she used to use on him when they were young. The same one Samantha used on her brothers. Roger closed his eyes and rubbed his forehead again. It still hurt. "It's late, Jodie, and I'm not up to playing twenty questions. Tell me who she is."

"Remember when you were in college? She stayed with us one summer while her parents were divorcing. You couldn't stand each other."

Roger focused on college and the girls he knew then. Several close friends came to mind. One of them had been Karen, his eventual wife.

"She soaped your car," Jodie continued, "and you called her Auntie Em."

"Em!" Roger shouted and jumped to his feet. The whole summer returned in all its nightmarish details. A young girl, not much older than Samantha was now, had come to stay during his summer vacation from college between junior and senior year. He remembered short spiky hair, long legs, braces and a mouth that spewed more profanity than he'd heard in his frat house. His mother claimed it was Em's way of dealing with the disorientation brought on by her parents' divorce.

Nice girls didn't talk like that. Certainly not the ones hanging out with his sister. He'd attempted to remedy the situation by washing Em's mouth out with soap. From that day on, she managed to soap his car several times a week no matter where he parked it, usually just before he needed it for an important occasion.

Her pranks cost him several dates and nearly destroyed his relationship with Karen.

With a lilt in her voice, Jodie asked, "Remember now?"

"Yes." He uttered the word slowly, with a hiss. Try as he might, Roger couldn't reconcile the woman he'd met today with the teenager he remembered.

"She was my very best friend, and you know what? Sam reminds me of her."

For a millisecond, Roger's entire body trembled. Losing his job and Sophia were nothing compared with the nightmare that suddenly loomed in his mind—a teenage daughter like Auntie Em! He wouldn't last the year.

"Want me to set up something? The four of us going out to dinner?"

"Not interested," he said as the room started to come back into focus.

"Not interested or afraid you might be?"

Roger took in a deep breath before saying, "Since when are you trying to fix me up with married women?"

"Oh, she's not married. Not anymore, anyway. She was only married a few years or so, then it broke up."

No wonder. With her personality she's lucky it lasted that long. "I'm still not interested."

"So, you're not coming to your nephew's birthday party?"

"It's tomorrow?" He smacked his forehead with his palm and winced.

"Yes. It begins at eleven. Don't be late. Timothy's really looking forward to seeing the twins." Jodie hung up.

"Damn!" Roger walked back into the hallway and slammed the receiver into its cradle. Of course he'd have to take his kids to their cousin's birthday party. Jodie knew that and planned to trap him in her matchmaking scheme. Well, no way.

After a formal introduction to Emmy Lou Masters Turner, he'd leave—preferably after soaping her car.

CHAPTER TWO

"You're not going like that," Roger said when his daughter walked into the kitchen. He looked away, afraid his surprise might be obvious on his features. The makeup, meticulously applied, made her look years older than thirteen. He placed his coffee cup in the dishwasher before turning back to face her. "Wash that gunk off your face. It makes you look…"

"Sophisticated?" Samantha offered.

"You're too young for that."

"You're the one who has to grow up." Her ruby-red lips curled, and she placed her hands on her hips. "This is what everyone looks like in high school."

"You're not in high school yet. And until you are…" *And until I have a chance to check out what goes on in high school…*

"You'd prefer hand-drawn daisies on my cheeks. Something childish. Well, I'm not a little girl anymore."

"Then stop acting like one. Get cleaned up so we can leave."

"I'm not going." She stood her ground, her head tilted to one side, the exact stance Karen had taken whenever she disagreed with him. Except for the slight wobble in her chin, Samantha remained defiant.

How did these discussions escalate into full-fledged wars? Roger took a deep breath and tried changing tactics. "Everyone will miss you, and you'll miss out on all the fun."

"Yeah, right. Like I really care about kids under ten and adults over thirty. No one my age will be there. I hate these get-togethers." With that she turned on her heel and ran out of the room.

"Samantha," Roger shouted, but she didn't respond. Well, he couldn't wait around. He turned to Sophia as she came through the patio door with the twins, who carried snorkels and swim fins.

The boys wore swimming trunks and T-shirts with Diamondback logos, which meant he'd be spending a good deal of the time playing lifeguard at the pool. Roger had on a shirt that matched the boys' and khaki shorts.

"Can you see that Samantha gets to the party? I've got to drive the boys over now, and she isn't ready." His jaw tightened. "And see if you can make her presentable."

Sophia nodded. "Sure. When I take the birthday cake. Don't you worry."

The phone began ringing as the twins ran for the front door. "Don't answer it, Dad," Chip shouted over his shoulder. "We'll be late."

It could be important. Roger hesitated by the hall phone, picked it up and immediately wished he hadn't.

"Hello, Millie," he said, trying to put a smile in his voice. He hadn't told his mother-in-law about the downsizing at work and had no desire to go into any details now.

"You know what day Monday is?" Before he could answer, she added, "Karen's birthday. Are you coming up?"

No way. He had taken the kids to visit their grandmother in May, on the anniversary of Karen's death. Black drapes had been hung around the living room, and the flames of dozens of scented candles had consumed all the oxygen. But the séance, with a spiritualist trying to communicate with Karen, had really caught him unawares.

Even though he'd removed the children as quickly as possible, the twins had had nightmares for the rest of the week. Samantha had been reluctant to leave.

Losing a daughter and husband in the same year had affected Millie's ability to cope. Although he sympathized, Roger wasn't about to subject his children to another harrowing experience.

"I'm sorry, that's out of the question, Millie. Too busy this weekend. We'll celebrate Karen's memory on Sunday." He might mention it, but had no other plans. "Maybe you could come down here?"

"And have my blood boil away? You know I can't tolerate a Phoenix summer."

That he did. Fortunately, he could count on her staying away for a good portion of the year. "Sorry to run, but the kids are waiting for me in the car. I'll talk to you soon." He shook away the disturbing feelings, something her conversations always created, and put down the phone.

"Grandma Millie?" Sophia asked from the kitchen doorway.

Roger nodded. "If she calls again, give her some excuse."

"No need. She won't talk to me. Can't understand my accent." Sophia sniffed and turned back to the kitchen.

IT WAS A brilliant, blue-sky Saturday morning when Em and her son drove toward Jodie's house. "What do I have to go for?" Sammy asked. "I don't know anybody."

Em smiled. "It's a party. You'll make lots of new friends." Sammy gave her an "I don't believe you" look in the rearview mirror and placed his chin on his fist. He stared at her through the baby-fine blond hair that fell over his forehead and eyes.

If only she could reach him, she'd finger his hair back. "Don't be such a Gloomy Gus."

Em pushed her left spaghetti strap into place. It had a tendency to flop off her shoulder, and she kept forgetting to shorten it. But she was wearing the only cool sundress she owned, and she had no intention of roasting today. "You'll have a great time, and if you're not—well, we'll leave."

"You always say that. But you start talkin' and we never go." He made his mouth droop as he glanced at her. So small and precious. Em wanted to pull over to the side of the road and give him a hug.

"I promise. You say the word and we're out."

The party invitation had come as a delightful surprise when she'd called Jodie the previous day. A bunch of seven-year-olds at play would help Sammy meet kids his own age. He hadn't made any friends since they moved from California, and he still had a month to go before school started.

Jodie had told her that Karen had died, and

Em empathized with the children's loss and with Roger. She knew from her own experience how difficult it was to be a single parent.

When they reached Jodie's house, Em pulled her car past the row of vehicles parked in front of the balloon-bedecked mailbox. Another white van, a duplicate of hers, pulled past her and parked. Before it came to a full stop, children poured out and ran down the sidewalk.

"C'mon, Ma." Sammy pushed open the door and joined the group, stabbing at the balloons on the way.

Em chuckled. Kids, how quickly they adjusted. She reached for her bag and the gift and stepped out into the heat, just as Roger walked toward her. He nodded at her, a curt acknowledgment of her presence, before passing with his arms loaded with gifts.

For several moments she stood there, her hand braced against the door, expecting a smile similar to the one he'd given her the previous day. He walked past her without a backward glance. Didn't he remember her from yesterday? She jerked her hand from the car's scorching surface.

"Idiot!" she scolded herself under her breath. "He's probably figured out who I am and doesn't want a thing to do with me." She shook her hand in an attempt to ease the burn, took a deep breath, flipped her sundress strap back into place and headed for the party.

The moment she reached the backyard, Sammy said, "Ma, can I go in the pool? Ya brought my suit, right? Chip and Chaz need me to help drown girls."

"Chip and Chaz? Oh—so you made some friends." Em searched through her bag and handed him his suit. Without answering, he turned and headed for the pool, waving it over his head. A moment later he disappeared into the house with several young boys.

Someone screamed. "Emmy Lou!" Em turned as Jodie, with outstretched arms, raced toward her. Her short dark hair was held back in several tiny butterfly snaps.

After a quick hug that nearly crushed the birthday present, Jodie hooked her arm in Em's and directed her toward the gift table. She waved and shouted at another group of people standing under a tent. "Harve, look here. I want you to meet one of my oldest and dearest friends."

In an aside to Em, Jodie added, "And if you ever need to get divorced again, call Harve. He's the best lawyer in the state."

The remark startled Em. She had no intention of marrying a second time. Once more

Jodie grabbed her arm, and they headed for the tent.

Introductions went on for several minutes as all the parents welcomed her to Phoenix. Jodie zeroed in on a few single parents, men and women, clustered around a tent pole, and pushed Em into the group. Most of their children would be attending the same school as Sammy, so Em asked questions about what she could expect.

After some pleasant conversation, Em began to relax with the help of a cool glass of lemonade. She hugged one corner of the tent's shade and watched Sammy frolicking in the pool with several children his age. She had slathered him with sunscreen before coming. Too much sun with his light skin…

She was about to venture over to the pool to check on him, when she saw Roger. He circled the pool, shouting warnings and avoiding the splashes aimed at him.

No man had a right to look that good. He hadn't changed much in the past fifteen years at all. His hair was shorter but still fell over his forehead in that delightful wave that made her fingers itch. How many times had she dreamed of pushing it aside and raining kisses…?

Stop it, Em. You've grown up. Get a life!

She returned her attention to Sammy. She

had a life. She had her son, her mother, a job and divorce papers that said she'd never have to pay another dime of her ex-husband's bills. Life was pretty darn close to perfect.

Sammy disappeared under the water, and for a moment she couldn't see him. One hand gripping her large bag, the other clutching her throat, Em started for the pool. A second later he came up—choking.

Instantly her heart started to race. Not another asthma attack. Before she could reach his side, Roger pulled him out of the water and began pounding his back.

"Stop that!" Em shouted. Her boy needed assistance in breathing, not bruises. She kneeled by Sammy's side and handed him his inhaler. But instead of taking it the way he usually did, the boy pushed her hand away.

"I'm okay," he said in a hoarse whisper. He looked up at her with pleading eyes that tore at her heart. He wanted so much to be like all the other kids, with no weaknesses that might make him different. But she'd seen minor incidents like these escalate without proper care. She wasn't about to risk another trip to the hospital.

She pushed the inhaler toward him again. He turned away. Frustrated by Sammy's reluctance, Em sat back on her heels, her full skirt billowing around her ankles.

"I think he just swallowed a little water," Roger said, in a low voice.

His calmness helped quiet her nerves. Maybe she had overreacted. Her son's coughing had stopped, and his new friends waited for him in the water. She dropped the inhaler back in her bag and sprang to her feet.

"Be careful. I'll be near the tent if you need me." Without another look in Roger's direction, she headed for the cool shade.

"You okay?" Jodie asked when she reached the group of adults. "You look all flushed."

"It's this Arizona sun. I haven't adjusted yet."

"I'll get the kids out of the water. It's time they downed some hot dogs and hamburgers."

Once Sammy was on dry ground, Em felt she could find a restroom and compose herself. But on her way to the house, one of the single parents, a divorced man she had recently met, intercepted her.

"You embarrassed the boy," the man said.

Momentarily stunned, Em stuttered a reply. "He…he has asthma."

"Come on. I saw what happened. He swallows a little water, and you come on like the Red Cross in an earthquake emergency." He chuckled. When she still remained silent, the man continued. "Boys don't like to be babied in front of their friends by their mothers."

"Thank you. I'll keep that in mind." Em took in a deep, calming breath and forced a smile despite the pain it caused in her cheeks and jaw. "Ben, isn't it?"

"Right. There's my son Carlie." He grinned, pointing to one of the boys in the pool. Em could pick him out by the fiery red hair and zinc ointment on his nose that duplicated his father's. "Jodie thought maybe we could, you know, have dinner or something."

"I'll have to get back to you on that." Holding herself erect, she pushed past him and went into the house.

Roger watched her walk away after overhearing the conversation. Ben didn't have a clue. The look she'd given him was enough to turn this heat into a frost, but Ben followed her movement, entranced, as though he still had a chance.

She certainly wasn't the Em Roger remembered. If he'd roused her ire fifteen years ago she'd have thrown him in the pool. Ben went unscathed, although his callous remark about her son deserved a good punch.

Roger watched the swish of her skirt, an intriguing bounce of colorful flowers over legs that went on forever. She had changed and all for the better. Who would have guessed it? Maybe there was hope for Samantha, after all.

"OH, I SURE could use a cigarette." Em pushed back a few strands of hair that had pulled loose from her ponytail and glared at herself in the bathroom mirror. That darn strap was down again. She shoved it into place.

"Men! What makes that jerk think I'd ever go out with him?" She planned to grab Jodie first chance she got and tell her not to provide any dates. She wasn't looking, and she certainly could do better than Ben!

"What does he know about my son and his problems? Nothing! Has he seen him in a seizure so bad he can't breathe? Has he had to rush him to a hospital?"

Em emptied her purse onto the sink vanity. She'd given cigarettes up years ago because they created problems for Sammy, but she carried gum or mints for the occasion when the craving became all consuming. This was definitely one of those occasions. No luck. She tossed the contents back into her purse and went outside.

The pool was empty. Everyone had assembled under the tent and strains of "Happy Birthday" floated toward her. The tent looked crowded, with Ben motioning her to join them.

The glaring sun made the rest of the yard totally uninviting.

She wanted more time to herself to regain her composure. If not, she might say something she'd later regret. Sammy sat with his friends at the picnic table, so she could afford to take a few more moments for herself.

The whiff of smoke had her spinning in several directions before she honed in on its source. A path led around the house. Em followed her nose to a small patio surrounded by walls of white stucco. Arms of leafy bougainvillea with magenta blossoms clung to the wall.

A young woman Em's height with a bob of brown curls smoked a cigarette. She wore a baggy man's white dress shirt that practically hid her shorts. These were former jeans, ragged out to create a fringe. It barely covered a rose tattoo on her thigh.

"Ahem," Em said, hoping not to startle her. The woman turned around and immediately stubbed out the cigarette against the wall. "Oh, I wish you hadn't done that. I came here specifically to enjoy the smoke."

"It's not good for you, you know."

Em had to chuckle. She was aware of all the dangers, but she never expected a lecture from another smoker. Especially not one sporting a tattoo.

"I know, and I've quit. It's just every now and then I get this agonizing urge."

"It's the nicotine." The woman flipped the pack and a cigarette came halfway out. "Want one?"

"Thanks." Em took it and bent over to accept a light. After a swift inhale she straightened, released the smoke and sighed. Magic. Already she could feel the tension drain away. But it wasn't worth the guilt she'd feel if Sammy found out. He had a sense of smell like a bloodhound and would surely notice the scent of smoke on her clothes and hair. One more puff and then she'd put the cigarette out.

About to toss it, Em paused when a door opened behind them. As Roger stepped onto the brick patio the woman next to her casually dropped the pack of cigarettes to the ground. The moment she saw him, Em's tension increased, and she took another long drag.

"HERE YOU ARE, Samantha," Roger said. He couldn't tolerate the makeup that made her look so old, but Sophia had said it was the only way she could get the girl to come with her. Why was it getting harder and harder to tow Samantha to family gatherings? "Don't you want to join the party?"

He noticed Em then, puffing on a cigarette

like a coal-burning locomotive. God, she had the worst habits. You'd think she'd be aware of all the health hazards. He bent down, picked up the discarded pack and handed it to her. "You dropped these." He used all his control not to crush the pack in his fist.

While taking the pack from him, Em glanced at Samantha, and he followed her gaze. The girl shook her head ever so slightly. Had he interrupted something? "Thanks," Em said, then slipped the pack into her skirt pocket.

She's probably up to two packs a day by now, he thought, recalling the summer when Em had turned Jodie onto the addiction. Suddenly, a frightening thought struck him, and he turned to his daughter. "She didn't offer you one, did she?"

"No, Dad. I offered them to her."

Sarcasm. That's all he got lately. Before making any remark, he paused. It was sarcasm, wasn't it? His attention turned to Em, who had started a choking fit.

"You okay?" he asked. He felt as though he should do something, swat her back, as she continued to choke. She moved away, possibly anticipating that he'd do just that.

She nodded and dropped the butt, crushing it beneath a dainty sandal. Everything about her was delicate. One of her straps had slipped

down her arm, and he drew his hands into fists
to avoid readjusting it for her.

"Smoking's a hard habit to break," Samantha said.

Em quickly nodded again. "Yes. I've been
working at it." Her voice was hoarse, as though
she could barely get enough air to speak. Smoking could do that to a person.

Vivid recollections of the lectures he'd given
Samantha about cancer came to mind. He
thought of repeating them to Em, but he had
no right to lecture her. Besides, he doubted if
she'd listen.

"So, this is your daughter?" Before he could
introduce them, Em offered her hand. "I'm
Emmy Lou Turner, but everyone calls me Em."
Except her ex-husband, who never gave in to
her preference. All the years they were married, he continued to call her Emmy Lou.

"Like the alphabet?" Samantha beamed,
showing off a set of braces. "Samantha Holden,
but you can call me S."

"Anything except Sam. She hates that name,"
Roger offered.

"Oh, really? My son's named Sammy."

"How old is he?" Samantha asked.

"Seven."

"Another little kid." Samantha's smile immediately disappeared. "Why can't we have anyone here my age?"

"How old are you?"

"Fourteen."

Roger didn't bother to correct her since she'd have a birthday in a few months.

"I was about your age when I met your father."

"Em was a handful," Roger said, recalling the many times they had fought.

"Maybe," she said, raising an eyebrow. "But I never got a tattoo."

Samantha covered her mouth and giggled, suddenly acting her age. Once again he wondered how she could do that, one minute the twenty-year-old femme fatale, the next his thirteen-year-old little girl? She licked her thumb and ran it over the pattern, smearing it across her leg. "Daddy won't let me get the real thing—yet."

"Ever," he said, emphasizing the point. So far she hadn't defied him on that, but she still threatened to pierce something—a nose, an eyebrow, her navel. Roger shuddered. What got into kids these days? How could he survive the next few years without a clue?

"You coming Samantha? You, too, Em. They're about to open presents."

"You go along, Dad. We'll be there in a minute."

Roger hesitated. He wasn't too sure he should leave Samantha alone with Em. She had been everything he didn't want his daughter to become. *Oh, for heaven's sake, I'm losing it. What possible damage can she do in a few short minutes?*

"Okay. But don't wait too long. You won't want to miss all the fun."

Em breathed a sigh of relief when he left, although she wasn't too pleased to be stranded with his daughter. His daughter! Samantha couldn't be more than thirteen or fourteen if Em's math was correct. And here Em thought she was bumming cigarettes from someone who could legally smoke them.

"Fun." The word came out like a curse. "As if a bunch of little boys tearing wrapping paper is a treat."

"I suppose you want your pack back, but frankly, I wouldn't feel right returning it to you," Em said as she pushed her strap back over her shoulder. A refreshing breeze began to stir the bougainvillea, and Em moved out of reach of the thorny branches. "You're not legally allowed to smoke."

"That's okay. You keep it. You need it more than me."

"I've quit, remember?"

"Yeah. Right." Samantha looked down at her feet and whispered, "Thanks."

"For what?"

She looked up and Em noticed the prettiest brown eyes—Roger's eyes. "For not telling my dad the cigarettes were mine. He's got this big thing about smoking because my mom died of cancer."

"As I recall, you told him they were yours."

"Like he listens. He only hears what he wants to hear, even if nobody says it. As if my mother's cancer had anything to do with smoking. She had breast cancer, not lung cancer or anything like that."

"Still, it's not good for us. He's right about that."

"Well, there's nothing to worry about. I'm not smoking anymore."

"Oh?"

"Yeah. I don't want to get so hooked I can't stop when I'm old." Samantha paused and a stricken look crossed her face. "Not that you're that old."

She might not rival Methuselah, but Em suddenly felt very old, very old indeed.

CHAPTER THREE

"DON'T CALL ME Sammy. It's a girl's name."

Em didn't give in to the urge to laugh, because her son looked so serious as they rode home from the party. "Why do you say that?"

"Chaz says it's his sister's name." He had talked nonstop about the twins he'd met. They would be attending the same school as her son, even though they were first graders, a grade behind Sammy.

"Oh, his sister must be Samantha. I met her today."

That meeting came back in all its clarity. Her embarrassment at learning the girl was Roger's daughter had sent her into a choking fit similar to her son's asthma attacks. She'd actually felt sorry for Roger. He showed such love and concern for his children, and hadn't had the slightest clue what that little vixen had been up to. Nonetheless, Em admired her spunk, even if it did mean Roger had a rough ride ahead of him.

"Well, I got other names."

That he did: Bradley Samuel Turner, Jr. Her

husband, Bradley, had chosen to use the baby's middle name because he never knew if she was talking to him or the baby when she said Brad. She had grown to like the name Sammy. It provided less of a reminder of her husband after he left.

"What do you want to be called? Brad or Bradley?"

"I want a nickname like Chaz or Chip. That's neat."

Remembering her alphabet discussion with Samantha, she tried another approach. "How do you spell junior?"

Sammy thought for a moment. "J.R."

"How's that for a nickname?"

He concentrated, chin on fist, then turned to her with a beaming smile. "I'm J.R. Wait till I tell Chaz."

Which would be sometime tomorrow. Sammy had pleaded to have them come over to the pool at their apartment on Sunday. She had agreed. Since Roger planned to drop the boys off, she wouldn't have to deal with him for any length of time. Now that she had seen him in the present, long-ago images of him had begun to dim, replaced by intriguing new ones. She wasn't sure how she felt about that.

"'LO, GRANDMA," SAMMY said as he dashed into his grandmother's apartment. Doris Masters moved out of his way and extended a cordless phone toward Em.

"Who's calling?"

Doris glanced at Sammy's retreating back before saying, "Bradley." As Em grasped the phone, her mother added, "Collect." Doris turned on her heel and followed her grandson.

Bradley? She had sent him her new address when she arrived in Phoenix so he'd have no excuse. His child support checks were already two months behind, and she could really use that money.

Taking a deep, fortifying breath, Em began, "Hi, Bradley. Would you like to speak to Sammy?"

She started to go after their son and stopped when Bradley said, "No. I need to speak to you. What's with all these stamped, self-addressed envelopes?"

My way of making it easy for you, she thought, but controlled the urge to say the words. Hadn't she always made it easy for him? Just like smoking, it was a hard habit to break.

"If it's for child support, you can forget it."

Em held on to the spaghetti strap of her dress, ready to flip it back onto her shoulder. "What are you talking about? You agreed...."

"I agreed to a lot of things, including you

getting total custody and taking the kid to Arizona. You want to get into that can of worms?"

Em tensed. The strap broke loose at one end, and now lay like a limp string in her hand.

"Bradley, things here are tight. Jobs in Arizona don't pay what they do in California. I've had to take temporary work...."

"You chose to leave the land of opportunity. Don't try pushing that one on me."

With a snap, Em freed the strap completely from the dress.

"Besides," Bradley continued, "at least you have a job."

"What are you talking about?" Em braced herself against the wall.

"I've been laid off, Emmy Lou. No job, no money, no medical insurance. You know what that's like, right?"

Slowly, Em slipped to the floor, her skirt making a swirl of flowers around her on the worn rug. She almost mentioned COBRA, the program that allowed people who lost their jobs to continue on their employer's health insurance. Instead, she bit her lip, hard. If he had no money, he might suggest she contribute to the payments, and she wasn't about to volunteer spending another dime on this lowlife. Saving him stopped once she got the divorce.

"Well, get another job, Bradley," Em said,

trying to restrain the frustration in her voice. How come every time she had to deal with her ex-husband, she felt as though she were free-falling through space? "With all that education…" She paused as a new thought struck home. "Unemployment insurance. You can send me money from that."

"Missed it by two weeks." Why wasn't there some worry in his voice? Concern for himself, if not for their son? "So, what kind of work did you find? With all your computer skills, it should be a breeze…."

With a flick of her thumb, Em disconnected the phone.

"You okay?"

Em looked up. Her mother stood above her, leaning against the green-striped wallpaper, arms crossed over her chest.

"I take it from that scowl, and your ruined dress, the conversation wasn't exactly pleasant."

Before pushing herself off the floor, Em glanced down at the ripped bodice, destroyed when she'd pulled out the strap. "When is it ever?"

"Care for some fresh lemonade? One of my friends has a lemon tree, and she gave me enough lemons to last the rest of the summer."

A look of worry passed over Doris's face as she reached to touch Em's lip. "Is that blood?"

Em passed the back of her hand over her mouth. "Yeah. I bit myself."

Doris turned and headed for the kitchen. "Take a seat at the table. I'll make us iced tea without the lemon. I don't think you'd like citrus juice on that wound right now."

Maybe she would. Intense pain might block out the conversation she just had with her ex. Em clenched her hands and struck them on the small dining room table as she took a seat by the window. For the first time, she noticed the strap was still wrapped around her fingers. Slowly, she unwound the delicate fabric.

"I really liked this dress," she said when her mother returned with the tea.

Doris placed two coasters on the wooden table before setting the tall glasses on top. "Take it off and put it in my room. I think I can fix it."

"Did I ever tell you what a wonder you are?" Em lifted her glass in a silent toast before touching the rim to her lips. The moisture stung momentarily but not enough to keep her from taking a long swallow.

Em and her mother had always remained close, talking on the phone and visiting whenever possible. When Em lost her job this past

spring, her mother had asked her and Sammy
to live with her in Phoenix. With Doris retir-
ing in June after thirty-five years of teaching
second grade, it meant Em wouldn't have to
put out extra money for daycare.

Deciding to accept the offer had been easy.
Nothing had gone too well for them in California. But they waited until Sammy finished
first grade, even though it put a strain on their
limited budget. Having come from an unstable
family herself, Em tried to ensure her son's life
was secure wherever possible.

"He's not sending any money," Em said without preamble. "Lost his job and health insurance." She chuckled, recalling her thoughts. "I
almost volunteered to pay for COBRA insurance. Can you believe it? I can't even afford it
for myself, and here I'm about to volunteer to
pay his."

"You've always been too generous."

"No more. I may end up biting my lip to
shreds," she said, pounding a fist on the table
again, "but he's never going to see another red
cent from me."

Doris pushed some strands of gray-blond
hair back over her ear. "So, did he mention
what college he's going to?"

"College? What college?"

"Before you showed up, he said he was back in college, working toward some degree."

"How can he pay for tuition, books…?"

"How did he pay for them before? He never held down a job, did he, before he walked out on you?"

Em sat back and stared at the ceiling. Some loose paint looked as if it might fall, but their landlord wasn't due to paint the place for several more months. "No, Ma, he didn't. Not while we were married, anyway. He always planned to once he finished college." Em thought a minute. "You don't suppose there's someone out there…."

"As much in love with him as you were?"

Em sucked on her lip a moment, wondering if it might be swelling. "No, I was going to say as gullible as me." Her lip must be swelling. The word barely made it out of her mouth. Or maybe she found it way too painful to admit that anyone could be conned into supporting a man while he attended one college after another and offered nothing in return.

"Why don't you contact your lawyer? Maybe he can do something."

"He's already bled me dry, and Bradley only has the assets I paid for." The car, stereo set and all the other items he'd charged to her credit cards. She ran a hand through her hair and pulled out the fancy elastic holding her ponytail.

For a fleeting second, Em recalled what Jodie had said about her husband. But Em couldn't afford to pay Harve, and she didn't want to accept his charity. Besides, Bradley could still threaten her with repealing the custody agreement. She didn't want to give him any reason to come after the one thing he knew she treasured.

"I'm accepting that job."

"Where you're a temp? I thought you said they didn't pay enough."

"The pay is doable. I'll get benefits immediately, and Sammy's start in six months. I haven't found anything better, and Metro stopped hiring."

For several moments they sipped their tea in quiet companionship. Em played with the torn strap on the table, making a coil first one way and then the other.

Finally, Doris said, "How was the party?" She placed the glass in front of her face, but it didn't hide the grin. "Was Roger there?"

Em nodded and pushed the fabric to the side.

"Did he finally wake up and realize how the two of you were meant for each other?"

Em tossed the cork coaster at her mother. "That was a long time ago."

"So, your fatal attraction has worn off?"

"He's still very attractive, but…I don't know. It's different." Em sighed and checked out the peeling paint on the ceiling again. "A lot of things have happened in my life since I had a childish crush on him."

"Anything new with Jodie?"

"She's the same old Jodie. I think she tried to set me up by introducing me to some single parents. One guy actually asked me for a date."

"And you said…?"

Em scrunched her nose and shook her head. "A real jerk."

"I think you just have a total dislike for men right now. That, too, will fade with time."

Not possible, Em thought as she continued, "Sammy made good friends with Roger's twin boys. They're coming over tomorrow for a swimming party."

"Sounds like fun. It should go a long way in helping Sammy adjust to life here."

"I'M TAKING THE boys over to Em's apartment to see her little boy," Roger told Samantha as he sent his sons off to the car. "You'll be all right till I get back?"

Sophia had the day off, and it meant Samantha would be all alone. Mentally, he ticked off the damage she could do in that time. Long dis-

tance calls to her cousin in England. At least
she couldn't get on the internet and buy out
China without his password.

"Can't I come, too?"

Roger's jaw dropped. Samantha had always
avoided her brothers every chance she got.
Now she asked to be included in something
that couldn't interest her at all. It had to be Em.
What spell had she cast over his daughter?

"Sure," he said, "but I wasn't planning to
stay. The boys are going to swim and then
watch a video." *Something that would probably make your skin crawl,* he almost added.

"That's okay. I'll help. Watching three boys
is a handful. I'll get my suit."

Still agape, Roger watched her rush up the
stairs. What had happened to her? This daughter, who put up a stink if he asked her to watch
her brothers while he showered, was volun-
teering to babysit? No way. Whatever she had
going with Em was going to stop right now.
Even if he had to stay around and supervise.

"Sounds like a good idea," he said as he followed Samantha up the stairs and passed her in
the hall. "I think I'll take my suit along, too."

Samantha paused by her door and regarded
him. "Dad, I thought you wanted the time alone
to get some paperwork done."

"All work and no play makes fathers very

dull. Besides, I can bring the work with me."
She shot him a look of disbelief before disappearing into her room.

What had he gotten himself into? He had yet to make all the schedules for the transfer to Seattle. A half dozen people had posted for other jobs; now, who would do their work? He had to review the remaining personnel and determine what jobs required immediate attention. And here he was blowing a chance at a peaceful day alone. Crazy. How could he accomplish these tasks at a noisy apartment complex while he baked in the hot sun?

But he had to go. He'd never be able to concentrate on his work knowing what he did about Em. He reminded himself again that in one summer she'd annihilated his sister's good family upbringing. Who knew what she was capable of doing now?

While he changed in his room, Roger talked to the picture of his wife, which held a prominent place on the white-washed oak dresser. "You wouldn't recognize Em," he said as he pulled on his gray plaid swim trunks. "She's grown up into quite a woman. Not that I'm interested, mind you. It's just that Samantha seems to like her.

"Remember what a pill Em was? Well, your daughter's another Em." Roger slipped on his loafers and a shirt, and walked over to the picture. Picking up the gold frame, he said, "I sure could use your help raising Samantha." He kissed the glass surface and whispered, "I miss you so much." With a heavy heart he returned the picture to the dresser and headed out the door.

Roger met Samantha in the front hall. "Dad, you're not wearing that!" When did she start talking like her mother?

He glanced in the hall mirror at his gray-plaid trunks. His white ones probably would look better, but he'd tossed them in the laundry last night. The colorful Hawaiian shirt had faded a little since Karen bought it for him on their delayed honeymoon to Oahu. Okay, so it looked a little weird, especially with the briefcase, but he was going for comfort, not to make a fashion statement.

"What will Em think? That I'm related to some geek?"

Roger dismissed the remark and opened the door. "This is me. You coming or not?" He had no intention of dressing to impress Em. This shirt reminded him of happy times with Karen. Furthermore, if Samantha found his clothes so despicable, she might decide to stay home and eliminate his need to stay at Em's. After yesterday's encounter with the cigarettes, he planned to keep his family's exposure to Em at a minimum.

THE BOYS FOUND Sammy and hit the pool the moment they arrived at the apartment complex. Samantha took off for Em, who was sitting under a ramada, a wooden roof that shaded a picnic table within easy access of the pool. She got up and headed toward him as he secured the safety gate. He stopped short and stared along with every other male in the area.

Her white suit was conservative, covered by a sheer, colorful blouse in blues that hugged her every time a breeze passed by. "Hello, Roger. Samantha says you're planning to work here." Her puzzled expression showed a concern he hadn't expected. "Maybe you'd prefer the apartment, where it's quieter."

"No, this will do fine." He placed his briefcase on the table. "I just have a few things to catch up on for the office." Not that he'd get anything done with so much distraction, but he didn't want to leave his children alone with her. Her attention was already back on the boys horsing around in the pool. It gave him a chance to observe her.

Several strands of blond hair had come loose from her ponytail. When had she decided to grow her hair long? It certainly was an improvement over the short spikes he remembered. He looked back at his sons, intending to keep an eye on them. They had a tendency to get rowdy if they thought they could get away with it.

At least he didn't have to worry about Samantha. She was sloshing in the pool with some kids her own age. Four years in high school followed by four more in college. How was he going to pay for that without a job?

Suddenly, the task before him took on enormous proportions. He had a presentation to make the next day. Roger sat down and began making a list of what he had to accomplish over the next six months.

"WOULD YOU CARE for some iced tea?" Em stood before him holding two glasses.

Roger accepted the offered glass. He hadn't even realized he was thirsty. After a long swallow, he forced himself to look away. The boys had disappeared. He half stood, searching the pool for any sign of them.

"They're taking a break, playing in the sandbox with some trucks and action figures. Mind if I sit here? It's the only shade left in the area."

"Go ahead," he said as he pushed papers to one side.

"I'll try not to disturb you."

"That's okay. It's time for me to take a break." Usually, when his children were around, one part of him was always tuned in to them. For some reason he had lost himself in his work, and left the supervision to Em. Was it instinct or something else that had trusted Em to watch out for them? The realization struck him as odd, considering how he felt about her potential influence. He looked around for his daughter.

"Samantha's playing cards with her friends in the other ramada." Em nodded to the other side of the pool.

"How did you know…?"

"It's the look you get. Sort of a fatherly, worried expression. I noticed it yesterday when you thought I was enticing her to smoke."

"Déjà vu. I remembered how you turned my sister into a smoker."

"I did what?" Her strident tone morphed into a long sigh. "Jodie Holden introduced me to every vice I ever had, including smoking."

"My sister?" Roger started to laugh at the absurdity. "She was a milquetoast until you came along and ruined her."

"You haven't a clue what she was really into." Em started to tap her fingers on the table. He glanced down to the movement and noticed that her nails, although polished in light pink, were short and practical, not the fake extensions in vivid colors Samantha often tried.

"Oh, no? When you showed up that summer, she started to drink, swear, smoke and carry on with the opposite sex."

Em pierced him with her blue eyes. "Just like you were doing?"

Roger paused. Just like him? "That's different," he said. "I was attending college at the time."

"No. What's different is you're male and we're female." Em sat straighter. Roger gave her his complete attention and doubted if anything other than a comet's entry into the atmosphere could distract him. "And according to you, we're supposed to abide by a stricter standard. Jodie chose not to, and I went along for the ride."

Roger placed his elbow on the table and braced his chin in his hand. Maybe Em was right. He'd never paid much attention to his sister until Em arrived on the scene. "Well, she never soaped my car."

A smile turned up the corners of Em's mouth. Her cheek threatened to dimple. "You deserved that."

He leaned across the table. "Thanks to you and those little stunts, Karen nearly broke up with me. She had a driving test on one of the days you soaped the windows, and we couldn't get it all off in time. She missed her appointment." He leaned back. "And I don't appreciate that self-satisfied smirk. You really created havoc with my love life."

"I was fourteen at the time. How old is Samantha?" Roger squinted at the ramada across the sun-drenched pool.

"She'll be fourteen in October, but she's been acting like someone in her twenties for the past year."

"And she could easily pass for eighteen." Em rose and took their empty glasses. "Looks like you've got your hands full." She beamed a smile on him warmer than the Arizona sun. "Want some more tea?"

He watched her walk away—the swing of her hips, the swish of that golden hair. Em had grown up into a very interesting woman. A very interesting woman, indeed.

CHAPTER FOUR

"THANKS FOR HELPING, Mom," Em said as Doris finished washing the dishes. Roger and the twins had stayed for lunch, a macaroni-and-cheese creation of her mother's that Sammy couldn't get enough of. Everyone else seemed to enjoy it, as well. The kitchen was small, with dark cabinets and barely enough room for the two to work. Em wiped the last plate and planted a kiss on her mother's cheek, a small thanks for all that she had done.

"Once I finish up here, I'll go back to my room and read," Doris said. "You go entertain Roger."

"I don't know." Em glanced through the kitchen doorway. "He's engrossed in some business he has to complete for tomorrow."

Doris placed a wet hand on her shoulder and pushed. "Go on. I remember when nothing could keep you from bugging him."

Em stayed put. "Was I that bad?" All those juvenile high jinks she had performed in an attempt to gain his attention. A tremble shook her head and shoulders. If only she could wash away her misguided antics.

Doris flipped back a strand of hair and sighed. "As I recall, you thought he walked on water."

"Well, I know better now." Another push from her mother sent her into the dining room. She had no desire to join the boys in the living room and watch another rerun of *Star Wars,* the video they had chosen. Samantha hadn't returned from having lunch with a girlfriend, so Em couldn't talk with her.

Despite the relatively pleasant time she and Roger had shared today, Em felt ill at ease. Maybe it was that ridiculous shirt he was wearing. It belonged on a bonfire. She had changed into white shorts and a red T-shirt, but obviously Roger hadn't bothered to bring anything extra.

"Can I get you something? More iced tea? A beer?"

Roger looked up from where he sat at the dining-room table and smiled. Except for one slightly protruding eyetooth, he had a perfect smile, one that made her feel all warm and cozy inside. "No thanks. Pull up a chair, unless you'd rather join the kids."

"I'd prefer adult company, if I'm not disturbing you."

Roger tilted his chair back and stretched his arms over his head. His Hawaiian shirt momentarily pulled tight across his chest before he dropped his hands back to the table. "Actually you might be able to give me some insight. I'm working on transfering work from my department at Metro to another office in Seattle. It means several people will be losing their jobs unless they can move to Seattle. I'd like some input from someone who's been there. Your mother mentioned you've been laid off before."

"Twice."

"Two times? That's got to be hell!"

"More like an endless roller-coaster ride." Em pulled out the wooden chair and sat next to him so she wouldn't be forced to look at that shirt.

"Tell me about it. The company's providing us with an agency that deals with outplacements, but I'm interested in hearing firsthand what actually helped to get you back to full employment."

He moved his arm, so that the short hairs tickled hers, and Em shifted slightly to avoid the contact. It was too disconcerting and she was trying to keep her mind focused on their discussion.

"The first time was the worst. About twenty of us were walked out of the building like criminals the day we received our notice. They gave us one month's severance and a printed list of possible employers we could find on the internet." She folded her hands on the table in front of her.

"And the second time?"

"Not so bad. I had learned there's no such thing as job security. Besides, this company made the transition bearable." She needed to do something with her hands. Em reached for a pen and inadvertently touched Roger's arm again. She pulled her hands into her lap.

"They expected everything to take two years to transfer," she continued, "and they did what they could to keep our morale up so we'd stick around. Anyone who stayed through the entire process would receive a large bonus package."

The space between Roger and her was decreasing, because Roger kept leaning toward her as though he wanted to catch everything she had to say. Em considered moving her chair a little farther away, but decided she liked the idea that he found her interesting.

"How did they keep you there?" Roger picked up a yellow legal pad and began making hen scratches.

"They offered training we'd need to make ourselves more saleable in the work world and gave us counseling as well as help in writing résumés and… Am I going too fast for you?" Roger stopped writing and looked up.

"No. This is great information. Go on."

"How are you going to read that?"

Roger dropped his pencil and propped his head on his hand again. "It takes a while, but I manage."

"Wait a minute." Em got up and returned after a moment with a laptop computer. At least this would keep her hands occupied. "I'll put it all down in a readable form. What else do you want to know?"

"What they did to make life bearable. Stuff like that."

Em typed as she talked. "They gave us unexpected breaks that cost them very little…."

"That's good," Roger said, straightening and pointing to the computer. "Put that down."

"Like one day they gave us the afternoon off to watch a video, a comedy, and they provided popcorn and pop."

"Didn't that cut down on production?"

Em typed in his question then added her answer. "No. Production improved. Most of us were glad to have some relief from the pressure that was always present." She was really getting into this, enjoying their exchange.

"What else?"

"Well…" She closed her eyes a moment to picture the scene. "They used incentives."

"To keep production at its peak?"

Em chuckled as she typed. "No, to keep us coming in every day. People who had collected sick time began to get ill Wednesday and recover by the next Tuesday. The company needed reliable workers, so everyone who didn't miss a day during the week got a little prize."

Roger placed his hands over his face and mumbled, "Oh, boy. Here it comes." He brushed his hands through his hair before sitting back. "What's it going to cost?"

"What's the cost of four or five days of pay for just one person out sick, not even counting the production cost or the strain on the other employees who have to fill in?"

Roger whistled softly before Em added, "We received prizes of tickets for movies or lunch passes. In a month of perfect attendance, we might get items equal to an hour and a half of our pay. No big deal for them, but a fun thing for us."

"Who decided these things?"

"Well, we had an agency working with HR and our supervisors worked closely with them. They constantly solicited our opinions. Also, those who'd made a month of perfect attendance had their names placed in a special drawing. Once it was a hundred-dollar gift certificate and another time a weekend at a dude ranch—big prizes that made us strive to stay."

"You ever win one?

"No, I never had perfect attendance." She'd often had to take time off to care for some emergency with Sammy.

Roger leaned over and looked at her screen. "You getting all that?" Once again, she found it disconcerting to have him so close. She misspelled a word and hastily corrected it. When he gazed at her with a look of total admiration, she loused up a whole sentence and quickly erased it.

"You know, I could use someone with your skills, but I can't add any more people except temps. Your mother mentioned you're a temp at your present job. Would you consider switching? I'd hire you on the spot."

Work for Roger? Today had been so enjoyable. Wouldn't more time with him be even better? Em ran her tongue over her bottom lip and felt the area still raw from yesterday's bite. Men. They could certainly louse up your life. Not likely anything would be different working with Roger.

She rushed to say, "But my job—"

"Weren't you over at Metro looking for work?" he interrupted.

"Yes, but when I heard about the layoffs at Metro, I accepted a permanent job for an excellent salary." The lie came so easily. She hoped it would become truth tomorrow once she applied for the job. "Unfortunately, the medical plan isn't the best."

He moved away but continued to stare at her. "You look healthy enough." She warmed under his scrutiny.

"I am, but Sammy suffers from asthma." She returned her attention to the computer and saved the file. "Their policy doesn't cover pre-existing conditions for the first six months."

"Too bad. Isn't he covered under your ex's plan?"

Without pausing to consider her words, Em rose and said, "Bradley doesn't work. I'll go attach this to my printer and get you a hard copy."

"Thanks." Noise from the other room increased. "It sounds like the galaxy has been saved. I'll round up the boys and get Samantha. I still have to type up my presentation before tomorrow's meeting." He punched the air with his index fingers, simulating his hunt-and-peck typing style.

"I could type it for you. If it's not sensitive or confidential."

"No, you've done enough already." He backed away toward the living room. "Thanks for a very nice day."

The moment had turned awkward, but Em couldn't figure out why. All she had done was volunteer to help, and Roger obviously needed all the help he could get.

ALONE AT HIS computer, Roger stared at his incomplete notes. It was after midnight, and he still couldn't get his mind to focus on the job at hand. It was too busy rehashing and remembering each exchange with Em.

The day had been perfect, much like the times he'd shared with his wife. More important than her typing skills, Em offered humor, something missing in his life. For a short time the pressure of his job and the needs of his children had been shared.

Oh, she would make a wonderful assistant. He leaned back and grasped his hands behind his head, remembering her reaction when he offered the temporary position. Was it the hesitation or the awkward movements that seemed out of character? But then, what did he know?

Roger picked up his notes and glanced at the picture of Karen's smiling face on his desk. It had been taken several years before her death. In this photo, too, she looked so lovely. So full of life. Who knew that in just a short while....

He'd enjoyed Em's friendly companionship. That's why he wouldn't pursue it. He didn't want to take advantage of her giving nature when he had nothing to give in return. Karen still remained the love of his life. He had nothing to offer anyone.

"YOU DON'T UNDERSTAND, Dad." Samantha stood by his desk, hands on hips. "I need clothes. I start high school in less than two weeks, and I don't have a thing to wear."

Frustrated by the interruption, Roger turned from his computer. Only two weeks? Where had the summer gone? The schedules he needed by the next day still weren't finished. After discussing Em's suggestions with the group hired to handle the outplacements, Roger had implemented several of them. They'd go a long way toward helping the transition run smoothly. If everything could be completed, he'd have his weekend free to take the boys camping, a chance to relax for a change. Shopping certainly wouldn't fill that bill.

Maybe she did need clothes. Lately, she wore only his discarded dress shirts and shorts made from torn jeans. "I do understand, Samantha.

It's just that I can't take you shopping until next weekend."

"By then there won't be a decent thing left in the stores."

"That's ridiculous." He looked back at his computer in despair. He'd lost the file he'd worked on all evening and had spent the past hour trying to regain the information. Nothing had gone right today.

"Why *can't* you take me this weekend?" Samantha droned on in a voice that rubbed his nerves raw. "Arizona Mills is having special sales and..."

He swiveled to face her and slammed his elbow against the computer in the process. He bit down on his tongue to keep from swearing. "You know why, Samantha. I'm taking the boys camping this..."

"The boys. The boys. That's all that matters to you. You don't care what happens to me. No one does."

He turned back to his computer. "Speak to Sophia."

"She's wrapped up in her wedding and her move to Tucson. She doesn't have any time for me."

Sophia planned to leave in two weeks, and he still had no idea how to replace her. Roger made a mental note to call an employment agency the next day. "How about Aunt Jodie?"

"She has other plans."

Roger closed his eyes and rubbed the lids in an attempt to relieve some of the pressure building behind them. Today, three more people left for different jobs, two transferred within the company and another just quit, accepting the offered severance. If only he could do that, leave right now and walk away with a severance based on all the years he'd spent at Metro. With a sigh, he knew he'd never do that. Completing this task at work had become a moral obligation.

"I'll spend the whole weekend with nothing to do," Samantha continued.

"Would you rather come with us to Prescott?"

"No. I'd rather go shopping!" she shouted as she stomped into the family room. A moment later he heard her heavy steps on the stairs. A door slammed. Damn. Roger leaned back in his seat and stared at his monitor.

Oh, if he could only ditch this whole mess. His mind was pulled in too many directions. One problem got solved and two jumped in to take its place. He still hadn't found someone to help ease the load. If only he could hire Em. He was certain she'd never lose a whole file, or if she did, she'd know how to recover it.

Every time he found a chore he'd normally put in an administrative assistant's competent hands, he thought of how well Em would handle it. No one in the group of displaced employees had demonstrated any of the skills he needed. Continuing to muse, he visualized Em recovering the file and giving him a chance for a full night's sleep instead of one with recurring nightmares.

He glanced across the desk and saw Karen staring at him. Would she think he was obsessing? Probably. She'd always managed to help him cope. Help him relax. Oh, he could really use one of her backrubs. Every nerve in his body longed for attention. Except for his morning swim, he hadn't even had a chance to exercise.

What would Karen's reaction be if he told her how his opinion of Em had changed? Instead of that teenaged brat, he saw an attractive woman with a delightful sense of humor. He mused a moment longer, remembering the pleasant afternoon they'd spent. He returned his attention to Karen's picture, and a sensation of guilt hit him unexpectedly. Ever since he'd met his wife, no other woman had captured his interest.

He and Karen had talked about how his life had to go on after her death. She had insisted he find someone to take her place and give their children the mothering they needed. Roger focused on Karen's smiling face. *But no other woman could fill my life the way you did. A man couldn't expect to experience heaven more than once in a lifetime.*

Roger chewed over his predicament. Okay, so Em was the first woman he'd even noticed since…since he'd met Karen. But he doubted Em could ever have any interest in him. For that matter, she acted nervous and preoccupied around him. Why? And he couldn't forget how much she'd hated him during that summer spent with his family. What had he done to create such animosity? One prank after another. If he had acted on his feelings at that time and strangled her, he'd probably still be in jail.

Roger stood and stretched. He had to find a way to retrieve that file so he could present it the next day. From the way Em handled her computer, he felt sure she would know what to do. She had offered to help. He scratched his head and tried to think how he could broach the subject. If she was willing to come here, he'd treat the whole thing as a business deal. Before he could change his mind, Roger reached for the yellow pad where he had scratched Em's number and dialed.

"You know anything about retrieving lost

data on a computer?" he asked the moment she
answered. "I had about four hours of work go
into never-never land, and I'm having an impossible time trying to find it."

"Is this Roger?" a hesitant voice asked.

He grabbed a hank of hair and pulled. "Yeah.
Sorry, Em, I..."

"This is Doris. I'll see if she's still up."

Roger glanced at his watch. Ten o'clock!
Why hadn't he checked the time before call-
ing? He was about to hang up, when Em said,
"Hi, Roger. Mom said your computer crashed."

"No. It's just a lost file. Listen, I'm sorry I
called. It's late and you have to go to work tomorrow."

"We both do. I may be able to help. What's
your address?"

Em busied herself in front of the bathroom mirror, removing the night cream she'd applied.
She stifled a yawn. If it was nothing more
than a lost file, she'd be back and in bed in no
time. She fiddled with removing several curlers
she'd put in before going to bed. The curls she'd
planned for the next day would have to wait.

"Aren't you primping a lot just to fix a computer?"

Em took a quick look at her mother leaning
against the bathroom doorjamb. "I don't want

to look as though I just got out of bed, Mom. Give me a break."

"You planning to go au natural?"

Em glanced down at the sleeveless T-shirt she used for sleeping. "I plan to change." Her mother hadn't shown this much interest in her attire since she was a teenager. Em glanced back at her mother, an edge to her reply. "Shouldn't you be in bed?"

Doris chuckled as she turned away. "He still walks on water."

Em stopped and stared at her image. Was she giving Roger's sudden need for her help too much importance? After all, more than ten days had gone by without a call. He had sent a card: a short, formal thank-you to tell her how much the boys had appreciated the swim party, the meal, and how much he'd appreciated her help. But nothing personal such as "I'd like to see more of you."

Something unknown, maybe common sense or karma, had kept her from taking that job with Roger. Close contact with him might have ended with her making a fool of herself. Too many of her friends had become involved in office romances and lived to regret it. Before she could reconsider and take the job Roger offered, she approached her boss and told him she'd like to accept the full-time position the company offered her. It was a done deal before the end of the week, with increased pay and eventual medical benefits for Sammy.

Right now, thanks to their sons, she had a fragile friendship with Roger. She wasn't about to ruin it and make a fool of herself. She'd provide the help he needed and get home as quickly as possible.

Em brushed her hair roughly, enough to make it sting with static electricity. She found the sports bra she had discarded earlier, pulled on a clean T-shirt and slipped into shorts. With a quick look in the mirror, she decided even her mother would approve.

THE WHITE STUCCO walls glared under the porch light as Roger paced outside his front door. Nervousness churned in his stomach. What if she couldn't recover his file? He told himself all this anxiety had to do with that possibility. He'd offer to pay her and usher her out.

How much should he offer? Immaterial. Whatever she charged would be worth it. He'd pay for it himself if he couldn't get reimbursed from petty cash. She was here to help him out of a jam. He hesitated. What if she felt offering her money was insulting?

Karen, Karen, what should I do? His silent query went unanswered.

The moment Em's car pulled into the driveway, Roger ran off the porch and opened her door. "I want to get this clear from the start, Em. I'm hiring you in a consultant capacity. Name your price."

"Fine," she said, stepping from the car.

Fine? No argument, no negotiations? Roger closed his eyes and rubbed his forehead.

"Headache?"

He opened his eyes. Em stood inches away. He took a deep breath and drew in her scent. Wrong move. "No," he said, barely able to get the word out. "Can I take that for you?" As he reached for her bag, he brushed her hand and nearly dropped the computer.

"Whoa, let me take that." Em pulled it away from him. About to put his hand on Em's back to direct her, he turned toward his house. The moment he saw Samantha standing at the door, looking every bit like her mother, he dropped his hand to his side.

"Oh, I need your help desperately, Em," Samantha said. She clasped her hands prayer fashion under her chin. "Dad won't take me shopping, and I don't have anything but rags to wear to school."

"Samantha, stop being so dramatic and get to bed." *Why was she still up?* He pushed past her into the house. "I told you I'll take you next weekend."

The girl uttered a strangled cry, shook her hands in the air and looked heavenward for help. How was he to deal with such antics? Couldn't she cut him some slack? He faced a few more important crises than her lack of wardrobe.

Em turned to him and said, "Why don't I go upstairs with Samantha while you get me a drink? Iced tea if you have any." She followed his daughter before he could offer a protest.

"Okay, what's going on?" Em asked when they reached the bedroom on the second floor. The room, decorated in frills and lace, seemed too immature for someone who had given up smoking at thirteen.

"Look at these." Samantha picked up an armload of clothes that had been strewn across her bed and tossed them in the air. "They're all out of style. I've grown two inches in the last year, and Dad hasn't even noticed."

Samantha lowered her voice and glanced toward the open door. "Besides," she said, pulling the bulky men's shirt out at the bust line, "My boobs are getting bigger and nothing looks right."

"Um, well…" Em cleared her throat, and glanced around the room in an attempt to gather her thoughts. This was way beyond what she'd expected. This weekend. What plans had she made this weekend? She turned back to the girl. "I can take you shopping Saturday, but you have to clear it with your father, first."

Samantha threw her arms around Em and nearly strangled her. "Oh, thank you, thank you, thank you. I'll see if I can get Daddy's credit cards."

"My what?" Roger asked from the doorway. He held out a tall glass of iced tea to Em.

While sipping the drink, she watched the adult and child move into their separate camps. She had no business interfering. Why hadn't she gone straight to the computer and avoided this scene?

"I told you I'd take you next week. You are not dragging Em away from her busy life."

The past few weeks of strain showed clearly on his face. A muscle twitched in his cheek as he spoke in hushed tones to his daughter. The whites of his eyes were no longer white but sunset pink. From Em's perspective, he looked overworked, overtired and emotionally over-extended.

"Oh, but *you* can?" Samantha scowled at him, hands on her hips. "It's eleven, Daddy. Why did you drag her over?"

Em tried not to react to the innuendo. After

all, Samantha was using every means possible to get her way. But Roger turned red as fury washed over his face. His jaw tightened. Had Samantha hit a nerve?

"Why don't you show me your computer, Roger? I'll see if I can find that file." Em headed out the door and paused in the hall. A moment later Roger joined her, grabbed the doorknob, and pulled the door shut with a force that rattled a picture on the wall.

"That girl is going to drive me to the nut house."

For the time being, at least, further confrontation had been averted. Em felt so relieved she started to chuckle.

"What's so funny?"

"This is nothing. Just wait till she starts to drive. Then you'll really get a ride to the nut house."

"No way." The tension in his jaw slowly began to ease. "I'll sell my car before I let her get behind the wheel."

CHAPTER FIVE

WHEN EM ENTERED Roger's office, a room connected to the hall and family room, she saw a photo of Karen displayed on his desk, and several others hung on the wall above the file cabinets, along with those of the children.

Fifteen years ago, Em had hated that woman. If Karen hadn't dominated Roger's time, he might have paid more attention to her. A stupid idea, Em realized. Why would any college student look at an awkward fourteen-year-old, especially when he had a beautiful girlfriend so handy?

Em's animosity had diminished over the years, but not totally. She propped her computer case in front of the desk picture to keep it out of view.

While she worked to find his lost information, memories of Samantha's insinuation kept troubling Em and destroying her concentration. Why had Roger waited until so late in the evening to call her? Did he have ulterior motives? Was he attracted to her?

The idea excited and frightened her at the same time. If these thoughts hadn't ruined her focus, she might have finished the job in half the time. Even so, it took fewer than fifteen minutes for Em to capture all the missing information and save it to Roger's desktop.

"I'm impressed," Roger said when she'd completed the task.

Was the pleasure in his eyes only because of her having saved his file? Once again that hank of hair falling over his forehead made her fingers itch to push it back. The late hour must be getting to her.

Em stood and collected her things, as Roger reached for his wallet. "How much do I owe you?"

"I'll send you a bill. I like to keep accurate records for my income tax."

"You do this a lot? Troubleshoot computer problems?" he said as he returned his wallet and walked into the hall.

"Yes. It's something I learned after one of the times I was laid off. The company provided computer lessons for us to hone our skills."

"Another thing I should consider."

She followed him into the hall and nearly collided with him when he stopped in front of the staircase.

He glanced up. "They should be asleep."

When he backed away, still keeping an eye on the upstairs landing, she followed quietly. He ushered her past the staircase and through the doorway onto the porch. She stopped short when the overhead light went off. Roger closed the door behind them, cutting off the hallway light. Why had he done that? She could break her neck if she tried to maneuver down the steps in the dark.

"I think Samantha's finally gone to sleep."

Em turned and tried to read his expression, but her eyes hadn't had enough time to adjust to the dimness. Now that they were out of the air-conditioned house, the night air surrounded her like a warm blanket.

"I want to apologize," he said.

"Could you do it with the light on? I'm afraid to move."

"Sure, but it will attract bugs. I'll turn it on again in a minute so you can get off the porch. I'm sorry for my actions back there. When I blew my top."

"You're apologizing to the wrong girl."

"I know and I'll talk to her later. I don't usually lose my temper so quickly," he continued in a whisper. "It's just—I feel I'm in a pressure cooker ready to explode. I don't have enough time—for my work, for my family."

He paused and sighed. "And I'm wasting an ungodly amount of it daydreaming."

As her eyes adjusted, Em could see him leaning against the house, his hands behind his back. When she lost her job, her own fears and insecurities had produced nightmares. She could have used a friend, a confidant to help her through the difficult times.

Roger was about to share something of himself in this intimate cloak of darkness, and she didn't want to miss any of it. Em placed her computer bag and purse near a wrought-iron bench and moved closer to him.

"Nightmares can…"

"Not nightmares, daydreams," he said, pushing away from the wall. He moved over to the bench and indicated she should take a seat. "I've been daydreaming about you taking a job as my assistant." He sat down next to her.

"That's impossible. I…" He still wanted her to work for him? He needed her that much? Maybe she should reconsider.

"I know. I know. It's just…none of the displaced people are working out. They don't have the computer skills needed. Oh, they can do the programs the company provides, but they can't cut and paste or create a proper letter." He paused. "How did you receive your initial training?"

What had started as a clandestine meeting with lights out and murmurs had turned into nothing more than a request for information. Em relaxed as all her romantic thoughts dissipated. She took a deep breath and began. "The head of our department invested in PC-training tapes. We took two-hour classes after work in the education department, where they had banks of computers."

"I could do that," Roger replied. "We have an in-house training center. I knew you'd have all the answers."

The words, whispered near her ear, sucked all the breath from her lungs. "That's me," she said, when she could find her voice, "a walking encyclopedia."

When he didn't add anything, she continued, "I also took courses at a local college that gave me extra skills. If I ever have more opportunities, I plan to take additional courses, possibly go into that field."

Moving ever so slightly, Em turned to face him. They were barely inches from each other as a light flicked on. They jumped apart. Em's foot hit her laptop, sending it skittering. She started after it.

"So, Dad, is she taking me shopping or not?" Samantha leaned against the doorjamb, arms folded across her chest, the exact image of Karen.

"How long have you been behind that door?"

"Long enough." She glared at him. A guilt Roger never anticipated made him wither under her gaze. He closed his eyes to shut off that stare. It was as though he had been caught cheating on Karen. It was a stupid, senseless thought, but one he couldn't suppress.

And Samantha knew she had found something to hold over his head. Blackmail, that's what it was. He had to give up his weekend camping with his sons, or his daughter would hold this transgression over him for the rest of her life.

"All right," he said, opening his eyes, "We'll go Saturday morning."

"I'd rather go with Em."

He couldn't win. Every time he agreed to one of her demands, Samantha switched to something new. He was about to lay the law down, once and for all, when Em touched his arm.

"It's okay. I enjoy shopping. Why don't you let me take her?"

Had he heard correctly? Em volunteered for what had to be the closest thing to hell— shopping in a mall on Saturday, when zillions of people needed to get prepared for school.

She was too helpful. How could he ever pay her back?

"You won't bring your son," Samantha said as she stepped onto the porch.

"Of course not." Em chuckled, a delightful sound that helped relieve the tension pulsating through Roger. "He hates shopping. My mother can watch him."

Both of them turned to Roger and waited. He ran his hands through his hair while he considered his alternatives. Em could solve a major problem for him, providing she controlled Samantha's spending. But what could he do in return? He snapped his fingers as a solution came to him.

"Fine. You can take my daughter for the day, if I can take your son for the weekend." Before she could protest, he continued, "Harve and I are taking our boys camping in Prescott, where it's cool. We have plenty of room for Sammy, and they all get along so well. How about it?" He scrutinized his daughter with a no-nonsense scowl. "That's the only way I'd consider letting you take Samantha."

"Dad!"

Em hesitated. "I'd have to check with Sammy."

Samantha hooked her arm in Em's. "Do it. He'll love Prescott, and you and I can shop till we drop."

EM FRETTED ALL the way home. What had she agreed to? Shopping had always been a pleasant pastime, so she didn't mind that. But could she tolerate Sammy going off on a camping trip without her?

They had never been separated overnight, even the few times his father had been scheduled for a weekend visit. Bradley always picked his son up on Saturday morning and deposited the disappointed boy home on the same night. He used the excuse that Sammy might suffer from a serious asthma attack, and Bradley didn't want to put the boy at risk.

The last time, Sammy had tried not to cry. "Dad doesn't have to worry. I know what to do," he said after Bradley left. Em offered the only comfort she could, a hug and assurance that she'd always be there for him. It did little good when the boy wanted a father's love and attention.

But that asthma problem was an issue she couldn't put aside. Could she trust Roger to care for Sammy if he was out of breath or coughed uncontrollably? Maybe she was worrying for nothing. Maybe her son wouldn't even want to go.

"HI, EM. IT'S JODIE. Can you believe how time flies? What's it been? Two weeks. I should have called you right after the party. Timothy loved the action figures you gave him. Even takes them to bed with him."

Em held the phone close to her ear so she could hear over the television. The three of them were watching a cartoon, and the noise carried through their small apartment.

"What'd you say?"

"I loved seeing you again, but we never got a chance to talk."

"Just a minute. I've got to find someplace quiet." Taking the cordless phone out the door, Em halted on the tiny veranda that served as their porch and entrance into the second-floor apartment. She settled on the white plastic chair that faced the garden and pool.

"That's better. Now at least I can hear you. What did you want to talk about?"

"Nothing special. Just thought maybe we could get together sometime. You free for lunch tomorrow?"

"Sure am. I wanted to talk to you, as well. Samantha and I are going shopping on Saturday when Roger and Harve take the boys camping. You care to join us?"

One of the tenants motioned to Em from poolside to join him. She waved and shook her head. The night was warm and balmy, perfect for an evening swim, but she had no desire to encourage any of the men she'd met at the apartment complex. Remembered tensions from her divorce kept her from seeking relationships with anyone.

"You're seeing Roger?"

The exuberance in Jodie's voice made Em pause as she returned her attention to the phone. For a moment, no words came to mind. Finally she said, "No. What gave you that idea?"

"You're taking my niece shopping, which means you've made inroads with Roger, bigtime. He never lets her out of his sight, let alone allows her to go off with a relative stranger."

"I'm not exactly a stranger. Besides, he offered to take Sammy camping with the boys. It was the least I could do to help." Em paused. She didn't like discussing Roger and the problems he might be having with his daughter. How could she steer the conversation in another direction? "So, do you want to join us for a shopping marathon?"

"I'd love to, but I can't. Sam already asked me, and I had to beg off. When Harve said he was taking Timothy camping this weekend, my friend and I booked ourselves into the Princess for a weekend of pampering. The spa has summer rates. Maybe you'd like to join us?"

"No. I'm committed to shopping with Samantha."

"You probably *will be* committed after a day with a teenager. Why not come just for Saturday night and Sunday? Have all your tense muscles massaged by some tanned Nordic god." Distracting noises on Jodie's end momentarily stopped the conversation.

The image of extravagance that Jodie had conjured appealed to Em. How nice to be able to have any cares massaged away and to spend a delightful weekend with friends. But she couldn't afford such luxuries, no matter how good the summer rates.

When Jodie came back on the phone, she said, "Harve's back. So, how about Saturday? Should I book you in with Eric or Finn? Either can uncoil a really tight muscle."

"Thanks, but I think not. What's Harve's take on these Nordic gods? Does he approve?"

"Oh, he says he doesn't mind if I read the menu as long as I eat at home. Right, dear?" The words were followed by what sounded like a kiss. "I've got to go. See you at noon tomorrow?"

"Where?"

"You pick a place."

"How about Applebee's, the one near my work?" Em provided an address.

When the line went dead abruptly, she placed the phone on a tiny plastic table, tilted the chair back and enjoyed the night air. The pink slowly left the sky. No matter how hot the summer day might be, the nights were delightfully cool. Only another month and even the daytime temperatures would start to fall.

The more she thought about meeting Jodie, the more Em realized how difficult it might be. During their years together as best friends, Em had never let on about how much she adored Jodie's brother. That crush seemed ridiculous now, yet she wasn't sure she cared to discuss it. Jodie might take it wrong and think Em still had feelings for Roger. Having seen Jodie in matchmaking mode, Em wanted to avoid giving her any ideas.

Well, the restaurant Em had chosen might help. The food was great, but it was crowded at noon, and the noise level too high to have any kind of intimate conversation.

The door opened behind Em, a light flicking over her before it closed again.

"Here you are," Doris said as she took the other chair. "Sammy's getting ready for bed. You haven't mentioned the camping trip?"

"No. I thought I'd do it tomorrow night. It will be less traumatic if he doesn't have too much time to think about it."

"For you or for him?"

Although the area held little light, Em could

still see the disapproval on her mother's face. "His asthma kicks in when he gets stressed."

"I've always felt one of the biggest joys in life was the anticipation of pleasant things. You're robbing him of that."

"His body can't distinguish between pleasant things and harmful things." Em fought to keep her voice even. "Stress is stress whether you win a million dollars or lose the same amount."

Her mother sighed. "So, who was on the phone? Roger have another computer glitch?"

Em was thankful for the change in topic. "No. It was Jodie. We're meeting for lunch tomorrow."

"You don't sound too pleased."

Her mother could always pick up on Em's moods. "She asked if something was going on between Roger and me."

"And you said...?"

"The truth. Nothing's going on."

"Remind yourself of that a few thousand times between now and then, and maybe you'll be able to convince her." Doris pushed away from her chair and stood. "Maybe you'll be able to convince yourself."

EM ARRIVED AT the restaurant in one of her new summer dresses, carrying a jacket in case the air-conditioning was too cold. She arrived a few minutes before twelve in the hope of getting a table ahead of everyone else working nearby who came out for lunch. Jodie was already there, drink in hand, sitting at the bar. She looked cool in shorts and a sleeveless jersey top in shades of blue. Her dark hair was pulled back and held with clips similar to what she had worn at the party.

"Hi. I thought I'd wait here until our table is ready. Have you tried their strawberry daiquiris?" Jodie took a long sip and sighed. "I could live on these."

"They're probably terribly healthy, as well. All that fruit." They both chuckled as the hostess indicated their table was ready and led them to a corner. The table next to them quickly filled with another couple.

"I'll have what she's having," Em said, when the waiter came over for drink orders. Although liquor usually zapped her energy, not a good thing when she had to return to work, it also served to bolster her courage. She needed all the fortification she could get in case their conversation turned to Roger.

"I'll take a water. This is enough extravagance for me," Jodie said, pointing to her half-finished daiquiri.

When the waiter left, Em thought of safe topics and asked, "How are your parents? I didn't see them at Timothy's party."

"They're doing fine. Daddy decided they needed to see the world, so he takes Mom on every cruise he can find. They're looking to sell their house and get a condo."

"You're kidding. That beautiful home?"

"It's way too big for them. They asked if Harve and I'd be interested, but I said no."

"I really loved that place." It had been Em's first experience in a real house, not the apartments she'd lived in all her life. In her youth, she'd believed only happy families lived in houses and the ones with problems lived in apartments. Nothing had proven her wrong. "Some of my best memories were reading in your mother's rose garden next to your grandparents' cottage. Or us spending endless nights talking in your bedroom. I can't see how you would want to give it up."

"I know, I love the place, as well. But, frankly, I'm afraid it would be too much work keeping up the extra house. We have no use for it, and I don't want the problems of renting it."

Jodie took a sip of her drink, then moved closer to Em and said in a conspiratorial whisper. "You know, when you were living with us that summer, I thought they were going to adopt you."

"You're kidding."

"Nope. No one told me why you were there, about the divorce and all. I thought they were finally giving me the sister I always wanted."

Jodie looked over the rim of her glass before placing it on the table. "We had some good times. Remember stealing Roger's beer? He would have killed us if he'd ever found out." She looked up and laughed. "My parents would have killed us." Jodie smiled and sat back in her seat. "I cried for a week after you left."

"So did I." But not for the same reason. Em had missed Jodie, but not as much as she'd missed Roger. She had kept him alive for years in her dreams, her diaries.

"You got out just in time, before the fireworks started."

Em's drink arrived at that moment, interrupting any further conversation. Em glanced at her watch. She only had forty-five minutes left in her lunch hour. Jodie's last statement intrigued her, but Em followed the same discipline that had kept her secret safe in the past. Too many questions about Roger might wave red flags. Jodie picked up the menu and didn't bother to give any more details, so Em let the subject drop.

"I have to head back soon," Em said. "New

job and all. Don't want to break too many rules."

"What do you do?"

"Payroll. I also create weekly, monthly and quarterly reports that show where all the money went. At least the job has some variety, not just working with endless figures."

"I'd love to go back to work once Timothy starts school. I met Harve when we took similar courses in college, but I wasn't interested in becoming a lawyer so I became a paralegal. With a few brush-up courses, I'm sure I could get back into it."

It didn't appear that Jodie planned to get back to their former topic, so after the waiter brought them water and took their orders, Em bolstered her nerve and asked, "What fireworks?"

Jodie looked confused.

"You mentioned there were fireworks after I left."

"Oh, that. Roger got into trouble."

Drugs, jail, and DUI all went through Em's mind. "What kind of trouble?"

"He and Karen had to get married."

Em sat back. "Oh."

"The whole thing turned into a regular soap opera. Karen's mother was livid." Jodie threw up a hand and hit the stained glass globe above the table. The two women next to them glanced at them pointedly before returning to their food. "She did everything she could to prevent the marriage, insisted the baby would be better off if they put it up for adoption."

Em felt sudden empathy for Karen. Give up your child? How could anyone suggest such a thing?

"They took off for Las Vegas and got married. Mom and Dad continued to pay for his education, but Karen's parents cut her off completely, so she never returned to school. My grandparents had moved into a retirement village by then, so the newlyweds took over the cottage. It wasn't until after Samantha came that Karen's mother even spoke to them again."

"So it all worked out."

"Right. Until Karen died. Roger took it so hard. He still refuses to date anyone." Jodie leaned across the table and grinned. "Until you came along, that is."

"I already told you, we're not dating. Our boys have become fast friends, that's all." Em took a long drink of her daiquiri just before their salads arrived and avoided making eye contact. "Roger included Sammy in this trip for the boys, and I volunteered to pay him back by taking Samantha shopping. That's it. Nothing romantic about that." She offered a quick smile before diving into her food.

After a deep sigh, Jodie said, "I used to wish you'd marry Roger. Then you could become my sister for real."

Em slowly chewed her food. So she hadn't been the only one with secret fantasies.

"I never could figure out the two of you. How come you hated each other so much?"

Em reached for her water to stem a choking fit. One of the women near her moved closer and asked if she needed help. Em shook her head.

Finally able to breathe again, she said, "We were water and oil."

"I guess. And now he's so strung up about Karen. I don't think he'll ever get over her."

Em pushed her salad away, her appetite suddenly gone.

CHAPTER SIX

"MILLIE, HOW ARE YOU?" Roger asked. The unexpected phone call from his mother-in-law made him sit straighter in his chair. A relationship that had started poorly back when he married her daughter hadn't progressed much since then.

If only he had an assistant. Then all his calls would be monitored, and he could avoid dealing with the frustration that usually followed a conversation with Millie. Roger leaned across his desk and jotted, "Check out displaced again for administrative assistants."

"I'm not bothering you at the office, am I?"

"No. Of course not. Is anything wrong?"

"Yes, something's wrong," Millie said in that authoritative voice that grated on his nerves. He pictured the woman, with her white curls and stiff spine, scolding him for some infraction, something she did regularly whenever they spoke.

"You've lost your job, and you're too proud to even ask for help. If it wasn't for my granddaughter, I'd never have known you were even in this predicament." She paused and added more solicitously, "I'm here for you, dear. You should know that." Another pause. "Especially now that your parents are gone."

His parents had left on a cruise, for heaven's sake. Millie made it sound as though they had died. Roger leaned across his desk again and drew the picture of his wife closer. "I—we appreciate your offer, but I'm fine."

"How can you say that," Millie asked, her tone getting more irritating, "when that Mexican woman is leaving? Who will you get to replace her?"

"You mean Sophia?"

"Whatever. It's just as well she's going. You know how I feel about her speaking Spanish to the children all the time. Why, the twins thought it was their native language for the first few years of their lives. It's downright un-American."

Roger placed his hand over the receiver and spoke to his wife's picture. "At least they won't have to bumble through a foreign language in high school the way we did." Karen smiled back, even though when alive she had usually warned him to be nice to her mother.

"What did you say?"

"Someone just came into my office. Was there anything else?"

"You'll need someone to watch the children. Why not send them to stay with me? They love Flagstaff, and it's so much cooler here," Millie continued. "Honestly, dear, who in their right mind can spend a summer in Phoenix and remain sane?"

"Millie, I—I'm sorry but the children are staying here with me. I'm working on getting a full-time nanny for them. I assure you, everything is fine. Got to go now. Thanks for calling."

Without waiting for a reply, Roger hung up the phone. He grabbed the pad and wrote down two more items to take care of, "Tell Samantha not to share all our problems with her grandmother" and "Look into getting a nanny."

The last thing he wanted was Millie influencing their lives.

"YES, YES, YES!" Sammy danced around the living room, not able to contain his joy about the camping trip. "Where we goin', Ma?"

"*You're* going—if you want to—with Chip and Chaz."

"Yes!" Sammy said as he pulled a fisted hand into his body to emphasize his agreement. "When?"

"Tomorrow morning…"

He stopped. "Why can't we go tonight?"

Em explained further, and his enthusiasm cooled. Her heart warmed. He'd miss her too much to go and leave her behind. "It's okay if you don't want to go."

"Oh, I'm goin'. What do you take on a campin' trip, anyway?" he inquired over his shoulder as he headed toward the room they shared. By the time she reached him, he already had half the contents of his drawer on his bed.

When Em returned to the kitchen, Doris asked, "So he likes the idea?"

"What do you think? I'm definitely low man on the totem pole where Chaz and Chip are concerned. I just hope Sammy sleeps well tonight."

"You worry too much."

"Of course I worry. Mothers do that." Em started to reach for the mail on the counter, but Doris intercepted her.

"That's mine," she said and slipped an opened envelope into her apron pocket. The logo on the envelope looked like the apartment complex's.

"They aren't raising the rent, are they?" Em asked, aware that their lease was up the end of August. She flipped through her credit card bill. Good, she had paid off enough that she could buy a few things when she went shopping with Samantha.

"Grandmothers, on the other hand, know that worrying never helped their own children one bit," Doris said, returning to the previous topic.

Em focused on her mother. "You worried about me?"

"Of course I did."

"When?" Her mother always seemed so consumed with her own problems.

"Too many times to recall."

"Name one."

Doris glanced at the ceiling as she leaned against the counter. "We really need a paint job in here. It wasn't done before I moved in. I should have insisted."

"Stop changing the subject, Mom. When did you worry about me?"

With a deep sigh, Doris pushed away from the counter and pointed to the dining room. "Let's sit."

Chuckling, Em followed her mother into the dimly lit room and took a seat. "Oh, so the list is so long and complicated we need to get comfortable."

Doris pulled a straight-backed chair from the table. "As if we could get comfortable on these.

You know how we acquired these chairs? Your grandmother…"

"Mom. You're fudging. We're not talking about chairs."

"Okay, okay." Focusing on the ceiling again, Doris continued, "Do you see that paint peeling up there?"

"Mom!"

Doris glanced at Em then quickly looked away. She paused long enough that Em felt she might not get to the subject at all. Could her mother be turning senile? After all, she was moving up in years. Em was about to prod her again, when Doris said, "I worried about how you were handling the divorce."

"Which divorce?"

"Mine."

"No you didn't," Em replied. Recalling those days when her parents screamed at each other brought back all the insecurities that had kept her awake at night. "You left me high and dry with the Holdens."

"Because I knew you couldn't handle the problems your father and I faced. I wanted you out of that battleground. You know how horrible a divorce can be. You went through the same thing with Bradley."

Em watched her mother's tapping fingers in silence for a few seconds. "It was nothing like that," she said in a tight whisper. "I would have stayed with Bradley through hell and back again to keep Sammy safe. Unlike you and Dad, we never argued. Never had so much as a discussion about problems in our marriage. One day he just packed his things and walked out."

"Another woman?"

"I wish. At least then I would have known what to fight."

"Never wish that. It's the worst thing in the world to know you can't satisfy the man you married, and he has to go and find it somewhere else."

Em straightened in her chair. Then her spine gave out, and she slumped on the table; she stretched out her arms to still her mother's tapping fingers. "I never knew."

Doris's grip tightened when she answered. "I wasn't about to share that with my teenaged daughter. That's why I sent you off with Betty and Dave Holden. They volunteered, and you'd always been good friends with Jodie. You talk about worrying. Here I was fighting for my sanity on the home front and worrying about you getting involved with Roger."

"Roger was in college. He considered me a pest."

"Right. And you started doing things to impress him, things you thought were grown-up. Things I had no control over."

Roger had mentioned something along those lines, as well. Em started chuckling again and patted her mother's hand. "Mom, you probably had good cause to worry. I was experimenting with a lot of things then."

"Drugs?"

Em pulled her hand away. "No. But I did have my first drink. Jodie and I confiscated a six pack of beer from Roger's stash. We each had three cans. To this day, every time I have a beer I remember that."

"And smoking. You started that, too."

Em leaned over and placed her head on her outstretched arms. Then she dragged herself back to a sitting position. "Right. Oh, how I wish I could stop. Jodie got me started, but she must have quit somewhere along the way."

"You saw her today, didn't you?"

"Yes."

"How is she?"

"Fine. She's off to some spa to get pampered for the weekend. Wanted me to join her after the shopping spree, but I can't afford that, even if the rates are cheaper in the summer." Em leaned back in her chair. "When am I ever going to stop worrying about money?"

Doris leaned over and tapped Em's hand.

"When you have some security in your own home. That's what we have to work toward, save toward."

Em scowled. "If only I could save something. I'm going to have to really control myself tomorrow. Don't want my credit card expenditures going through the roof again. Did you want me to buy anything for you?" When her mother didn't respond, Em looked up. Doris was gazing out the dining-room window. "Mom?"

Doris looked back at her daughter and sighed. "What?"

"Is something wrong?"

"Oh, I'm probably having a senior moment. I've been known to have them on occasion."

As far as Em was concerned, her mother had had several since they started their conversation. What could be distracting her? It wasn't like her at all to lose her train of thought.

"You know, I always believed I'd enjoy retirement. Frankly, I'm getting bored. Once Sammy starts school, I think I'll look for something to fill my time." With that, Doris pushed away from the table and crammed her hands in her apron pockets as she headed for her room.

Where did that come from? Em wondered. She was about to follow her mother and ask what had set her off, when the top letter in the stack of mail caught her attention. It was one of the self-addressed envelopes she'd sent to Bradley.

Em tore it open. She hoped he had reconsidered and decided to send her a check. Several slips of paper fell to the floor, and she reached down to pick them up.

"Receipts?" Four of them for books and other items purchased at a college. A note was scribbled on the back of one, "Please send payment. You always took care of them in the past. B."

"Over your dead body!" she shouted, and stuffed the papers in her pocket.

"You sure this isn't a bother?" Roger asked after pulling into the apartment complex's parking lot Saturday morning. Em deposited Sammy's sleeping bag by the curb. "Samantha can be a real pill."

"No. I love shopping. Really. You're the one with your hands full." She planned to pick up the girl as soon as everyone left for Prescott.

"This I can handle." Roger looked around and a broad smile replaced the worry lines that had recently dominated his face. "It gives me a break from work and all the rest of my headaches."

"I never even asked. Do you need food? Anything?"

"No, we've got the preparations down to a science." He reached into his pocket and pulled out a credit card. "Here. Samantha's allowed to sign on this card. Within limitations, of course. Under the circumstances, I don't want her to go overboard and leave me with a bill that compares to the national debt."

Em glanced down at the girl's signature and suddenly felt mischievous. She drew the credit card closer to her face, raised an eyebrow and grinned. "We are going to have fun with this."

When he attempted to grab the card, she placed it behind her back. Her yelp turned into a giggle when Roger pulled her against his chest, as he fought to wrestle the plastic away. She tried to wiggle free, yet she was enjoying the tussle and the strength in his arms, which bound her to him. Laughter bubbled forth then died in her throat. She stopped moving as Roger's arms tightened around her, the card forgotten.

"You've got the most infectious giggle, Auntie Em," he said, close to her mouth, his breath a breeze of fresh mint.

She inhaled deeply and focused on his eyes. "No one's called me that in decades." Wrapped in his arms, she felt so warm, safe and comfortable. She didn't want him to let her go.

"Mom!" Sammy said as he butted against her leg. "Come on. We gotta get goin'."

Reluctantly, Em moved out of Roger's hold. "You remember what we talked about?" she said, turning to her son and squatting to his level.

"Yeah. It's in my backpack. Big deal." He looked longingly toward Roger's white van, where the boys and Harve were waiting.

She grasped her son's narrow shoulders. "You can handle it, right, buddy?"

Sammy responded to the urgency in her voice with a serious scowl. He nodded, and she gave him a quick hug. Before she'd completely straightened, Sammy had bounded off to join his friends.

Em pulled out a typed paper from her pocket. "He has all the inhalers for his asthma and knows how to use them. Here's a list of the symptoms and possible problems." She held the paper out to Roger. "My number's there and—"

Roger grasped her hand and slowly pulled out the paper, sending a tingling sensation along her arm. "You are a worrywart, Auntie Em." He continued to hold her hand while placing the paper in his shirt pocket. "He'll be fine."

They stood there for several moments until the boys started a deafening roar.

"Let's get goin'."

"Come on, Dad."

Harve had moved into the driver's seat and revved the motor. "Gee whiz. You going to talk all morning?"

Roger took the passenger seat in the van. He waved. Em stood there, returning the wave until they'd disappeared down the street.

HOURS LATER, EM elbowed through throngs of shoppers at the Arizona Mills mall. Loaded down with shopping bags, she longed to rest her aching feet. No chance of that. If she didn't keep moving, she might lose Samantha and her friend in the crowd.

Samantha had begged Em for permission to bring her best friend, Amy, along. She had no one to take her shopping, either, plus Samantha couldn't make a decision without her friend's approval. Still in the shopping spirit at that point, Em had agreed.

They had spent a good hour trying on bras to be sure Samantha had the right fit. For some reason, nothing appealed to her. By the time they were ready to leave the third store, Em lost her cool.

"I thought this was a number one priority."

"Not everyone has to wear one. Didn't people in your day burn them?"

"That was in my mother's day," Em said, surprised that Samantha had picked up that little bit of history. "Besides, they only destroyed one bra, not their whole collection. And you're getting to where you really need one."

It still surprised Em that Samantha had totally skipped the training bra in the smaller sizes. She was nearly as developed as Em, who had contended with a baby and breast milk.

"Well, I don't need one." Samantha started for the exit and had reached the main thoroughfare that connected the stores, before Em grabbed her arm and pulled her back.

"Yes, you do. You're starting high school shortly. You can't disguise this any longer."

Samantha's eyes bulged and her mouth began to twitch. *I've gone too far,* Em thought as tears welled in the girl's eyes. "I'm sorry, honey. I didn't mean to…"

"Bras can give you breast cancer," Samantha said through tight lips.

"What? Where did you…?"

"Grandma Millie told me. She said that's how my mother got it."

Grandma Millie had to be Karen's mother, since Em knew Roger's parents. Why would the woman tell a child that? Em pulled the distressed girl into her arms as the crowds of people elbowed past.

"I don't think that's true. At least, I've never heard of it." Em pushed her away a little so she could see her face. "And did you know men can get it, too, and they don't even wear bras."

"She's kidding, right?" Amy nudged Samantha with a cross-eyed scowl. "It only happens to women."

"I'm not up on every aspect of the disease, but I know I've worn one since I was your age and so has my mother. Neither of us has had any problems." When Samantha still didn't look convinced, Em continued, "Listen, I'll go on the internet tonight and see what I can find out about this."

"Find out how many men get it," Amy interjected.

Why had she even brought men into the picture? Em thought as she moved to get out of the main thoroughfare. "But you have to buy one today. We can toss it if we find they're the major cause of cancer." When Samantha still didn't reply, Em felt exasperated. "Okay?" she asked, her voice rising. "One day can't possibly cause any harm."

Finally, Samantha nodded and slowly turned to reenter the store.

Em made her buy several. This way, Samantha wouldn't have to wash one out every night.

Samantha stood straighter and displayed a

confidence that had been lacking before they'd started their shopping spree.

Now, as Em tried to keep up with the girls, she wished she hadn't agreed to bring Amy along. The two infused each other with energy, something that had left Em hours ago. By the time she caught up with them, they were examining gold earrings in a jewelry store. "We're getting our ears pierced," Samantha informed Em. "They can do it right here."

"Oh, no you're not." Em placed her packages on the floor next to her feet. "Your father would kill me if I let you."

"No, he won't, honest. We've talked about it, and he thinks it's a great idea."

"Well, he hasn't talked about it with me."

Immediately, Samantha pressed her lips together and glared at the ceiling.

"Well, I'm getting mine done." Amy motioned to the clerk before Em could respond.

"You're not, either," Em replied, shooing the clerk away. "As long as I'm in charge, you two won't do anything to your bodies without your parents' permission." She picked up her bags. "Come on. Let's get something to eat."

The two girls whispered behind their hands and shot dirty looks at her. Now that they were no longer speaking to her, they lagged behind. Em slowed to a crawl, creating traffic congestion around her. She had no intention of losing them. When they arrived at the food court, the girls bounded in front of her, searching for a place to sit.

Amy zoomed in on the only free table, beating out several other patrons with trays of food, and deposited her bundles. Despite the glares aimed at them, Em appreciated the chance to rest her feet. She plopped down among their packages.

Amy nudged Samantha. "Ask her."

Samantha swatted her back. "No!"

"Ask me what?" Both girls stared at Em, but neither one spoke. Finally, she inquired, "What do you want to eat?"

With a furtive look toward Amy, Samantha leaned across the table. "Are you and Daddy doing it?"

Em scowled. Teenagers. She didn't understand half of their vocabulary. "Doing what?"

"You know." Samantha cupped her hands around her mouth and whispered, "Sex."

The remark was so unexpected Em didn't respond at first. When she could find her voice, she said, "No, we're not. Do you want pizza or sandwiches?"

Samantha sat back. "You've been kissing."

"No we haven't."

"I saw you on the front porch."

Amy moved forward. "We learned in sex education that one thing can lead to the other." She started a nervous giggle then stopped when Samantha punched her arm.

Em drew in a deep breath and whooshed it through her lips. So this was what they'd been talking about since leaving the jewelry shop. Her sex life. Now, there was a topic for curing insomnia. However, until she satisfied their curiosity, they'd probably never get to the food. Em dived into the unfamiliar waters with trepidation.

"You did not see us kissing because we weren't." They had been close, inches apart. *Would* Roger have kissed her if Samantha hadn't shown up so unexpectedly? "We were talking, nothing more. Besides, intimacy between two people requires love and commitment and should be saved until marriage."

The girls looked at each other and said simultaneously, "Yeah, right."

What did she expect? Her ideas were considered old-fashioned when she'd voiced them to Bradley some ten years earlier. Why would today's teenagers support her view? "It's what I believe and practice." Em stood. "Now, are you going to tell me what you want or take potluck?"

"Well, it's not what my father practices."

Em sat down. She never thought of Roger as a person who fooled around. Where would his daughter get that idea?

Samantha leaned across the table again. She looked to the right and left before whispering, "I'm not stupid." She grimaced. "No five-month preemie weighs nearly nine pounds."

Em expelled all the air in her lungs. "Your parents told you that?"

Samantha shook her head and stared at the table. "They never talked about it at all. And when I asked, they said I was cute and lovable and everything they ever wanted."

"Well, I'm sure that's true."

"No, it's not." Samantha's eyes bulged as she looked up at Em. "I was a mistake. They had to get married."

Someone had to provide her with this nonsense. If it wasn't her parents, then who…? "Did your Grandma Millie tell you this?" Em asked.

Samantha pressed her lips together and nodded. Even though Em hadn't met Millie, loathing seeped through her. How could a woman tell such stories to her own grandchild?

"I knew both your parents before they married. They were devoted to each other and planned to spend the rest of their lives together." Em recalled how jealous she had been.

Theirs was a relationship she had longed for, if not with Roger then with someone like him. When she met Bradley, she thought she had met that someone. She hadn't.

"You coming when you did gave them the chance they wanted to be together sooner than they planned. I'm sure they were always grateful for that."

Tears welled in Samantha's eyes. Em reached over and placed her hand on the girl's. "Your father is intimate only with someone he loves and cares about, and I only 'do it' when I'm married. So, you have absolutely nothing to worry about." She gave Samantha's hand a squeeze. "Now, can we eat?"

The topic didn't come up again, although it replayed itself in Em's mind. Roger still loved Karen. It was obvious in the pictures he had throughout the house, in his response to his daughter when she caught them on the porch. Even from the grave, Karen was still a force to reckon with.

CHAPTER SEVEN

"Now what do we do with them?" Roger asked Harve. The boys had set up tents at Lynx Lake in Prescott, gone fishing, played tag, eaten and kicked a soccer ball around. Now they were chasing one another in a loud and frenzied game of Cops and Robbers. Any suggestion that they calm down or play something quiet made no impression.

"I'm all for tying them to a tree."

"I've got a better idea." Roger stood and stretched. "Let's take them for a hike up Thumb Butte."

"Are you kidding?"

"Come on. You need the exercise, and it will tire everyone out."

"I'm already tired out." Harve motioned for Roger to retake his seat on the cloth folding chair. "Your sister wants the lowdown on what's going on with you and the kid's mother. And you know her—she won't be satisfied unless I come home with a full report."

"Nothing's going on."

Harve guffawed. "Yeah, right. I saw you holding each other this morning. That was definitely something."

"It wasn't." Roger stared into the distance, remembering how much fun he'd had teasing Em. He controlled his voice and the smile that played around his lips. "I mean it."

"Well, think of something or I will. Jodie made a promise to Karen...."

Roger snapped his head toward Harve. "She what?"

"Before Karen died she made Jodie promise to find someone for you."

Roger sat back. "So that's why she's on my case all the time."

"Right. And if you want her off it, start something up with Em. That doesn't seem like it'd be any problem."

Roger eyed him before turning his attention back to the boys. "Yeah, so I like her. But..." He paused, glanced at Harve then looked away. "You're going to think I'm crazy."

"Probably." When Roger didn't continue, Harve probed, "So, what's this big dilemma you have?"

Roger blew out his breath loudly before saying, "Guilt."

"Guilt? You are crazy. You figure Karen's going to care?"

"Of course not. It's just…I can't seem to get past it."

Harve leaned closer. "You planning to never date again for the rest of your life?"

"No." Thoughts of Em had destroyed his concentration on numerous occasions. Roger took a deep breath and exhaled before adding, "The timing's not right. Over the next six months, I'll be in Seattle most of the time. And then I've got no job, no prospects."

"I didn't say you had to marry her. Date her once or twice." Harve gave him a whack on the arm and leaned back in his chair. "Make your sister happy."

Amusement bubbled as Roger replied, "What did my sister ever see in you?"

"What every woman wants." Harve grinned and turned to Roger. "Love and commitment." He sat up and said, "So, should I tell Jodie you're going to ask Em out?"

Roger made a fist and shook it in front of his brother-in-law's face. "You do and you'll be wearing this. Now, come on. Get off your butt. We have to do something with those boys before they destroy the campsite."

"Okay," Harve said, as he pushed himself out of the folding chair. "Except next time you get a bright idea to go camping, don't bother to invite me along. I've aged ten years since this morning."

But before they could call the boys in, a buzz sounded from Roger's pocket. He took out his cell phone and checked the number. "Oh, for Pete's sake. It's Millie. What could she want this time?" he said, debating whether to answer.

"Your mother-in-law?" When Roger didn't reply, Harve continued. "It could be important."

"Everything with that woman is important. She makes mountains out of molehills." Reluctantly, he clicked on the receiver.

"How come you're in Prescott?" Millie said as soon as Roger greeted her.

"How did you know I was here?"

"Your Spanish woman told me, and I'm really disappointed, Roger. You could have brought the boys here to camp. You know it's cooler in Flagstaff and not that much farther."

As usual, the whine in Millie's voice set him off, but he tried to keep his tone level. "It was a spur-of-the-minute thing, and several friends came along with us. I wouldn't want to put you out."

"Well, you certainly could have dropped Samantha off. I would have loved to take her shopping. We have marvelous stores here. I really don't understand why you don't include me more in your plans."

Roger considered the extra hour it would have taken to deliver his daughter to her grandmother. The time wasted as well as the difference in their tastes and ages. Samantha would never have settled for that. Still trying to be diplomatic, Roger said, "I apologize. Maybe next time."

"And don't forget about my offer to watch the children. I expect to hear from you on that."

As soon as Roger disconnected, Harve asked, "Problem?"

"Millie wants to take care of the kids when Sophia leaves."

Harve laughed. "Millie? You've got to be kidding."

"I wish." Roger replaced the phone in his pocket. "I sure hope I don't get that desperate," he mumbled before rounding up the boys.

AN HOUR LATER they parked in the pine forest beneath Thumb Butte. "Let's take the steep trail," Harve's son said when they stood at a fork in the path.

Roger placed a hand on Timothy's shoulder and directed him to the gentler, slower course. "We don't want to tire the younger boys out, sport. We'll follow the other trail when we come down."

As the boys raced off ahead of them, Harve caught up. "Right. We don't want to slow the younger boys down. Ha! If I have a heart attack today, I'm suing you for every dime you own."

"Stop the lawyer talk and enjoy the clean air." Roger filled his lungs with the fresh scent of pine. He loved the tall trees and the rough terrain. "This reminds me of the outskirts of Seattle. The boys would really enjoy it there—hiking, sailing, fishing."

"Maybe you can take them for a vacation, once your life returns to normal," Harve suggested.

Harve *would* have to remind him of his problems, just when Roger had finally put them out of his mind. He hurried ahead, adding, "Wait till you see the view. Spectacular."

While Harve trudged behind, Roger cautioned the boys not to get too far ahead. But he had nothing to worry about. Fatigue had finally gotten to them. Sammy lagged behind and the twins slowed to stay with him. Roger was about to pass them and catch up with his nephew, when the unnatural sound of Sammy's breathing stopped him.

"You all right?"

When Sammy didn't answer, Roger dropped

to one knee and grabbed the boy's shoulders. His face had turned pasty. Cold sweat dampened Roger's brow as Sammy pulled in another ragged breath.

"Your medication! Where is it?"

Panic flashed through Sammy's eyes. "My backpack," he wheezed.

One of the twins spoke up. "He left it in the van. Want me to go get it?"

"No, son. You stay here." Roger swatted his shirt pocket, searching for Em's note. He'd perused it earlier, and could remember only one of the details: if Sammy didn't respond to his medication, get him to a hospital. His nephew rejoined them just as Harve came into sight.

"You guys stick together," Roger said to the group, "while I carry him back to the van." He hoisted Sammy into his arms and started down the trail.

"Harve, stay with the boys. Follow the trail up and meet me back at the van when you're done." Already his mind raced ahead. "If we're not there…" He paused. "Take my phone, just in case."

"That's okay. I've got my own," Harve said, patting his back pocket. He gave Sammy a thumbs-up as he touched him on the shoulder. "Hang in there, kid. You're in good hands."

Sammy's tortured breathing rattled in Roger's ear, and he tried not to show the terror he felt every time the boy drew a breath. All the way down the slope to the van, Roger chastised himself for not taking Em's concerns seriously. He'd always considered asthma nothing more than an excuse—something wimps used to get out of doing what they didn't want to do. But Sammy was no wimp. He horsed around with as much gusto as all the other boys combined.

Once they reached the van, Roger found two inhalers in the boy's backpack. At least the boy knew exactly what to do and handled the inhalers with ease. Sammy tried one and, when that didn't provide any relief, Roger handed him the other. He willed the boy to breathe and found his own breath catching in his throat.

Abandoning the inhalers, Roger placed Sammy in the van and roared off. He stopped a patrol car and asked the police officer where he could find the nearest hospital. Fifteen minutes later he was in the emergency room at the Medical Center in Prescott.

HARVE'S LAST WORDS stuck in Roger's mind as he stared at his hands, *You're in good hands*. Roger slammed a fist into his palm then dragged both hands through his hair. How could this beautiful day have gone so wrong? How could he jeopardize a boy's life by being so callous? What was he going to tell Em? That he'd lost her note somewhere in the parking lot? Of all the stupid... Afraid no one would take care of Sammy without Em's permission note, he'd said the first thing that came to mind... "Please help my son, he can't breathe." A nurse approached, and Roger hurried to get an update.

"Your son will be fine, Mr. Holden," the heavy woman said when he reached her. Roger gripped the back of his neck where the tension had settled.

"You sure?"

"He's a brave little boy, and he's responding well to the medication. We do want to keep him overnight, though, just to make sure everything's all right. We're taking him to a room now. We'll put a cot in there for you as well if you'd like to spend the night with him."

Tension around his neck and shoulders eased. Sammy was going to live. For a while there, Roger thought no one so small with such difficulty breathing could ever pull through. He pulled the stout woman into a bear hug. "Thank you. I'll be back in a minute."

Roger raced to the waiting room, where the boys lounged in a semistupor. Fortunately, Harve had been able to call a taxi so they hadn't been waiting forever at the park.

Harve rose to his feet. "How's he doing?"

"Fine. Fine. Did you reach Em, yet?"

"I got her mother. She'll have Em call as soon as she gets home."

"Did you tell her?"

"No. Said the boy was homesick and wanted to talk to her. Figured I'd keep it vague and let you tell her when you knew more."

"I better get back to her. She should know what happened. At least now I can give her some good news."

"Okay if we leave? They're finally ready for bed. I know I am."

Harve jingled the keys and the boys responded by slowly getting to their feet and rallying around him. While Timothy stayed with his father, the twins came over and wrapped their arms around Roger's legs.

One of them looked up. "Will he be all right, Daddy?"

Roger squeezed the twins against his body, thankful that they were healthy. "He'll be fine."

Harve tapped him on the arm. "You staying here for the night?"

Roger nodded.

"You got my cell-phone number?"

Roger nodded again.

"Give me a call if anything…"

"You'll be the first." With a nod and a wave,

Roger turned and headed for a quiet corner where he could call Em.

He sat on his haunches, taking deep breaths, pumping himself up for the call. Finally, he dialed the numbers and waited while the phone rang.

"Hello, Doris. I need to talk to Em. Has she returned yet?"

"No. Is there a problem? Harve called before...."

Roger slumped on the floor and leaned against the wall. "Sammy had an attack...."

"Oh, my God! Is he...?"

"He's fine. We're at the hospital, and he's responding to the medication. I need to contact Em."

"Well, she hasn't returned yet. Have you phoned your place? She took Samantha shopping."

Roger glanced at his watch. They should have finished that chore hours ago. When he'd phoned earlier, no one had answered, and he hadn't left a message on the machine. Where could they all be?

"I'll try my place again, but if she comes home, have her call me. And tell her not to worry. Sammy's fine. They just need to watch him overnight." He rose to his feet and gave

Doris the numbers for the hospital and his cell phone.

A moment later he dialed his home. Sophia answered. Roger closed his eyes in relief. At least someone was there.

"Have you seen Em?"

"Oh, yes," Sophia said in her thick accent. "She's here. We're watching videos. Nice lady. You should have her over for dinner one time before I go. I make enchiladas."

"Put her on, please," Roger said, "I need to speak to her." How could he break it to her gently, the least traumatic way, so she wouldn't panic? He'd pondered it since he'd witnessed Sammy's first ragged breath. Nothing he thought of could diminish the fear she'd experience once he explained what happened. When Em came on the line, he searched for words.

"There's a problem."

"With Sammy? Tell me."

"He's in the hospital," he blurted and waited for the hysteria.

"Which one?" No crying, no emotion, just a calm voice asking a simple question. When he told her, she said, "I'm driving up."

"No. It's two hours away, and there's no need. I'll bring him home as soon as he's released tomorrow morning."

"I'll see you in two hours."

The line went dead. Em might not be show-ing it now, but by the time she reached Prescott, she'd be a basket case. He'd seen it happen with Karen, who had had difficulty handling every problem from her pregnancy with Samantha to her terminal bout with cancer.

Em would blame him for Sammy's condi-tion. And he deserved every rotten thing she could spew at him.

EM DROVE NORTH on I-17, cursing the seventy-five-miles-per-hour speed limit. She acceler-ated. Roger said Sammy was okay. She'd focus on that. He's okay. Still, the hospital would cost a fortune, and all she had was a pittance in her checking account. She'd have to use her credit card and return everything she'd bought today so the card wouldn't max out.

The doctor had warned her that altitude could make normal exertion a problem for Sammy's lungs. Why hadn't some warning light gone off in her brain when Roger had mentioned Prescott, the mile-high city? *Be-cause, you damn fool, you knew how much Sammy would enjoy such an outing.*

When the speed limit on the turnoff to Prescott dropped to sixty-five, she could barely tolerate the snail's pace. But her having an acci-dent would do Sammy little good, so she stayed within the speed limit. By concentrating on her driving, she kept the panic from creeping into her throat and cutting off her oxygen. Thanks to the GPS in her cell phone, she had no trouble finding the Medical Center, but it was 10:00 p.m. by the time she walked through the door. She found Roger sitting in the waiting room, leaning forward, his hands folded between his knees. He jumped up the moment he saw her.

"Em. He's doing fine. You shouldn't have come."

"Where is he? I need to see him."

Roger looked worn-out, worse than she felt, his dark-brown hair unkempt as though he'd used his fingers to comb it. Her heart warmed to him for all that he'd gone through for the sake of her son's health.

"Em, there are things we need to discuss."

"Later. What room's he in?" She swept past him.

"I'll show you," he said, catching up to her.

They stopped inside the door. Sammy looked so small in the large bed. Her little boy, her joy in life. She ran to his bedside and stood over him, watching for any signs of distress. His breathing was slow and natural.

She turned to Roger, who had come up beside her. "Thanks, for everything," she whispered. "You probably saved his life." Her voice caught in her throat, and she pressed her lips together.

When he pulled her into his arms and held her close, she crushed her face against his chest for a moment and drew the mixture of soap and sweat deep into her lungs, taking strength from his embrace. But she mustn't think like that now. She pushed away and leaned over Sammy's bed.

When she ran her fingers through his blond hair, he stirred. He opened his eyes and smiled. "Oh, Sammy. I'm sorry, honey. I didn't mean to wake you."

"S'okay. Don't call me Sammy, Ma."

"Sorry," she said, unable to control her grin. He had to be better if he was correcting her. "I'll try and remember, J.R." To see him breathing without a wheeze or hacking cough was wonderful.

"No. Not that name. Call me The Bus." He accentuated the two words as though they held equal weight.

"The what?"

"The Bus, like this guy on the football team."

Roger leaned closer. "The Pittsburgh Steelers." He did a little finger wave at Sammy, who grinned back.

Em looked at Sammy with a confused frown. "Why do you want to be called The Bus?"

"Cause he has asthma, too, and I'm goin' to be just like him. Right, Dad?"

Em's spine went rigid. One day away from her and her son had fixated on Roger. Or had Roger instructed him to call him Dad? "Did you tell him to call you that?"

Roger shrugged. "It's something a sports announcer mentioned last season. I thought…"

"That's not what I'm referring to. We've got to talk." She moved back to Sammy and kissed him on the forehead. "I'll be here all night, and I'll drive you home tomorrow."

"Can't I go home with Dad and my brothers?"

Em seethed, but she kept her face calm. "We'll talk about it tomorrow."

She grabbed hold of Roger's elbow and spun him around. The moment they were safely past the nurses' station she lit into him. "How could you?"

"So the kid wants to be called The Bus. It got his mind off his problems. Next week he'll want to be called something else."

"I don't care about that!" she said, raising her voice and poking him in the chest. "He called you Dad, and you didn't blink an eye."

Roger grabbed her hand and placed a finger over his lips as he glanced from side to side. "I told him to."

Appalled, Em stood motionless. "You told him? How can you play with my child's emotions that way?"

"Em, listen," Roger said as he released her hand and grasped her arms above her elbows. "He knows it's just for today."

"You have no idea what you've started. His father never paid this much attention to him—taking him camping, dealing with his sickness. He's fixated on you, and the trauma this will create…"

"He's a bright kid. He knows it's so we could fool the hospital. Otherwise, they might not have taken him in."

"Why would you have to fool the hospital? I gave you permission in my note to stand in for me in any emergency." She felt anger building in her body, ready to explode through her pores. "Where's my note?" She struggled to get free of his grip, but he held tight.

"I was reading it and then…I must have lost it. In the parking lot, I think. That's the last time I saw it."

"You told him to lie!" Em used all her strength to shrug out of his grip and move away. "You filled out papers saying he's your son. That's fraud." She covered her face and gasped, trying her best not to burst into tears.

"I don't believe this," Roger said, starting

to pace in front of her. "You're calm as can be about your son's near-death emergency, and you fall apart over my getting him into the hospital."

Once Sammy's emergency was over, she could focus on other problems. And Roger obviously had no idea what problems he faced. "It's illegal. You could lose your insurance. You have no idea how devastating that can be."

"There's nothing to worry about. I paid with my credit card so it won't go through the insurance. No fraud there, and I only did that to get him admitted. You're here now, so you can tell them verbally I had your permission if the question ever comes up."

"Well, you're not paying for it—I am. I'll do it right now." She whirled and headed down the hall, anywhere just to get away from him. Now that she no longer had to remain strong, she didn't want Roger to see her lose all her control and bawl like a baby.

"Tomorrow, Em, tomorrow when we take him home," he said right near her ear. She felt the gentle pressure of his hands on her shoulders and stopped.

"You're not taking him home. I am." Still defiant, she spat the words through tight lips. He eased closer. His body, when it pressed against her, destroyed the last of her willpower.

"Harve's driving the boys home in the morning," he said as he turned her around and enclosed her in his comforting arms. "I'm coming with you." His lips moved against her forehead and along her ear. All her control slipped away, and she convulsed with the tears she had kept dammed up inside her.

He held her tightly to him as she cried. "Let it out, Em," he whispered in her ear. "Let it all out."

CHAPTER EIGHT

EM LAY ON the cot set up by Sammy's bed. She held his hand, watched his small form, and thanked God for his even breathing. How many times had she monitored him in the past, waiting for a change that might mean another attack? How many times would she repeat this same vigil in the future?

"How's he doing?" Roger whispered.

She released Sammy's hand and turned to see Roger's face in the dim light. "Better," she said as she raised herself to a sitting position and dropped her bare feet to the floor.

"Don't get up. I didn't mean to disturb you."

"Where have you been? Did they get a cot for you, too?"

Roger flipped around and pointed to the hall. "No. I've been talking to Harve."

"He's here?" It had to be close to midnight. She got off the cot and stretched. Oh, it felt good to relieve those tense muscles.

"No. He's camping with the boys. We've been talking on our cell phones to keep everyone up to date. The boys were really worried. We all were."

"Sammy's okay. He'll need a lot of rest, but he's doing fine." Em paused. "I should never have let him come. The elevation is too high for him. I should have realized it." She pressed her knuckles against her lips as she gazed down on her precious little boy.

Roger came up behind her and began to gently massage her shoulders. She leaned into him, enjoying the healing touch. "How are *you* holding up?" he asked.

"Fine."

"Not if you're kicking yourself for being a bad parent every time Sammy gets an attack. Things happen, and we just have to handle them the best way we can."

She felt his warm breath near her ear reassuring her. If only she could relax and forget her troubles. His manipulating her shoulders was going a long way toward that.

"Come and sit over here," he said, and led her to one of the chairs. He took the other and pulled it closer so that the armrests touched. "How was your day with my daughter?"

Em started to chuckle. "Interesting, to say the least."

"Am I in hock for one or two million dollars?"

Sammy stirred and Em leaned closer to Roger so she could keep her voice low. "Actually, you got off cheap. Samantha watched the prices very closely and only bought things on sale. And I managed to bring her home safe and sound without any tattoos or body piercings."

"What!"

Em quickly placed a finger over Roger's lips to avoid any further outbursts. "She wanted her ears pierced, but I put my foot down. That's something she'll have to discuss with you. And," Em continued, not allowing him to interrupt, "she got some bras. I also found out why she has avoided it until now. Someone told her bras cause breast cancer."

Roger pulled Em's hand from his face and cupped it between his hands. "Who would say such nonsense?" he asked, his forehead turning into a mass of furrows.

"I looked it up on the internet and there actually are people who believe it. However, I think it came from her Grandma Millie."

With an exaggerated sigh, Roger slumped against the chair, pulling Em's hand against his chest. "Karen's mother. She means well but she's a few cards shy of a full deck." He placed his free arm around Em's shoulders, drawing her closer.

A nurse entered to check on Sammy. "He's

doing well," she said as she paused by Em and Roger. "I didn't know both parents would be here. I'll see to having another cot brought in."

Em nodded. Good. He'd have a place to sleep, as well. She yawned and placed one foot on her knee. Her feet still ached from hiking around the shopping center. She began massaging her foot.

"Here, let me do that." Roger released her other hand and removed his arm from her shoulders. Grasping her foot with both hands, he started to knead it with expert fingers.

"You're good."

"I've had lots of practice."

"Karen?" Em asked.

Roger nodded. "It helped her relax."

After giving her several minutes of pure pleasure, Roger released that foot and reached for the other one. When he was done, Em curled up in the chair and leaned against him, their heads touching. Her eyes drooped shut. Such comfort. She couldn't remember the last time she had felt so content or so safe.

As Em drifted to sleep against his cheek, Roger held on to the moment. Their quiet talk while he massaged her feet had gone a long way to relax him, as well. He needed that intimacy, the feel of another person. He'd missed it so much.

He remembered the nurse's remark and a grin started that he couldn't suppress. Auntie Em as his wife. Either Em had been too tired to pay any attention to the nurse's comment, or it hadn't affected her.

How well she fit against him. He noted her soft hair and how nice it felt touching his face, its pleasant smell. Herbs probably, as in the commercials. He moved his lips against her forehead. So smooth. So cool.

Maybe he should wake her. She needed sleep, after all, and the cot would provide the most comfort. But he didn't move. He liked the warm body snuggling against him.

He awoke when the nurse came in to check again on Sammy. Roger's arm had gone to sleep and his neck had a crick that required massaging. Once the nurse left, he lifted Em and placed her on her cot. He leaned over and kissed her on the cheek.

"Good night, Auntie Em," he whispered before heading for his own cot. But sleep refused to come. He stayed awake, listening to her even breathing.

THE FOLLOWING MORNING, Em woke to someone gently pulling her hand. At first she thought it might be Roger, but when she opened her eyes, Sammy grinned back at her.

"Hi, Mom." He had powdered sugar around his mouth and a definite jelly stain on his shirt.

"Hi, yourself." When had she climbed onto the cot? Em pulled herself to a sitting position and glanced around the room. Roger's folded cot stood near the door. Where had he slept?

A box of doughnuts sat on the table.

"Who brought those?" she asked.

"Chip and Chaz," Roger said from the doorway. "It was our camping breakfast, and the boys brought the box over before they headed home."

Doughnuts, really? Em realized she should have looked into this camping business more thoroughly. What else had they had for meals?

"And heading home is what we should do. Right, sport?" Roger slapped the top of a wheelchair and indicated Sammy should take a seat.

Later, when Em went to pay the bill, she said, "I want to pay for the entire medical bill with this." Why was the woman looking so intently at her credit card?

"Aren't you Mrs. Holden? This says Turner. And your husband gave his credit card to us yesterday."

"My husband?" The word still conjured up Bradley, and for a moment, Em tried to sort out the mixed signals bouncing in her brain. Had someone contacted Bradley? Had the nurse really called her Mrs. Holden?

Em glanced in Roger's direction. What stories had he told these people? What problems would he face if she told the truth?

Willing herself to stay calm, Em decided to be honest. "Sammy is my son and Mr. Holden had my permission…" She paused and took a deep breath. "…to act on my behalf in an emergency. Which he did, and I'm very grateful. But all the expenses are mine." Em pushed her credit card toward the woman again. This time she took it without further comment.

When Roger placed a hand on Em's shoulder, she nearly jumped. Her purse skittered to the floor, and Roger bent over to retrieve it.

"You sure you can cover it all?" he asked.

Em looked at the printed bill and nodded. She'd be fine as long as she didn't eat anything for the next month. She'd manage. Her son was safe, recovering. All because of Roger. Together they pushed Sammy out to the parking lot."I want to thank you for last night," she said, when they reached her van. "That massage…it really helped me unwind. I…"

"It worked for me, too." Roger opened the door for Sammy. "It brought back so many happy memories with Karen."

Em's jaw tightened, and she made an attempt

to swallow the lump that had materialized when he mentioned his wife. His dead wife.

EM DROVE THE scenic road through Skull Valley rather than head back to Phoenix on I-17. Not because she wanted to. She'd have preferred the faster route, so she could get Sammy home quickly. But someone rushing into the hospital had mentioned that an accident had tied I-17 into a horrendous traffic jam. That could entail hours of delay. Either way, it meant too many hours with Roger.

Fortunately, he had folded his arms across his chest, slumped against the passenger door and fallen asleep. At least she wouldn't have to provide conversation. Right now, she couldn't get any words past the tightness in her throat.

Once they began their trip, Em focused on the awesome stretch of valleys surrounded by distant mountains. They reflected her life. Soaring spectacular heights such as last night's closeness with Roger, and plunges into deep ravines when he spoke of times with his wife. Em was alive. Couldn't he respond to that?

She had no intention of continuing this roller-coaster ride. If he couldn't forget Karen, so be it. Em had managed the past fifteen years without his warmth and caresses; she could manage at least that many in the future. Besides, all that pretending to be his wife at the hospital had little to do with reality. She'd never hook up with anyone who had lost his job. Bradley had taught her that lesson. No way would she support another man, let alone one with three children.

The road curved back and forth, often on the rim of a precipice. Sammy slept in the seat behind her. At least he was getting the rest he needed. Concentrating on the task of driving helped take her mind off her worries. Except for a few curves that required she slow down, the trip into Phoenix was uneventful.

ROGER WASN'T ENJOYING the journey, however. He sat only a couple of feet from Em with his eyes closed. Was the cool air fanning his cheek from the air conditioner or from the iceberg driving the van? He'd never seen anyone shut down the way Em had when he'd mentioned Karen. Shades dropped, lights went out, all because he said something about pleasant memories with his wife.

What he'd meant to say… What he should have said… Damn it. He hadn't been thinking of Karen at all when he'd held Em in his arms.

He had enjoyed the feel of Em, her hair against his face, the light sound of her breathing. All those things that he had enjoyed with

Karen had reappeared with another person. He never thought it could happen again. What a bungled mess. How could he ever repair the terrible crack he had created? Crack, nothing. He'd created a hole the size of the Grand Canyon.

He continued to pretend sleep, even after Sammy woke and began a nonstop discussion of the previous day. He mentioned The Bus, and despite Roger's foul mood, he smiled to himself.

"Sammy, give it a break." No way was Em going to call him The Bus. "Mr. Holden's trying to sleep."

Roger straightened and turned to face her. "It's okay. I was just thinking."

Sammy leaned over Roger's seat and said, "We goin' campin' again sometime, Dad?"

"Get your seat belt back on," Em shouted.

Sammy mumbled something about her, but Em was too furious to respond. The road was now curving dangerously. Otherwise, she would have directed all her anger at Roger. She hadn't confronted him about calling Sammy his son. Not in the boy's presence, anyway. Yet the animosity she felt over the deception still smoldered beneath the surface.

"You have to stop using that dad stuff, sport. Your mother doesn't like it."

Em pulled into the first safe turnoff she could find and stopped the car. "Don't you make me out to be the villain," she said, unsnapping her seat belt and focusing all her frustration on Roger. "You take care of this here and now or your head will be one more added to Skull Valley."

She pushed open the car door, grabbed her purse and got out. Oh, how she needed a cigarette right now. Something to calm her, or she might very well carry out her threat.

Em headed down the road at a fair clip with the intention of lighting up once she got past one of the boulders. She rummaged through her purse, looking for the cigarettes Samantha had given her. She stopped, pulled out the pack and stared at it. After Sammy's attack, how could she even consider such a thing? With a quick toss, the pack flew into the air, then dropped cigarettes among the brambles that lined the road. Slowly, she turned and headed back.

Em waited a good distance from the car, concentrating on one of the jagged mountains that rimmed the valley they were now in. Why did she have to bump into Roger at Metro? Every current problem in her life stemmed from that one chance encounter.

Something small and warm slipped into her

hand. She looked down into the upturned face of a contrite Sammy. "Sorry, Ma," he said and squeezed her hand. She squeezed back.

"We're not going to have this problem again?"

Sammy sighed. "Nope. Mr. Holden says I only have one dad. Besides, he's got too many kids callin' him that now."

Relief flooded Em. At least she wouldn't have to deal with that problem on a daily basis. She wasn't too sure what Sammy understood about the lying part, but she could wait and cover that problem later. She picked him up and wrapped him in a bear hug. "I love you."

"Me, too." He planted a wet kiss on her nose before wiggling down and running to the car.

Roger waited, draped over the open passenger door. He smiled and said, "Sorry, Ma," before slipping back into the front seat.

Darn him. She wanted to punch him and hug him at the same time. She decided to relax and put all the trauma behind them. It was a beautiful day in the cool mountain air. She could afford to be generous.

A few minutes later, he said, "Em, I have a problem you might be able to help me with. Sophia is leaving."

"I know. She told me about remarrying and going back to Tucson when I met her yesterday. She'll be hard to replace. Samantha adores her."

"Her departure is going to be hard on everyone. Sophia's been part of the family since the twins were born. You know anyone good with kids looking for a live-in job?"

Em thought a moment and shook her head. "I can ask my mother, though. She might know someone."

"Why don't you ask Grandma to do it? She's great with kids," Sammy said near her ear.

"You get back into that seat belt, and I don't want to see you out of it again." She checked the rearview mirror just to make sure he followed her order. He muttered again. Maybe she had been too harsh, but his suggestion hit a nerve. They couldn't afford the apartment if her mother moved out.

"Wasn't your mother a teacher before she retired?"

"Yes" came from the backseat. "And she's gettin' bored, Ma. She told me the other day…"

"Sammy, you stay out of this. Grandma is not going back to work." Just saying the words brought a niggling doubt to her mind. Hadn't her mother said something the other day? No. She'd never want a full-time job that didn't end when the school bell rang.

"You don't want her to work?" Roger asked.

"That's not the point. She spent thirty-five years teaching second graders. She's earned a break, a chance to enjoy life and play for a change."

"She can play with us," Sammy piped in. "We need someone to pitch the baseball, and she's good at it."

"Oh, she's a good baseball player. Sounds like perfect credentials for the job."

"Roger, please. Drop the subject. I can't afford the rent and other expenses on my own. If she moves out…"

"I understand." He crossed his arms over his chest and stared out the front window.

"I don't just lose money, I lose family, our first real family in years," Em said, raising her voice despite her attempt to control it.

Roger remained silent for a long time, and Em felt relieved that the subject had died. She concentrated on driving down the steep mountain road that brought them into the valley north of Wickenburg. Sammy had remained close-lipped, too, and she checked the rearview mirror. He had fallen asleep again.

ROGER MUSED OVER their conversation. Em might need financial support and a baby-sitter for Sammy, but right now he was desperate. He needed someone to look after the kids while he was away at work, provide meals and keep the house in order, especially during those times when he'd have to travel to Seattle. He'd contacted agencies to help with his selection, but none of the applicants gave him the confidence he needed.

And he certainly wouldn't consider Millie. If he didn't find someone soon, she'd be hounding him about it, insisting she could replace Sophia. How could he tell her no without hurting her feelings? As much as he disliked the woman, he didn't want to alienate her.

Doris would be perfect. As his mother's best friend, he'd met her on several occasions. Their last encounter at Em's apartment had made a favorable impression on him as well, and as a former teacher, she was well suited to take care of children.

As long as he was working, he could help Em financially. By next summer, his severance would kick in. That should be enough time to straighten out his life. And Sammy could come to his house after school until Em picked him up. It was the most logical solution. But he didn't dare spring it on Em while she was driving and risk an early grave.

After they crossed over the wide dry bed of the Hassayampa River, Roger said, "I'm getting hungry." He turned around in his seat. "What about you?" Sammy opened his eyes and gave him a drowsy smile. Roger had to control the urge to add "son," the word that came so naturally to his lips when he spoke to his own boys. That particular endearing term would send Em ballistic again. Boy, she could make the biggest deal out of nothing.

When they pulled to a stop in the parking lot of a fast-food restaurant, he decided to spring his decision on her. "I'm going to speak to your mother, Em. Doris might go for the idea of living with my family, and I have to hire someone I can trust. I'll figure out something to cover your expenses and take care of Sammy while you're at work."

"You'll work it out? Oh, that's just great!" If Em wasn't restrained in her seat.... She looked furious. Roger opened the door, ready to make a quick exit.

"Think about it, Em. She'll have her own suite with a private entrance. We'll work it so everyone's happy. What do you say? At least let me ask her."

Sammy appeared and hung over the seat, cutting off eye contact with Em. "Can we come and live with you, too?"

Roger didn't know how to reply, so he remained motionless while Sammy continued.

"I can sleep with Chip and Chaz, and Mom can stay with Grandma. Then we won't need that old apartment anymore." Sammy snapped his mouth shut into a self-satisfied grin, tossed his hands in the air and waited for a response.

The boy had a practical mind, a solution to every problem, and what he said made logical sense. Roger snuck a peek at Em. From her expression, he knew she didn't care for the idea at all.

"Oh, boy." Roger got out and stood by the car door. "Let's get something to eat." He opened the back door and grabbed Sammy's hand. "We're going to need nourishment to handle the fallout."

CHAPTER NINE

ROGER AND SAMMY walked hand in hand into the restaurant without a backward glance at Em. *Fallout? Exactly what did Roger mean by that?* She started to chuckle, thankful the two men in her life weren't able to hear her laughing, because they could never understand what she considered so funny.

The expression on Sammy's face had been precious. He believed he had come up with a solution equal to that of solving world hunger. It was so completely off the wall that it couldn't be taken seriously. Yet, Roger actually believed she'd be upset with her son's innocent remark.

Em opened the door of the car and got out into the hot air. Already she missed the cooler weather they'd left behind in Prescott.

Once in the restaurant, she started to chuckle again and put her hand over her mouth to try to control her laughter. Roger raised one eyebrow as she approached.

"Don't worry. I'm not going to blow up."

"Really? You like the idea then?"

Em laughed outright, unable to hold it in any longer. "No. I just think we're wasting a lot of energy. My mother hasn't even been approached about your offer, so we're arguing over a moot point."

"What's a mood point?" Sammy asked.

Without correcting his pronunciation, she said, "Something that's not worth worrying about because it will never happen."

Roger picked up their tray, loaded with wrapped food, and headed for a table. "Well, if you're not going to loan me your mother, will you help me check out the applicants?" He sat down and began distributing the food. "The agency is sending over two prospects I have to interview. I'd appreciate any input you can give me."

"Why not ask Samantha to help?"

Roger sat back, his jaw dropping a bit before he closed his mouth. "You got to be kidding. I should ask for a thirteen-year-old's opinion about something this important?"

"Yes. She knows what has to be done. Besides, you'll want her to work with the person and not create a problem. If she's involved in the process, she'll be more inclined toward making it work."

Roger popped a French fry in his mouth and winked at her son. "I like Sammy's idea better."

"In your dreams."

"Is she going to blow up now?"

"Boom!" Em said as she threw her arms out to imitate an explosion. "I just blew up." Sammy started to giggle, and Roger joined in.

At that moment Em realized she'd never been happier, laughing with the two of them. Her son was well, after a harrowing experience, and she sat across from the man of her dreams, someone who treated her son as though he were his own. Sammy had a companionship he'd never experienced with his own father. If only this could go on forever.

She yearned for this man to love and cherish them both, make them part of his own. But she could never replace Karen. His dead wife stood between them, preventing any permanent relationship. Fifteen years ago, Em had tried to break the bond between them and failed miserably. What chance did she have now that the bond had grown stronger?

Em's thoughts sobered her, but she refused to let them dampen her present mood. At least she had these few precious moments of happiness to treasure.

"WHAT'S THIS MOOD thing that makes you explode?" her mother asked Em the Monday after she returned from Prescott. They were preparing supper, and Em finished placing the dishes on the table before reaching for the silverware.

"You been talking to Sammy?"

"Not exactly. He talks nonstop with his new friends on the phone, and this mood thing kept coming up. When I asked him about it, he said it makes you explode. It have something to do with his trip to the hospital?"

"No."

"If I'm prying…?"

"No, it's not that. Sammy's mispronouncing m-o-o-t, for moot point, involving a silly tiff I had with Roger. It became a joke."

"So—what's the joke? I like a good laugh."

Should Em explain? What if her mother liked the idea of taking care of someone else's children in a large home? Em collapsed on the dining room chair and indicated her mother should do the same. Doris gingerly took the seat opposite her. "You're not going to explode, are you?"

Em chuckled and reached for her mother's hand. "No, but this whole blowup business involves you."

Doris pulled her hand free and placed it on her cheek. "Me? What did I do?"

Em stretched across the table and took her hand again. "Nothing, Mom. It's just that Sammy said—you were thinking about getting a job. You're bored home alone."

Doris laughed as she patted her daughter's hand. "That boy picks up on everything."

"Then you do want to go back to work?"

"Oh, Em, I looked forward to early retirement, but I miss the kids, the routine." She smiled and leaned across the table. "Sammy and I have such fun together, but once he's off to school..." Doris sat back and looked around the room. "How many times can I clean this small apartment?"

A chill ran down Em's spine. Maybe working for Roger would suit her mother's needs. It certainly would provide enough activity, as well as enough children, to fill her day. "I never realized you were unhappy."

"Oh, posh." Doris waved dismissively and got up from the table. "I'm not complaining. This is a wonderful time in my life, and I have loads of options. I'll put in my application to do substitute teaching. They always need people, and I can work out my schedule to be home when Sammy's here. Now, let's put dinner on the table before it gets cold."

Em rose from the table, unwilling to tell her mother anything more about Roger's need for a housekeeper. It could be a moot point, again, since Roger was interviewing candidates tonight. If one worked out, there'd be no need to look for anyone else. But if it didn't... Roger had little time left, and her mother did want a job.

When Em joined her mother to help with the dishes, Doris pointed a sudsy finger at several crushed pieces of paper. "I did the laundry today. Those things were stuffed in one of your pockets. Anything you want to keep?"

Em put the dishtowel down and reached for the receipts her ex had sent her. She sighed disgustedly. "Bradley expects me to pay for his college expenses. Look at this." Em flipped over the one with his writing. "Can you believe it?"

Doris squinted at the papers then returned to her dishes. "Are you going to?"

"Are you kidding?" With a flick of her wrist, Em sent the papers toward the wastepaper basket. Only one made it, and she had to bend over to pick up the rest. "I don't owe that creep a dime." This time she deposited the receipts in the receptacle.

"Give me five," Doris said, her hand raised. Em slapped her hand, sending soap suds in every direction.

That evening, Em stayed dressed in her business attire of beige silk suit and turquoise shell, which she'd worn to work that day. She wanted to look professional while helping Roger with his interviews. Could she be objective? Her

own financial fears and mixed emotions mud-
dled her thoughts as she approached Roger's
home.

DURING THE FIRST interview, the candidate took
herself out of the running. She wanted her
weekends free, an impossibility under the present circumstances. Roger walked the woman
to the door, thanked her and returned to the
living room, where Em and Samantha sat on
the couch.

Sophia had dismissed herself early from the
interview, saying too many cooks spoiled the
soup. He didn't bother to argue. Four of them
tossing questions could be intimidating to anyone seeking the job.

Em had said little. She looked untouchable,
her hair pulled to the back of her head in the
same style she'd worn the first time he'd run
into her at Metro. Whereas he and Samantha
were both dressed in shorts and knit T-shirts,
Em wore a suit. On several occasions he noticed her taking a furtive glance at Karen's portrait. Em looked about as uncomfortable as he
felt under Karen's watchful gaze. How come
the picture never bothered him before? He'd
take it down the first opportunity he had and
give it back to Millie.

He had almost mentioned Millie's offer to

Samantha. But he didn't know what her reaction might be, and he wasn't willing to take the risk in case she might like the idea. Roger shook his head in an attempt to chase his mother-in-law from his thoughts.

He'd had no contact at all with Em until she showed up tonight. Was this cold and controlled woman the same one who had fallen asleep in his arms?

"I still don't see why you don't hire me," Samantha said when he returned to his easy chair. "I get home before the boys, and Sophia taught me how to cook all sorts of things."

"No." The topic had been broached many times. But Samantha wouldn't take no for an answer, and her insistence had become quite annoying.

"I can do the laundry and vacuum, and you don't have to pay me as much as you pay her, and I can move into her apartment so the boys don't have to share a room anymore."

"Samantha, I said no."

Samantha turned to Em. "What do you think?"

Roger grasped the arms of his chair. He was the deciding voice in this house. Yet, if he insisted on his way, it usually sent Samantha running to her room in a huff. Would Em back him? He tried desperately to make eye contact with her, but she avoided looking at him.

Em smiled and reached across the short distance to pat Samantha's hand. "I think you did a great job tonight helping your father, and in an emergency you'd pitch in and do all those things you mentioned. But you don't want a full-time you-have-to-do-it-every-minute job. An apartment of your own and the money aren't worth it."

Roger released the arms of the chair and started to breathe again. He hadn't realized how important it was to have Em agree with him.

"Are too," Samantha muttered.

"Not if you have no time to spend the money, and the only thing you do in your new room is sleep. No friends, no parties, no movies, no TV. You'd be giving up your life." Em looked in his direction but quickly looked away.

He wanted to let her know how much he appreciated what she said. It duplicated what he felt, and Samantha accepted it without further remarks or tantrums. How could this woman accomplish so much with such ease? He wanted to take Em in his arms and thank her. He'd also enjoy pulling that hair free so she'd look like the Em he knew.

Why wouldn't she look at him?

The doorbell rang. Reluctantly, Roger went to answer it. He sincerely hoped this new candidate would fit the bill. He didn't have the stamina to go through more interviews.

Samantha asked numerous questions during the interview and chatted amicably about daytime soaps and the evening TV programs. Since she and the woman hit it off so well, Roger figured this had to be the one. But Samantha dismissed her as soon as she went out the door. "The lady watches too much TV. When will she do her work?"

"You've got a point," Roger said as he pulled his hand through his hair. "But I've contacted every reputable agency, and every person they suggest has a flaw. We'll have to go with this one."

Samantha tossed her hands in the air and gave him a dirty look. "What do you have me here for if you don't even value my opinion?"

"I do value it, and you're probably right, but we've got no more time and no other people to interview. Unless…" He paused and glanced at Karen's portrait before returning his attention to his daughter. "I wanted to avoid it but…your grandmother said she'd like to fill in once Sophia leaves."

"Nana Betty!" Samantha jumped to her feet. "Oh, that would be great."

"No. Grandma Millie," Roger said without a scrap of enthusiasm. If only he could con his mother into staying with his children. Life certainly would be simpler, but his parents weren't expected back from their Australian cruise until mid-September.

Samantha screwed her face into a scowl and plopped down on the couch again, arms folded across her chest. "She treats me like a two-year-old. And I don't like Flagstaff. I'd rather stay in Phoenix with my friends."

The remark caught Roger totally off guard. Of course, Millie would expect them to stay with her in Flagstaff. Having his children in another city would complicate his life even more. Different schools. Longer commutes. Roger ran his hand through his hair in frustration. Now what was he supposed to do?

"I'll talk to that last candidate. We'll work something out with her."

"Okay," Samantha said with a sigh. "At least I'll have someone to watch TV with."

Em stood. "I think I'd better be heading home. It's getting late. Roger, would you walk me to the door?"

"Oh, here it comes. Kissy, kissy." Samantha propelled herself off the couch and paused under the wide arch that separated the living room from the hallway. "Don't do anything

you wouldn't want me to do." She scooted up
the stairs and disappeared before Em reached
the hall.

Kissy, kissy indeed. Where did his daughter
get such ideas? As much as he'd like to, he and
Em had never kissed except for a peck on the
cheek. And it didn't look as if he'd ever have
the chance.

Maybe if he apologized…

Yeah, right. Just be grateful she wants to
talk.

SAMANTHA'S REMARKS WERE downright laugh-
able, Em thought. With Karen's image domi-
nating the whole room, she hadn't been able
to talk to him, let alone imagine Roger kissing her. She had to focus on what she planned
to say—Roger had to know her mother might
consider the job, even though it would create
problems for her and Sammy.

"What's the matter, Em? You haven't been
your usual bubbly self." Roger stopped by the
door, holding on to the doorknob, limiting her
space. "Are you angry with me?"

"No." Em closed her eyes and ran her hand
across her forehead. Why must he stand so
close?

"What's the problem, then?"

"My mother."

"Doris? What's wrong?" Alarm rang in his voice, and she opened her eyes to see the deep concern reflected in his.

"Mom might be interested in your housekeeper position." She expected some delight, but not the hearty laughter that percolated from deep inside his chest.

"She is?"

"She might be. She wants more things to occupy her time, and she's lonely for children."

"Well, call her and tell her she's hired," he said with unqualified joy in his voice. "I want this settled tonight."

"I haven't mentioned it, yet, so it's not a sure thing."

Immediately he sobered. "You still don't want her to take the job. Is that what's had you so uptight tonight?"

"I wasn't uptight. I…"

"Sweetheart, take my word for it," he said as he attempted to wrap an arm around her. Em moved out of his reach. "You were very uptight, and I'd like to remedy the situation."

"How? By rubbing my feet, cuddling in a chair?" The words spewed out from someplace deep inside her, lacking any inhibition. "You've got enough memories of Karen in this house. I don't have to provide you with more."

Surprise and a sudden flush covered Roger's face.

"I'm sorry," Em said.

"Don't be. I deserved it. You don't know how many times I wished I could take back what I said at the hospital and tell you what I really meant."

"Which was?" Hope lingered just a little out of reach.

Roger held up a hand: a stop signal. "I have to say this first, so don't go ballistic."

Em chuckled. "I never go ballistic and I don't explode. Usually," she added as an afterthought. "Go on," she said when he continued to stare at her without comment.

"I loved Karen very much. I never thought anyone could take her place. Our time together, you and me," he pointed to her and himself before raising his hand again and reiterating that signal to stop, "was so special. It reminded me of what I missed with Karen but I... I'm not saying this right." He dropped his hand and eyed his feet.

"I made you think of Karen."

His head shot up. "No! I was thinking of you, and how *you* made me feel." When Em didn't respond, he continued, "I like being with you."

Em gazed at the purse she clutched. "I like being with you, too." She caught her lower lip with her teeth and looked up at him. "This might come as a surprise. Remember when I stayed with Jodie that summer?"

Roger nodded, his forehead furrowed.

"I had a crush on you back then." She could barely believe her confession. He remained immobile.

An eternity passed. "You liked me?"

Em nodded.

"That's why you deflated my tires and poured paint in my shoes, because you liked me?"

She nodded again. On her last day with the Holdens, she had tried anything she could think of to make him notice her. And he did, chasing her down the street with vows of death and destruction. If he hadn't tripped...

They'd never seen each other again until that day at Metro.

"If I had caught you that day..."

Em quickly added, "You have to remember I was Samantha's age at the time. How else could I gain your attention? I was a little naive...."

"A little?"

"Okay, a lot. You didn't hurt yourself when you fell, did you?"

Roger chortled. "It's a bit late, but thanks for asking. After four weeks in the hospital..."

"No!"

He laughed outright. "Here's a point to keep

in mind for future reference." He decreased the space between them. "I respond much more favorably when a person is nice to me."

Em grinned. "I'll try to be nice."

"And I'll try to say what I mean." Roger glanced up, moved closer to her ear and whispered, "We have an audience."

Grasping one of her hands, he started down the hall, still watching the top of the stairs. "It's time you were all in bed," he shouted.

Em looked up and saw the twins in their underwear, peeking through the railing. They didn't move.

"I'm sending Sophia up there, and I don't want anyone coming down the stairs." He walked toward the living room, where they had interviewed the women. "That should give us some privacy."

"Oh, really. What do you have in mind?" Em stopped just outside the archway. "Not in there," she said, unwilling to see that portrait of Karen again.

Sophia was coming out of the kitchen. "I'll take care of the boys."

"Okay, If I show Em your suite? We're going to offer her mother your job, and I'd like to show Em what the rooms are like."

"Oh, that's so good." She reached for Em's hand and pressed it before adding, "Of course. Just don't mind the mess. I've been packing."

CHAPTER TEN

"I LOVE THAT woman," Roger said, as he led Em into Sophia's suite. "That door takes you into a hallway connected to the outside, the garage and the laundry room." He opened another door into a small sitting room. "Doris will have her own TV and phone." He continued to the bathroom. "A standing shower as well as a tub." Still on the move, Roger walked through the bathroom into an oversize bedroom. "What do you think? There's a walk-in closet, but I don't want to disturb Sophia's things."

Em gazed in awe at the peach-colored walls. "You have more room in here than we have in our entire apartment."

Instead of going into the bathroom again, Roger directed her though another door back into the sitting room. He pointed to the blue chintz couch. "Have a seat. I want to hear all about this crush you had on me. I'm what, six, seven years older than you? Why on earth would a teenage girl have any interest in someone so much older? Is that typical? Could Samantha go for college guys?" He placed his arm over the back of the couch and leaned against the cushions.

Em sat, but didn't relax, afraid she'd end up with Roger's arm around her shoulders if she got too comfortable. And although that idea had some perks, it also made her uneasy. "I don't know about Samantha's interest in boys. She and Amy didn't share any of that with me."

"But when you were fourteen, college boys appealed to you?"

Em felt flustered. Why had she ever decided to share her thoughts as a teenager with Roger? "Let's put it this way. Age wasn't anything I considered. I thought you were cute."

Roger leaned back and laughed, swatting his thigh with an open hand. He sat up. "Don't be offended, but you didn't appeal to me at all." He moved closer. "However, you've improved over the years. I particularly like it when you wear your hair down." He reached up and stopped. "Mind if I...?"

Em offered no resistance and one by one, he pulled the hairpins from her French twist. She closed her eyes. He ran his fingers through her hair. "Smells nice."

Moving back against the cushions, he asked, "What do you suppose Samantha meant by kissy, kissy?"

Since it didn't appear he planned to kiss her, Em opened her eyes."Probably a reference to our discussion while shopping." He needed to know Samantha's thoughts about her birth.

"Tell me. Obviously, I haven't a clue what goes through a teenage girl's mind."

"The girls wanted to know if you and I were having sex." Em looked down at her hands, afraid her face had turned scarlet from the heat she felt rising there.

"What?" The word blasted from his lungs, and he momentarily left the couch, only to bounce back roughly against the cushions. "Where did that come from? Do they even know anything about what it entails? You and I…." He shook his head. "Oh, great. I'll have to talk to Samantha."

"There's more." She looked at him out of the corner of her eye.

He stared at her with disbelief.

"When this kissy thing came up, Amy said it could lead…there." Em made a gesture with her hand, unwilling to continue using the word the girls had used. "I told them not to worry. I don't do that unless I'm married." She paused, waiting for a reaction. Nothing. "And that's when your daughter said, 'That's not what my father does,' or something to that effect."

He sat forward, leaning toward Em. "She

thinks I fool around?" He flopped back again, this time massaging his forehead with both hands. "Where did she get that idea?"

"You got Karen pregnant before marriage."

His movement stilled, and he gazed at the far wall.

"She knows it, and it bothered her." Em leaned toward him and placed her hand on his arm. "I told her that her birth was a happy thing, something that brought you and Karen closer together."

When she removed her hand, he looked at her. "That's it?"

"She knows she wasn't a preemie, and she broached the subject when she thought we might be fooling around."

"Now I know what she meant when she said, 'Don't do anything you don't want me to do.'"

"Raising kids is hard."

"What's harder," Roger added, "is living by the rules we want them to follow." He stood, indicating their conversation had ended. As they left Sophia's suite, he asked, "In your teenage fantasies, did we ever kiss?"

"What do you think?" She glanced his way, having no intention of divulging her fantasies.

When they reached the door to the porch, he opened it and walked Em to her car. "I figured we could give that kissy, kissy business a try just to prove it doesn't lead to sex."

Em laughed and opened the door to her car. "Shame on you, Roger. You should know that's exactly where it goes." She was still laughing as she drove off.

"So YOU LIKE this Miss Em?" Sophia asked as she poured his coffee the next morning.

Roger regarded her, not too sure he knew what she was talking about. Except for removing those hairpins, they hadn't done anything that Sophia could question. And that hadn't even happened in front of her.

"I was showing her your room, Sophia."

"And she likes it?"

"I think so." He thought back to his conversation with Em and couldn't recall if she'd said anything about the suite. He'd spent most of the night planning how he'd approach his daughter about the subject he and Em had discussed.

Sophia sat down opposite him, a grin extending from ear to ear. "This Miss Em is the one, eh? Nice lady. The children like her. If she came to live here, it would solve all your problems. You can drive to Tucson, and we'll make it a double wedding." She got up and danced around, swinging her hips and snapping her fingers. "In Tucson, we know how to party. You think about it."

Roger stood, leaned across the table, and nearly upset his coffee. "Wait a minute, Sophia. You've got it wrong. We're not getting married." The idea was preposterous. Him and Auntie Em? Okay, so she was wonderful. And she was great with kids—hers, his and Karen's.

Roger took his seat as a cold sweat broke out on his forehead. Karen. She hadn't been in his thoughts much over the past few days. How could that be? Even after her death, she had been so much a part of him.

"It's not right," Sophia said. Roger looked up to see her glaring down at him, hands on hips. "A man needs a woman. One who's alive, like Miss Em. But you have to do it right for the children. You keep Miss Karen in here," she said, hitting her chest with a fist, "but you make room for Miss Em, too."

Sophia returned to the sink then paused. She turned and shook her index finger at him. "You do the right thing or you'll be one sorry hombre. Miss Em won't wait around forever."

"This is nice of you to treat me to dinner, Roger," Doris said as he escorted her and Em into Red Lobster. "But I might as well warn you, I won't reconsider, even after eating the most expensive lobster they have to offer."

He might be wasting time and money if Doris wasn't about to change her mind, but at least it gave him another chance to see Em. She looked lovely tonight, her hair loose over her back and shoulders.

Sophia's remarks about marriage had him considering the possibility. He certainly needed someone to take charge when he couldn't be around. Em not only created a wonderful relationship of trust and respect with his daughter but also understood the needs of his boys. Those attributes alone would be enough to make the commitment worthwhile.

All he could see were benefits for himself and his children. What could he possibly offer Em? Why would she want to saddle herself with three children and a man with an unsure future?

He turned to Doris once their orders were taken. "When Em called me this morning, she mentioned you were offended that I hadn't asked you myself."

"That's not why I said no."

"Well, what is? I really wish you'd reconsider. Last night I had nightmares about the last woman I interviewed taking every TV in our house and locking herself in her room. There's got to be some way I can convince you to take the job, even if it's only temporary."

Both he and Em placed their arms on the table and leaned toward Doris.

Doris took a deep breath and blew the air out before replying. She glanced at her daughter then directed her remarks to Roger. "Em moved to Phoenix for two reasons—to help me pay the rent so we could save and eventually buy our own place and so I could see my grandson grow up. If I'm off taking care of your kids, I'll never see my Sammy."

"But you will. Sammy will walk home with my boys, and Em can pick him up here when she gets out of work."

"Then there's the money. What you pay me won't equal what I can earn as a substitute teacher. How will we ever save for our own place?"

"But, Ma, you could end up working all day in the classroom. It would be just like it was before you retired, only you'd be going from one classroom to another. You'd be exhausted. And I can come over on weekends to help. Clean, baby-sit, whatever, so you can rest. I can manage the rent and in a few months I'll be due a raise."

Doris reached for her purse and pulled out an envelope. "I was hoping to cover this myself, but next month the rent goes up." She handed the envelope to her daughter.

Roger watched the play of emotions over Em's face, the intense concentration followed by a look of dismay. "Can they do this?" she asked. "It says we have to sign a two-year lease or vacate the apartment." Em pushed the paper across the table, and Roger fought a desire to pick it up and read for himself. "We could never afford that. I'll just have to find another place to live."

"And take Sammy away from his friends? You won't find anything in this area for less, and I'd have no way of watching him after school if he couldn't walk home with Roger's boys." Doris turned her attention to Roger. "So, I'm sorry, but you'll just have to find someone else."

"There is another possibility," Roger said as he rubbed his chin and gazed at the colorful fishes adorning the wall.

Doris placed her elbows on the table and leaned in. "What's that?"

"We could take Sammy's suggestion."

"No," Em said, emphatically. "It's out of the question." He couldn't tell if Em was startled or annoyed, but it definitely intrigued Doris.

"What suggestion?"

Em tossed her napkin on the table and looked

everywhere but at him. "It won't work. How could you bring it up, especially after..."

"What happened?" Doris asked but received no answer.

Roger was more inclined to agree with Em. After last night, he wasn't sure he could keep his distance if she resided in the same house. "Maybe you're right."

"Am I part of this discussion or not?" Doris asked, her voice taking on a tone that turned heads around in the restaurant. "Tell me what you two are talking about, or you can eat the lobster by yourself."

Roger sat back against the bench seat. "Sammy suggested all of you move into my place. He'd stay with the twins, and you and Em could share the apartment."

"I tell you, that boy is a marvel." Doris beamed as she reached out to grip Em's arm.

"You like the idea?" Roger asked. When Em continued to stare at her mother in open-mouthed dismay, Roger reached over and patted her hand. "See, she likes the idea."

"I still could substitute teach," Doris continued, "and you could help with the housework so I'd have enough energy left to watch the kids. We both save on rent, and you save on childcare. In no time at all, we can have enough for our own little house and forget paying some landlord a fortune." Doris reached over and grasped Roger's hand.

"So you'll do it?" he asked.

Em still hadn't looked at him. Roger slipped his hand over hers so that the three of them connected.

"It's up to Em."

Em glanced up, her eyes liquid pools of blue. Was she about to cry? He squeezed her hand in an attempt to offer support.

"I don't know if I can," she said, and he knew her doubt had nothing to do with her ability to move into a new home. The new circumstances he and Em would find themselves in had to weigh on her as much as they did on him.

THE LAST WEEKEND in August hit record temperatures of over 115 degrees. Even with the aid of a moving company, it took Em and her mother the full two days to remove all their belongings. Most of their furniture had to take up temporary residence in Roger's three-car garage, next to the only car that still fit in there—a red Mustang convertible. Jodie and Harve volunteered to keep the boys at their house until Sunday night so they wouldn't be underfoot.

Several times as they were packing, Em dived into the apartment complex's pool without bothering to change out of shorts and into her swim suit. The dips in the pool helped regulate her body temperature and the packing kept her mind occupied. But nothing controlled her emotions on their roller-coaster ride.

She experienced a dizzying high whenever she thought about living in the same house with Roger, seeing him every day.

And then she considered Karen's ghost in the house, and it gave her pause. Karen had been a deciding voice in planning the house. Her choice of plants landscaped the yard. Her decorating genius had turned the cold, white walls into a house of warmth and sunshine. Pictures of her dominated the photos grouped on the mantel. Even in death, the woman's presence was tangible.

And that portrait of her in the living room. Em would have to pass it every time she headed for the quarters she and her mother would share.

Finally down to moving the last carload of clothes, Em pulled into Roger's driveway late Sunday afternoon. She found Samantha huddled near the front steps, crying. Em rushed to her side. "Are you all right?"

Samantha stood and wiped at her cheeks. Nearly Em's height, she looked straight at Em with Roger's brown eyes and burst into tears again. Em threw her arms around the girl and gave her a comforting hug. "What's the matter, honey?"

"I'm going to miss her."

"Sophia?"

Samantha nodded, banging her wet chin on Em's shoulder. "And we can't even go to her wedding. Daddy says he's too busy." Samantha's tone became even more regretful. "It's only in Tucson. That's just two hours away."

"It's closer to three."

Samantha shrugged. "Could you take us?"

Em backed out of the embrace. Was the girl trying to manipulate her? "I wasn't invited."

"Oh, but that's no problem. Sophia really likes you," Samantha said with unchecked excitement, all tears having evaporated.

"I think not." She wasn't about to butt in on a decision Roger had made.

Immediately, Samantha's face turned sourpuss.

Em opened the sliding door of her minivan. "Can you help me carry in some clothes?"

Samantha folded her arms across her chest and glowered.

Roger dashed out of the house wearing only white shorts and sandals. He looked drained from moving one woman out the day before and two women in today. Every time Em saw him, he was taking something from her mother's arms so she wouldn't strain herself. "Need any help here?"

Em smiled and waved him off. "Thanks, but Samantha volunteered." He turned and headed back to the house, so he missed Samantha sticking out her tongue. Em chuckled, pulled out an armload of clothes and held them out to the girl. "The sooner we start, the sooner you get back to your own life." Samantha grabbed up the items and headed for the house, as well.

Em sighed. With this kind of help she'd have to spend hours ironing her clothes before she could wear them. When she reached the bedroom she'd be sharing with her mother, Samantha was standing in front of the mirror, holding up a short black evening dress with rhinestone spaghetti straps.

"I'll bet we're about the same size," Samantha said. "Can I borrow this?"

"Not for another ten years," Roger said from the doorway. Samantha gave him a disgruntled look before hanging it in the closet. With head held high, she left them alone, the first time since they had started the move.

He dropped two suitcases next to one of the double beds. One was Sophia's original bed and the other had come with Doris. "This does it. The last from your mother's car." He plopped onto one of the beds, fell back and looked as though he might never get up. "The boys should be back soon, and I've ordered pizza."

Em moved some of the clothes so that she could sit near him. "Samantha asked me to take her to Tucson next weekend."

"I hope you said no. I don't want her to start working one of us against the other."

"I did, but I can understand her wanting to attend the wedding. Sophia has been an important part of her life."

"I know, and I'd love to take her myself." Roger reached for Em's hand. "You're really good with Samantha. Everything *I* say to her turns into a confrontation."

"I understand where she's coming from because I was like her once."

"And you turned out okay."

"You seem surprised."

"I am." He chuckled. "I was really awful to you back then, wasn't I?"

"I was probably a pain in the neck."

"That you were." He grinned that delightful way that showed off his slightly protruding eyetooth. "But I sure do like the way you turned out."

CHAPTER ELEVEN

"PIZZA'S HERE."

Em drifted out of a deep sleep, barely aware of her mother's voice.

"Pizza's here," Doris said again.

The bed moved, and Em reluctantly opened her eyes. Her dream had been so beautiful. One where Roger held her, caressed her.

"Em," her mother said in a sharp voice.

Em woke fully then, all disorientation gone, and quickly sat up. Her mother stood near the bed, arms folded over her chest, while Roger slowly brought himself to a sitting position.

When Doris continued to stand by them, Em said, "We heard you, Mom. We'll be right there." She got off the bed, reached for Roger's hand, and pulled him to his feet. When he stumbled and placed an arm around her shoulders for balance, she started to laugh. "How long were we asleep?"

"Are you two through billing and cooing? 'Cause I've got something to say."

Em returned her attention to her mother as

Roger removed his arm. "What's the matter, Mom?" Em asked, amusement still bubbling in her voice. "You look annoyed."

"Because I am." Doris placed her hands on her hips, and scowled.

"Did the boys get back?" Roger asked.

"Oh, the boys got back fine. First thing they did was go looking for the two of you. As soon as they found you, they came running out and said you were having sex. Since they're young and might not know what they were talking about, I thought I'd check. Samantha beat me to it."

Roger started to laugh. "Well, clearly, we weren't."

Doris pressed her lips together in obvious fury. When Em touched Roger's arm in an attempt to stop him from creating more problems, he asked, "What's the big deal? We weren't doing anything inappropriate"

"The big deal is I don't want you in these quarters again," Doris said, pointing at Roger. "We set the boundaries right now. There will be no sign of impropriety while I'm running this place. A lot could be said with two unmarried people sharing the same house, especially when they're as friendly as you are."

"But…" Roger started.

"No buts about it, young man," Doris said

in a tone meant to stop second graders in their tracks, "or I pack up my things and move out this minute."

Roger's jaw dropped, and he eyed Em. "She's right," Em replied, not willing to look directly at her mother.

"Okay." Roger tossed his hands in the air and headed for the door. He paused and turned. "This is your inner sanctum, and I won't violate it again. However, I will have a talk with the boys. It's time they knew a little more about the birds and the bees."

"Weren't you a little rough on him, Mom?" Em said, after Roger left the room. "You know darn well the whole thing was innocent."

"It's the perceived impropriety I'm worried about. I'm not about to have my daughter the subject of gossipmongers." Doris picked up several items of clothing off the chair and deposited them in a drawer. "And, no, I don't think I was too hard on him. Whenever I started my classes each year, I made it perfectly clear from the beginning what the rules were. It saved me and my students a lot of grief."

Em took another pile of clothes and began to sort them for the drawers. They had a lot to straighten up before they could use the beds. "You go get your pizza," Doris said. "I'll finish up in here."

On her way out, Em stopped to give her mother a hug. "Thanks, Mom. And I promise. Roger and I will be good." Em paused by the door. "Just out of curiosity—where would you have gone if we hadn't agreed to abide by your rules?"

Doris tossed a pair of jeans at her daughter, but Em managed to duck before they hit her.

The moment Em reached the group in the kitchen Sammy rushed over to her, and she picked him up. It seemed like ages since she'd last seen him. "Oh, you taste good," Em said after kissing his tomato-sauce-stained cheek. "I'll eat you instead of the pizza." Sammy wiggled free.

"You want to see my—our room?" He grabbed her hand with sticky fingers and started to drag her away.

"Could it wait a minute, sport?" Roger asked. "Your mother's probably hungry."

Sammy grudgingly let go of Em's hand and returned to the table. Em opened a pizza box and took out a slice covered with pepperoni. "What, no anchovies?" A chorus of ughs greeted her along with some gruesome faces.

"You eat that stuff?" Samantha asked.

Em grinned. "It's my favorite. Right, sport?" Sammy held his head back and pinched his nose. "Say, I like the name 'sport.' Why don't you try that for a nickname?"

"Can't. He," Sammy said, pointing at Roger, "calls everyone sport."

"True, but I can limit its use to you, if you prefer."

"Nah." Sammy got up from the table. "I'm going to my room and get my things ready for school."

"Oh, my goodness, school!" Em said as she stuffed the last of her pizza in her mouth. "It starts tomorrow." She stood and began cleaning the table. "How about the rest of you? Everyone ready?"

The sounds of little feet pounding up the stairs brought Doris out of her room. "Slow down," she shouted before heading after the boys at a slower pace.

"I think Mom's about to give her second lecture of the day," Em said. She sat down at the kitchen table with another piece of pizza topped with gooey cheese. Roger moved to the seat across from her, propped an elbow on the table and supported his head in his hand.

"Is my sitting within reaching distance of you, staring at you while you eat, appropriate?"

"Definitely scandalous. What will the children think?"

Roger grinned, sat up and stretched. A long

string of cheese slipped off her pizza slice, and she gathered it up with her tongue, all the while watching Roger as he focused on her task. He licked his own lips before adding, "I'm going to go talk to them."

"I sure would like to be a bug on the wall when you tell them about the birds and the bees."

Roger stood, and walked around the wooden table. "I'll bet you would. Sleep well. I'll see you in the morning."

Em sat for several minutes enjoying his last words. She'd see him in the morning, every morning for as long as her mother was needed here.

"Dad, pleeease," Samantha whined. It was Thursday. Em and her family had moved in Sunday, and little had changed. His daughter still refused to cut him any slack or relent on the badgering.

"No."

"Everyone's doing it. Pierced ears are the best."

"I said no." Roger looked across the table at Em. Why didn't she take his side? Instead, she cleared the evening's meal from the table, pretending uninterest, yet he knew she heard every word.

Work today had been a disaster. Two more people had quit. His new assistant, Carnation, her name the choice of parents who'd been hippies, had spent most of the day in the ladies' room with morning sickness. As one of the displaced workers, she'd traded her job taking calls from customers for administrative experience. What he needed more than anything was someone to back him up for a change, so he didn't have to do everything on his own.

"I'm a dinosaur," Samantha continued. "Look. Everyone wears them." She pointed at Doris. "When did you get your ears pierced, Mrs. Masters?"

Frowning, Doris turned around. "I'm not sure. I think I was in my forties." She shrugged and continued with the dishes.

The corners of Samantha's mouth drooped.

"You're not even fourteen," he said as Samantha pushed away from the table. A hard day at the office followed by his daughter's daily tantrums was wearing thin. When she headed for the hall, he shouted, "And just where do you think you're going? Help with the dishes."

"I've got homework."

"It's not her night to help." Em placed several items on a tray at the other end of the table.

"Since when?" And now Em was defending her. Wasn't anyone on his side?

Em hoisted the tray. "Since we made up a work chart. This way everyone does the work, not just the girls." She started for the dishwasher. "You're scheduled for some time later this week."

"Me!" Roger stood so abruptly his chair skittered across the tiled floor. "I work. I pay the bills. Why do you think I hired a housekeeper?"

"Everyone here works, either at a paying job or at school," Doris said over her shoulder. "The chart's on the back of the closet door. Everything's negotiable. Reschedule if you can trade off with someone else."

Roger immediately marched to the closet door. There, on poster board in neat script, was a chart with everyone's name and responsibility for each day. The twins had already earned a star each for completing their daily chores. He glanced at Doris and caught her grinning at him.

"That's what you get when you hire an old schoolteacher to run your house."

Returning his attention to the chart, he saw his kitchen duty was scheduled for tomorrow. He'd manage somehow to stay late at the office. It would be worth it. Kitchen duty, indeed. He hadn't had that chore since he quit his job at McDonald's.

CLOSETED IN HIS home office, Roger worked on the information Carnation had failed to supply. New trainees at the plant in Seattle were starting the Tuesday after Labor Day, so he had to have all the details finished before taking off Monday night for Seattle. At least he got to spend this weekend home with his family.

Several employees had volunteered to train the new people in Seattle, and a few talked about transferring. Rumor had it that he might be considered for the position at the new and expanded division. He liked the idea, but wasn't about to pin all his hopes on it. The way things were going, nothing could be counted on as a sure bet.

When a knock sounded on his door, Roger looked up from the graph he'd been preparing. "Yes?"

The door opened, and Em stood there.

"Can I interrupt you a minute?"

Roger smiled, clasped his hands behind his head and leaned back in his chair to examine his visitor. Blond hair hung down to her shoulders. Was she wearing it that way because he'd mentioned he liked it down? Doris peered over her daughter's shoulder, and Roger abruptly sat up.

"Sure." He turned to the paperwork before him and pushed it into a pile on the side. "What's the problem?"

The two women came in and stood by his desk. "Something needs to be done about Samantha."

Immediately, Roger stiffened. Damn. "She's not getting her ears pierced, and I don't want to hear of it again."

"That's not the problem." Em leaned over and touched his arm. "It's more important than that." Roger ground his teeth and stood. He grabbed up a handful of papers and walked over to the filing cabinet.

"What is it, then?"

"She really misses Sophia and wants to attend her wedding."

"Nope. I've already had this discussion. I can't afford the time." Roger opened a cabinet drawer and stuffed the papers into the first file that lay there. He returned his attention to Doris and restricted Em to his peripheral vision.

"That may have been true earlier," Em said, "but you put off your trip to Seattle until after the Labor Day weekend."

"Yes, but I can't cancel the work."

Roger clung to the open drawer as Em positioned herself on the edge of his desk. "But you have Carnation now. She should have lessened the load." Em was rearranging his pencils or something. How on earth was he supposed to concentrate on the subject at hand with her distracting him?

"Carnation is pregnant. She's not working out as well as I'd hoped."

Doris headed for the door. "I'll leave you two to talk. The news is coming on, and I want to find out what I missed." He noticed she didn't close the door. Probably meant to keep an eye on him in case he planned to seduce her daughter.

Well, they had walked in on him, not the other way around, and this was his space. Roger crossed to the door, intending to close it, then decided to leave it ajar. No sense in hoisting red flags. He didn't need Doris the Bull charging in to protect her daughter from him. Once resettled in his chair, he regarded the woman perched on his desk.

"What are you grinning about?" Em asked.

"I'm surprised the headmistress allows you to be alone with me in my inner sanctum."

Em giggled. "So am I."

He rotated his head and rubbed his neck.

Em came around the desk and placed her hands on his shoulders, massaging the muscles. "I think tonight she hoped you'd be more inclined to agree with her if she offered me as bait."

Roger closed his eyes and moved his head to get the full benefit of her magic fingers. "Well, it won't work. I'm way too strong willed to fall for such temptations, no matter how pretty the package."

Em's infectious giggle started again. "Right." She stopped massaging his shoulders. "I'll let her know."

He caught her hand as she walked past him. "You giving up so easily?" He drew her back to his chair. "I'm a reasonable man. I'll at least listen before saying no."

"Mom thinks Samantha needs to attend the wedding. Sort of a closure. In many ways, Sophia has been a mother figure for her these past few years."

"And you agree?"

"Yes and no."

"Explain."

"Yes, because it would help Samantha, but no, because you don't need any additional pressure on you right now."

"What do you suggest?"

"I can take Samantha. It's only a day trip if we start early in the morning, and you can have the time free to complete whatever you need to do."

"You'd go through all that just to keep peace?"

Em pushed his hair off his forehead with several light sweeps of her hand. He momentarily closed his eyes, enjoying her touch. Unfortunately, she didn't get more personal.

"Will your mother go, too?" he asked.

"No. She's taking all the boys to a birthday party, so they won't bother you."

Roger mulled over the idea but couldn't make a decision. He moved his legs and got up, forcing Em to step away.

"Tell your mother I'll think about it."

"And when can we expect Your Majesty's decision?" she asked from the door.

"Tomorrow morning. I'll sleep on it tonight."

"WHAT DID HE say?" Doris asked the moment Em came back into the sitting room that adjoined their bedroom.

"He'll think about it and give us his decision tomorrow."

Doris clucked her tongue and shook her head. She pushed a needle into her crewelwork and pulled the wool with a vengeance. "Well, what did he say about Samantha? Did he agree this is important for her?"

"No. He's thinking about me taking Samantha so he can stay home and work." Her mother dropped her crewel embroidery on her lap. "It's the best solution, Mom. He's under a lot of pressure right now."

Doris gathered the various colored yarns she had spread out on the arm of the chair and put everything into her needlework bag. Without saying another word, she got up and headed for the door that led to the hall.

"Where you going?"

"I'm going to speak to Roger myself. You obviously never got to the heart of the matter."

After Doris flounced out of the room Em flopped against the back of the chair and rapped the arm. Darn. This was Roger's household, his children. Her mother shouldn't interfere.

Just as Em considered going after her mother, Doris reentered the room. "Well, did he agree?"

Doris paused. "He didn't give me a chance to explain." Doris raised her chin and looked away. "That poor girl. She's doing everything she can to attract her father's attention, and he only sees her as a nuisance."

"You're not giving him enough credit. Roger's very concerned. He just doesn't know how to handle her."

"Well, I do. And he won't listen to me."

Em pushed to her feet and walked over to her mother. Placing her hands on her shoulders, Em forced Doris to look at her. "It's his house,

Mom. We're guests here. He has to make the decisions about his children, no matter what we may think."

MAYBE HE'D BEEN rude in dismissing Doris that way, but Roger couldn't tolerate one more person's opinion concerning his daughter. Of course, Em's opinion had been more of a pleasing distraction, one he didn't mind at all. It wasn't until Em left that he noticed the picture of Karen lying facedown on his desk.

Roger went to his door and looked both ways before heading to the formal living room. Once there, he removed Karen's portrait and slipped it behind the couch. He'd have to decide what to do with it, but he wouldn't worry about it tonight.

He went back into his office, picked up Karen's picture, kissed it, then placed it in the bottom drawer of his desk. Two pictures of Karen out of view. He thought about that a moment. To his surprise he found her absence no longer hurt. Not that he'd ever forget her, but the anguish he'd felt for so long over her death had lost its sharp edge.

Heading down the tiled hall, he stretched his tired arms over his head. Oh, that massage had felt good. He smiled as he passed the hallway to Em's suite. At least she should feel more comfortable in the house now that Karen wasn't so visible.

A muffled noise caused him to stop before he reached his bedroom door. It sounded almost like a wounded animal. Strange. They had no pets despite the boys' numerous requests for a dog. Roger tracked the sound to his daughter's bedroom. Was she hiding something in there?

He grabbed the doorknob, intending to push the door open and catch her unawares. Some instinct warned him to knock first. After a few soft knocks, the sound stopped. "Who…who is it?" a weak voice asked.

"It's me, Samantha. Can I come in?" When she didn't answer, Roger opened the door. Her light was out. "You in bed?"

"Of course," she said. Sniffles and a hiccup followed her reply. He felt around for the surface of the bed and sat on the edge near her head. The sheet felt damp.

"So, you still want to go to Sophia's wedding?"

Sniffle.

"I'm not sure if I remember the time. Four in the afternoon on Saturday or Sunday?"

"Sat…Saturday."

"Let me see," Roger said, adjusting his position so that the headboard would support his back. "If we leave before one, we should make it in plenty of time."

A sudden movement brought Samantha right next to him. "Noon, Daddy, no later than twelve. We could have trouble on the road or something, and we don't want to be late."

"Noon, it is."

A deafening squeal by his ear, was followed by a body slam and a neck-breaking hug. "Oh, thank you, thank you, thank you." Samantha plastered several wet kisses on his nose and chin before he could grab her face between his hands. Without further words, he planted a kiss on her forehead, got up and headed for the door.

Roger wiped away the tears in his eyes before leaving her room. A momentary affliction. But the smile stayed with him for most of the night.

CHAPTER TWELVE

"How do I look?" Roger asked Em Saturday morning when he came into the kitchen. His white dress shirt had vertical pleats and white embroidery across the front. Black lizard cowboy boots peeked out from under flared pant legs.

"Very Spanish. As Sophia would say, you one good-looking hombre." He certainly was, with that dark hair falling across his forehead. She squeezed her fingers together to avoid touching him and returned to sorting laundry.

"The boys left already?"

Em nodded as he headed for the refrigerator. He pulled out a container of orange juice and lifted it to his mouth.

"A glass, Mr. Holden."

"There's only a swallow left, Ms. Turner."

He drank it down, tossed the container into the trash and wiped his mouth with the back of his hand before taking a seat at the table. "I was hoping the twins would come to the wedding. Sophia has practically raised them the past few years."

"Clowns and water balloons are much more fun when you're six."

"I suppose. What are you doing today?"

"Let's see. Mom left me a list." Em glanced at the paper on the table. "The laundry, some shopping and stripping the beds. If I'm really good, I could earn three gold stars."

"You're going to work all day?"

"Well, this is the *Labor Day* weekend." She picked up one of the boy's shirts and threw it in the pile of dark colors. Roger grabbed her hand and pulled her away from her chore.

"You are not staying here. You're driving to Tucson with us."

Em dug in her heels and caught the edge of the door frame before he could drag her any farther.

"I wasn't invited."

"I'm inviting you."

"I have work to do."

"I'm the boss here, and you've got no work to do in my house."

"I don't work for you, I work for my mother, and she gave me a whole list."

Roger placed his hand above hers and leaned toward her. "Do you want to dress yourself or shall I do it?"

Em was considering the possibility, when Samantha took that moment to walk down the stairs. She reached the bottom and twirled, sending her bright red skirt pinwheeling. "What do you think? All I need is castanets, right?" She stepped dramatically to the left, one arm arched over her head.

"You are gorgeous," Em said, slipping away from Roger. "Let me see that blouse." She took Samantha's hands and held them to the side for a better view. "I love it." The white peasant blouse had colorful flowers embroidered around the neckline, accented with red blanket stitches.

"Now, if I had pierced ears," Samantha said as she looked past Em at her father, "I could wear some really nice hoop earrings Sophia gave me."

Roger leaned against the wall, his arms folded over his chest. "Nothing could improve your appearance. But we have a problem." He pushed away from the wall. "Em doesn't have a thing to wear, and we need to hurry so we can leave on time."

"You're coming," Samantha shouted in unrestrained delight. "I know just the thing." She grabbed Em's hand and pulled her down the hall. Em glanced over her shoulder as

Roger washed the self-satisfied expression from his face.

"This one," Samantha said. She removed a dress from its hanger, a dress Em would never consider wearing.

"No."

"No?" Samantha discarded it on the bed and pulled out another.

Em pushed her aside. "Before you destroy my entire wardrobe, let me show you what might work." She took out her latest purchase, one she had intended to return if her finances didn't improve. With a flourish, she slipped off the plastic sleeve.

"What do you think?" The blue sheath had cap sleeves that could be worn on the shoulder or off. She had hoped one day to wear it on a special occasion, and what could be more special than a wedding?

"Perfect," Samantha said with eyes about to pop from their sockets. "Can I wear it one day? I think it would fit me, too." She looked up at Em and grinned. "I know. When I'm older. But that day will come. You watch. I'm getting older by the minute."

THEY HAD A choice of three cars: Roger's minivan, Em's minivan or Roger's red Mustang convertible. Samantha insisted no self-respecting person would be caught dead going to a wedding in a minivan. Because her hair was short and the constant breeze would not muss her hairdo, she sat in the back, with Em in the bucket seat next to him.

Nothing could have delighted Roger more than being in the car with Em and his daughter. Em's presence had to be the reason Samantha talked nonstop. He knew she could talk, because she often tied up his phone for hours at a time, but he'd never had the pleasure of being included in the conversations. All their communication had been in the form of confrontations.

They had barely reached the outskirts of Chandler, just south of Phoenix, when the sky darkened, and he had to stop. Before the first drops of rain fell, they managed to get the top up. It dampened Samantha's mood.

"Why couldn't the monsoon wait?" Samantha moaned as they continued their drive.

"We need the rain," Em added.

"Maybe it will be over by the time we reach Tucson. Summer storms don't generally last too long." But it did. The rain continued with such force that Roger had to pull off the road and wait until the intense downpour abated.

Samantha scowled. "We're going to be late."

"I'm more concerned that we'll be swept up in a flash flood and carried off to Mexico."

"Right. Then I'll never get my ears pierced."

Roger couldn't help but chuckle. Even the thought of death in a raging river couldn't dissuade his daughter from wanting to drill holes in her ears.

"You got a birthday coming up?"

Samantha bounced out of her slumped position and placed her arms on the back of their seat. "Yes. The end of next month. Can I get them pierced then?"

"I'm getting a little annoyed with that topic. What do you want to do for your birthday? Nana Betty and Grandpa Dave will be back by then. You want a party?"

"Besides getting my ears pierced, I'd like a boy-girl party."

Just then a flash of lightning hit a tree on the side of the road, followed by a boom. The car shook, Samantha screamed and everyone caught their breath. Em moved closer, and he grabbed her hand.

"Whew, did you see that?" Samantha asked.

"Yes, it was God voicing his opinion about your boy-girl party. I tend to agree with him."

"Da-a-ad!" Samantha smacked his shoulder. "I'm a freshman in high school. I don't want clowns making balloon animals and relatives pinching my cheeks. I want a grown-up party with booze and pot and sex—like you and Em used to have when you were my age."

He turned around, agitated as thoughts of her doing just that disturbed his reason. She was laughing, of all things, teasing him. And it felt so good. How wonderful not to have a constant fight. Em squeezed his hand.

"If I agree to this boy-girl thing, it will be chaperoned. No liquor. No smoking. No sex. And no drugs of any kind."

"Oh, Daddy," Samantha screamed as she wrapped her arms around his neck and cut off his windpipe. "You are the greatest." With that she sat back in her seat and began counting on her fingers, naming all the people she planned to invite.

At that moment, he felt like the greatest. Holding hands with Em, the rain pelting the canvas top, his daughter in blissful happiness in the backseat. What more could a man want?

"THAT'S IT. THAT'S IT," Samantha shouted as they drove down the highway past Tucson. "People call the church the White Dove of the Desert. Isn't it beautiful? Sophia says they go to services here all the time, and she always wanted to be married here."

Samantha picked up one of the black lace

mantillas they'd brought and placed it over her head. Em reached for hers, folded it and tucked it into her purse.

Once Roger parked the car, Samantha opened the door and took off. "There they are." She waved, held tightly to her head covering and ran toward the people gathered in front of the church. Immediately, she stopped, turned and pointed to the sky.

"Look. It's blessed." A rainbow arched over the San Xavier Mission and disappeared between the two white towers. A spectacular moment, Em thought. It would probably appear on postcards and advertisements in the future, although even a rainbow couldn't improve on the whitewashed beauty of the two towers framing the adobe sanctuary.

Roger came around and held the door open for Em. "Not exactly what I'd pick for a ceremony. This is a tourist haven. Half the people here aren't even invited to the wedding."

"I know. A chapel in Las Vegas is so much better."

Roger guffawed. "Especially when Elvis is reading the vows."

Em stared at him, not able to visualize prim and proper Karen going along with such a charade. "You're kidding."

"No," he said with a chuckle. "We did it right

in a real church several years later, when we could afford the honeymoon."

He placed a hand at the small of her back and directed her toward the entrance to the church. Avoiding the large puddles that dotted the parking area was a challenge in itself, but at least the rain had stopped. Em looked for the rainbow. It had already disappeared.

"I CRIED, SOPHIA. I couldn't help it. You looked so beautiful. Did you see the rainbow?"

Roger watched as Sophia took his daughter into her arms and hugged her. How difficult this must be for them both. Sophia had been a confidante, a friend as well as a sometime mother. And yet Samantha was handling it well. She was maturing so quickly.

Sophia brushed away tears from Samantha's cheeks. "I'm so happy you come," she said, grasping Roger's hand. She released him and turned to Em. "And Miss Em, it's good to see you again. This gringo treating you well? I told him he better or else." Sophia grasped Em's hands but gave Roger an evil look. Turning back to Em, Sophia said, "You like my church? I can make arrangements with the priest so you can use it, too."

"Your church is lovely," Em said. Roger recognized the hesitation in her voice. Of course he had never mentioned Sophia's suggestion that they make it a double wedding. Roger placed his hand at the small of Em's back, pressuring her to move down the line. Finally, Sophia released her, and they were able to slip past the rest of the wedding party.

"Doesn't Sophia look nice?" Samantha said as Roger led her and Em back to the car. "What is this, her third marriage?"

"Right, at least, I think so." Roger didn't care to continue discussing the marriage. Not when Em appeared to be mulling over Sophia's comments about the church. At any moment he could expect some lightbulb to go off, and he'd have to do some explaining, something he'd rather avoid until they were alone.

"Do you think she wore the same wedding dress each time?" Samantha asked, as she got into the backseat of the car.

"It's not done, usually. We'll have to ask her, and also if she had all three weddings in this same beautiful church." Em's words, spoken softly, oozed sugar. Obviously Sophia's remark hadn't slipped past her, despite his effort to hurry her into the car. "It is a beautiful church, don't you agree?" She drew the words out and practically blew them against his cheek before she slipped onto her seat. "Am I right, or am I right?"

Roger glanced at his daughter and saw her forehead pucker in thought. No way would he mention his conversation with Sophia with his daughter listening in.

Steeling his voice so Em would get the hint not to pursue the subject, he said, "And you told her, of course, you liked her church. Who wouldn't love all those lovely statues and ornate decorations?"

"That I did." Em grinned and buckled her seat belt. As he walked over to his side of the car he knew he hadn't heard the last on the subject. Between now and the next time it came up, he'd have to think of some kind of explanation.

THEY REACHED THE reception, a garden affair held in back of a Mexican restaurant. The men were dressed in black jackets and pants with shirts similar to Roger's. At least he was in style, and he felt comfortable. The women wore dresses in vivid primary colors, similar to Em's bright blue but in no way as form fitting. Despite the heat, everyone appeared to be enjoying the celebration.

"She's quite grown-up," Em said as they watched Samantha talk to a group of adults. They were standing under the large leaves of a mulberry tree that shaded them from the bright sun. All signs of the earlier storm had disappeared, except for the increased humidity.

"She's mastered the Spanish language. Something I've never been able to do," Em continued.

"It's all due to Sophia. The boys talk like natives. I hear them using Spanish even when they're by themselves. You watch. Sammy will pick it up, too."

Em shook her head. "Not if Sophia isn't around. My mother believes in mastering your own language first, and you know how strict she can be."

They headed toward a table set with drinks. Em picked up a glass of lemonade, and Roger reached for a bottle of Mexican beer, floating in a tub filled with ice.

Roger sighed. "Yes. But she can help them deal with the real world. I worry so much about the perils out there, and how Samantha will handle them."

Em sipped her lemonade before saying, "Are you sure you're not worrying about her repeating your mistakes?"

"We all make mistakes." Roger flipped the cap off the bottle and slipped a wedge of lime into the opening. "I'm sure she'll make plenty of her own." He turned to her, the bottle close to his lips. "Did you ever make any…mistakes, that is?" When she didn't answer, he added, "Besides having that crush on me?"

"My goodness, Roger. Are you going to fixate on that forever?"

Em laughed and headed toward the buffet tables, and Roger chuckled.

Em always made him laugh, one attribute he really appreciated. But although she knew almost everything about him and his life with Karen, he knew nothing about her life or her marriage. What kind of fool hadn't been able to appreciate such a gem? He followed her over to the buffet and picked up one of the sturdy paper plates.

The tables were piled high with enchiladas, salads, refried beans and tortillas. Roger took a sample of everything from burritos to *chile rellenos* and topped the lot off with a good helping of guacamole. Em did the same, and he wondered how her dress would expand to accommodate the food.

They headed for one of the tables under a white tent and sat next to a mariachi band, the only spot available. The exuberant music made conversation impossible, but the food was delicious, and they devoted the time to eating.

"WOULD YOU CARE to dance, *señorita?*" Roger held out his hand, and Em grasped it.

Stars sparkled in the cloudless night sky. Strings of tiny white Christmas lights, strung under the tent and wrapped around the tree trunks, offered a warm romantic glow. Sophia and José had left moments before, and the crowd had begun to disperse. Em and Roger had danced several times since they arrived at the reception, but this song was a slow one and possibly the last of the evening.

"Did I tell you how wonderful you look, *señorita?*" Roger pulled her close so that they were cheek to cheek.

"Why thank you, *señor,*" Em whispered against his ear. "However, I believe I should be called *señora* for my age and station in life. Samantha is a *señorita.*"

Roger pushed away so that his face was directly in front of her, his nose touching hers. "I think the only thing that counts is that you're single. There have to be at least a dozen hombres here who would like to escort this particular *señorita* to her home." She had spent a good deal of the time dancing with other guests. "I'll probably have to fight them all off."

Em collapsed in laughter and buried her face in Roger's shoulder. He pulled her closer. Oh, how good he felt. She moved her face so that her lips pressed against his neck. He smelled good, too. She breathed deeply as he planted a kiss against her ear.

They had had such a lovely day, a perfect day. Only one niggling point kept repeating itself—Sophia saying she could use the church. The only thing that could refer to was marriage, and obviously, something to do with marrying Roger. Why had that idea popped into the woman's head, and why did she bring it up when she did?

"Roger?" Em said as she moved away slightly.

"You're going to ask me, aren't you?"

She moved farther away, allowing enough distance to see his features in the dim light. "No, you're going to tell me why Sophia assumed you and I would get married in her church."

Roger blew into her hair and twirled her around a few times before answering. "You remember that night I showed you her room?"

Em nodded.

"The next day, she told me you were a wonderful woman and I was an idiot." He paused. "She spent the whole morning lecturing me on how I shouldn't let you get away."

"Oh, my." Em buried her head in his shoulder again, this time to hide her embarrassment.

"That's when she suggested a double wedding."

Em looked up. "You're kidding."

Roger backed away, his eyebrows raised in shock. "Listen, I haven't enough imagination to come up with that on my own." He swung her around as the music came to a halt. "And I wasn't about to bring it up in front of..." He nodded in Samantha's direction. "We can't talk now and I'd appreciate..."

Em walked out of his embrace and headed toward Samantha without answering him. "It's about time to go." She smiled at the young man who had been talking to the girl. "We've got a long drive."

Samantha pouted and said a lingering good-bye.

Em turned to see Roger watching her. Did he expect some comment? Something to the effect that she'd never make the mistake of believing he'd want to marry her? After all, they both knew he was already married to a ghost.

CHAPTER THIRTEEN

LABOR DAY. Was it ever. Up at dawn assembling figures for all the old problems that would be handled by the staff left in Phoenix. More charts on the training that had to take place in Seattle.

Roger had gone to his office on Sunday to make sure he had all the information he needed for his trip. Everything was downloaded onto a laptop. Carnation had made all the arrangements for airline tickets and hotel reservations for the six people who would be involved in training the staff in Seattle. If her morning sickness didn't cripple her completely, she'd be able to handle the local office while he was gone. She'd come a long way doing her job, and he now depended on her.

Nothing more had to be done.

Except for a brief time at breakfast and supper, he'd barely seen anyone in the household. Thanks to Doris, he had no worries about the children, and with Em's help on Monday, he was able to finish everything he needed for work. He packed his computer and suitcases, leaving enough time to relax by the pool before his trip to the airport. Em planned to join him. Since Samantha was off with a girlfriend, only Doris and the boys remained, all of them enjoying the pool.

It meant he'd have no time alone with Em. He'd wanted to find out more about her. Find out why she'd clammed up after he explained what Sophia had implied. Again, he must have explained it all wrong. One minute Em was cozying up in his arms, the next she was barely talking to him. Certainly nothing personal. Once again he realized that, despite their living in the same house, he knew very little about her or her past life, outside of that crush she'd had on him. Every time he remembered that, it instantly brought a smile.

Earlier she had given him another shoulder massage, something he not only enjoyed but also hoped to give in return. He'd picked up the sunblock she always used on Sammy. Eyes closed, Roger waited impatiently on the chaise lounge for her to join them.

"I brought us each a spicy tomato juice," Em said, in front of him.

Roger opened his eyes and slowly sat up. The white one-piece bathing suit she always wore was gone. Instead she had on a blue bikini, one he hadn't seen before.

"New bathing suit?" He took the offered drink and stirred the red liquid with the celery stalk before taking a sip. He avoided further comment on the suit, knowing any interest he showed might wave red flags. He glanced over at Doris, who sat under an umbrella attached to her chair with a towel covering her legs.

She eyed him with that schoolmarm stare. Although they hadn't had any further discussions about proper adult behavior, he'd made doubly sure never to do or say anything that could create problems. He sighed and raised his glass at her. She gave him a smile before turning back to the boys playing in the shallow end of the pool.

Em sat on the other lounge next to him. "Yes. Macy's had all their suits greatly reduced, and I can never pass up a bargain."

Roger casually lifted the sunblock. "With more skin exposed, you really should use this to protect yourself."

Em squinted up at the cloudless sky. "You're probably right." She sat up and took the sunblock from him. "Mom, could you put this on my shoulders?"

Doris turned to her with an expression of annoyance, removed the towel and looked about ready to get out of her chair.

Gathering his courage, Roger sat forward. "I can do it." He put his drink on the cement and stood as Doris sat back in her chair. "Those dangerous rays can be lethal. Move over and I'll put some on your back, too." He flipped the lounge chair down so that it went flat.

Em glanced at him and chuckled, but she scooted over and lay on her stomach so he could sit down behind her. "You want to help me with the strings? I don't want to get this stuff all over your new suit." When she didn't do as he requested, he added, "Okay, I'll protect your suit from the UV rays, too."

She moved her hand around and undid her top.

Roger edged her hair out of the way and glanced back at Doris. "Can't do more than protect you from the UV rays with the school-marm watching."

"Right!" Doris called. "You step out of line, and I'll send you to the principal's office."

Em laughed as he squirted the liquid on her back. Slowly he moved the moisture around, careful not to do anything that could antagonize Doris. "You've given me several back rubs. This is payback."

When he was finished, Roger stood. "You can fix the ties. I'm going for a swim."

He walked over to the pool edge and dived into water the temperature of a bath. He swam underwater to the shallow end, where the three boys batted a giant balloon around. After playing with them for a few minutes, he looked back and saw Em approaching the pool.

Phoenix had over 300 days of sunshine each year, Roger mused while swimming back to where she was standing. Seattle probably had an equivalent amount in clouds and rain. His thoughts drifted back to Em as he surfaced. Would she like Seattle?

"Would you care for your refreshment?" She held out the drink he had left behind.

He took a sip of the spiced tomato juice while he trod water. "Mmm. Hits the spot." When he finished, Roger placed the plastic glass on the cement and waved to Em to come in. She slipped into the water and joined him.

"Did you enjoy the wedding?" Roger asked. "We haven't had any time to talk about it." Maybe he could find out what he'd said, what had offended her. Em moved over to the side of the pool, where she could hang on to the edge and not have to tread water.

"My ears still hurt." Roger joined her.

"I know. Samantha talked nonstop and that

band was a little loud." Em drew her finger across his lips. "Looks like a permanent smile carved here. Couldn't have been all that bad."

"It was wonderful. And I'm so glad you could be there. I particularly liked the dancing. Maybe we could try that again, sometime."

Em looked away. "It was nice." She pushed off from the edge and began swimming the length of the pool. Being alone with Roger heightened her awareness of him. Better to work out the frustration that produced in physical exertion and avoid any possibility of getting personal. That backrub using the sunblock had been way too…personal. Roger kept pace with her, and they swam back and forth several times before he stopped in the deep end and grasped her hand to pull her to the edge.

"Em, look at me," Roger said softly.

The chlorine water stung her eyes, and she rubbed them.

"I'll be gone for at least two weeks."

"I know. Mom's worked everything out. Nothing to worry about."

"I've been thinking a lot about that wedding, the fun we had."

"It was nice," she repeated, pulling her hand free and kicking off from the wall. She headed for the stairs to get out. Roger was right behind her. Why so much talk about the wedding? Did he want to talk about what he'd discussed with Sophia? Marriage. A wedding at the church. The thought seemed so farfetched, yet she couldn't get it out of her mind, and it made her uncomfortable.

He followed her out of the pool, over to the towels on the chaise lounge. "It was better than nice."

Her mother had gone inside, taking the boys with her, so they were alone.

"Maybe we could go out on a date when I get back. You know, dinner, dancing. Just the two of us." When she dropped the towel, Roger enclosed her in his arms and brushed his lips against hers in a tentative kiss. She was about to relax and return the kiss, their first kiss, when he added, "Did you notice, I removed Karen's picture from the living room wall?"

Again with Karen! Em stiffened and attempted to move away, but Roger held firmly to her arms. When she continued to push against him, he let her go. "Will you at least let me talk?"

"I've got things to do, and I'm not interested in your great life with Karen."

He reached for her hand and wouldn't let it go when she tried to pull free. "I know that. I also know you're uncomfortable in the living room with her portrait. I took it down and put it behind the couch. I'm going to give it to her mother the next time I see her."

Em looked at the stucco walls, the palm tree, the patio furniture. Everywhere except at Roger.

"I want you to be comfortable in this house, Em. I just want to make it easier for you."

She faced him, the muscles in her jaw still tense. "Thank you. Now may I go?"

He released her hand. She didn't look back but could see Roger in the patio doors. Before she opened them, Roger collapsed on the chaise lounge and pulled the towel up to his face. Em was sick of hearing about Karen. Would he never be able to move on with his life?

EM WAS BY the front door, dressed in shorts. "Your carriage awaits, sire." She opened the door. The white van with its airport logo stood by the curb. Roger picked up his bags.

"Do you always call the airport shuttle?" she asked.

"Sure. It beats leaving the car at the airport."

"I could drive you."

Spending more time with Em. Now that had some intriguing possibilities. "Maybe next trip. I'll give you a call when I'm coming back."

She followed him to the porch steps. "Any last-minute instructions?"

Roger hesitated. He didn't want to leave but could think of nothing else to extend his stay.

The guy driving the van gave one honk of the horn.

"You sure your mother can handle everything?"

"Are you kidding? Mom could take on the presidency and never break a sweat."

Roger dropped his luggage and reached for Em. "I'll miss you." She came easily into his arms for a warm hug, interrupted by two beeps from the van's horn.

He picked up his bags, ran to the van and deposited them in the back before taking his seat. "Looks like the wife's going to miss you," the man next to him said. With a quick nod to acknowledge his companion, Roger glanced out the window.

Em stood leaning against the porch wall, waving.

But the reference to his wife bothered Roger. Not in the same way it would have a month ago. Karen's face no longer had the same clarity. More and more, Em's image had begun to replace it. His wife. Maybe Sophia had it right. He had to make room in his heart for Em.

"Here's my list."

Em was drinking coffee at the kitchen table

the following Saturday morning when Samantha came in and handed her a paper with names of boys and girls she wanted to come to her party. "A few of the guys are sophomores and one's a junior. You don't think Dad's going to make a big deal about that, do you?"

Em glanced down at what appeared to be twenty-plus names. Amy was at the top of the list. A few names had been crossed out. Em placed her coffee cup on the table and considered the possibilities. She wished there had been more time to discuss the party with Roger, so she wouldn't have to make so many of these decisions herself.

During the week, he had called often but usually he was exhausted from dealing with the problems at work. When she'd brought up the subject of the party, he had asked her to handle it. She planned to do just that, keeping it within his guidelines. That meant it would fall short of Samantha's expectations.

"We'll have to make out invitations and confirm with your father how many guests you can have."

"I already asked them all. The ones crossed out can't come."

"Samantha, you're getting ahead of yourself here. We haven't even discussed this. What if your father doesn't want such a big crowd?"

"I'm not telling people I already asked they can't come. This is my party, Em. Don't go spoiling it."

We're back to the cantankerous teenager, Em thought as she watched Samantha pace the kitchen tile in agitation. A lot of attitude had developed since her father left, and Em was at a loss to discover the cause. Any progress she had made with the girl seemed to backslide daily. Was it her new school? Her friends? Her birthday expectations?

"I'm not spoiling it. But there will be rules you'll have to abide by. This isn't going to be a free-for-all where you can just do what you want."

"No, but you can?" Samantha stopped, placed her hands on her hips and glared at Em. "What are you talking about?"

"You're doing it with my father!"

Were they back to that business about sex? Except for that furtive kiss Roger gave her at the pool , they'd barely touched. And Samantha hadn't even been around. Em nearly rose from her chair. "Explain yourself. I haven't the slightest idea what you're talking about."

"Yes, you do. I saw you dancing, making out at the wedding. You can't tell me it stops when you enter our house."

With a push, Em glided away from the table

and stood to face her accuser. "That's exactly what I'm telling you. And don't think you can make me the target when you can't get your own way. There will be rules set down for this party or there won't be one."

Without comment, Samantha turned and walked into the hall. "You hear me?" Em called after her, but Samantha didn't respond.

Em flopped down in her chair in disgust. "You sure handled that well," she mumbled. How was she supposed to approach Roger with this new development? And why was Samantha attacking her that way?

"Problems?" Doris asked as she took the seat across from Em. "I saw the youngest lady of the house going off in a huff. Didn't even say hello."

"She's planning this party for more than twenty kids."

"She sure is going to make out. A party for her friends on Saturday night and one for the relatives on Sunday."

Although Samantha's accusations had hurt her deeply, Em didn't want to reveal her real concerns to her mother. Instead, she broached another subject that had also been bothering her. "How will Roger afford it? I mean, two parties. He's losing his job, yet he hasn't curtailed his spending one bit."

"Don't you start worrying about his finances, too. It's Roger's problem, not yours. By the way, I got a note from Betty that went to our old address. She and Dave will be docking in Los Angeles, and they plan to be here for their granddaughter's birthday."

"Won't they be surprised when they learn we're living with their son." Em picked up the remains of her coffee and tossed it in the sink.

"Not as surprised as Samantha's other grandmother was. She's been downright rude whenever I've answered the phone. She's actually hung up on me a few times when she heard my voice."

"Why is she calling?"

"To talk to Samantha. They go at it for quite some time, almost every day, although I don't think the girl initiates the calls."

"Maybe she's just trying to find out what Samantha would like for her birthday."

"Maybe."

The doorbell rang and Doris went to answer. A few moments later she shouted, "Samantha. It's Amy."

The more Em thought about it, the less she liked the idea of running two parties. Roger had instructed her to take the cash he'd set aside for emergencies and use it for his daughter's party. If Samantha didn't cooperate, the whole thing could become a nightmare. But things had to be settled. No time like the present, Em decided, as she headed toward Samantha's room.

"I WANT A tent like the one Sophia had with tiny white lights." Samantha sat cross-legged on the floor of her room with Amy settled on the bed. Em propped herself on the floor against the wall and took notes on what appeared to be a debutante's debut.

"And a DJ?" Amy added.

"Right. Did you get that?" Samantha motioned to Em, who reluctantly wrote it down.

"This will be the best party ever. Everyone will wish they had been invited."

Em looked at the expanded list. Everyone *had* been invited. This was coasting into something totally out of control, and even though it could alienate Samantha forever, Em had to put a stop to it. She tossed a roll of bills onto the floor near Samantha's foot.

"This is how much we have to spend, and your father said it won't be a dime over that."

Samantha picked up the money, and Amy jumped down to help count it. "Wow! This is going to be outrageous."

"Now, we find out what all the things on

your list will cost and determine what will be possible."

Fifteen minutes later, they discovered most everything on the list had to be eliminated. The DJ alone would consume all the money.

"How important is food? Music? Lights? Games? Do you want swimming? You want it outside or in the family room? I need some input here, girls. Do you want casual clothes or dress up?" No response.

The two girls stared dejectedly at the paper in front of them, and the dark lines crossing out most of the items they had requested. Samantha looked about ready to cry.

"Come on now. What's the most important thing?"

"Food," Amy said. "Everyone likes pizza."

"Okay. Pizza it is. I'll find where we can get the best deal."

"I don't like pizza." Samantha's scowl spoke volumes as she sat back and folded her arms over her chest.

"What do you suggest?"

"I like subs, like those long ones that come in a box."

"Good suggestion. How about we go half subs and half pizzas?"

A glimmer of a smile tweaked the corners of Samantha's mouth. "But no anchovies."

NO ANCHOVIES, Em wrote boldly across the paper. "What do you want to drink?"

"Vodka!" Amy shouted.

Em glanced at Samantha. "Do you want to suggest something?"

They settled on a cooler full of a variety of pop, water and fruit juice. The party would be held late afternoon to early evening, and would definitely end at 9:00 p.m. Christmas lights, now packed away in the garage, could be strung to provide the festive quality. Since they'd be setting up her father's ancient sound system on the patio, Amy said they could use her iPod and dock for the dancing, which was a must and would take place after swimming and the meal.

With the girls' help, Em designed invitations on her computer, and by late that day, all the plans were complete. Never had she spent a more exhausting day.

SUNDAY AFTERNOON WAS tranquil, a nice change from her previous day. Amy had stayed overnight, so now the two girls watched the music channels in the family room to determine what songs they wanted for the party. At least Em didn't have to contribute her own ideas. She still preferred music from the 80s to any of the modern tunes.

Doris had taken over Roger's office so that she could review plans for a second-grade class—her first substitute assignment. The teacher's father had died, and she'd be out for a week.

After a supervised swim, the boys had retired to their bedroom to play different games on their Xbox. Now Em had nothing to do but relax on her own. She thumbed through the mail that had arrived the previous day. Credit card statement. Telephone bill. Another letter from Bradley using her self-addressed stamped envelopes with her old address crossed out and the new one added by the post office.

This envelope was twice as thick as the previous one. Em tore it open. Copies of the bills she had torn up plus new ones fell over the kitchen table.

"What the...?" She read the handwritten note several times. "This is to inform you that I have not received payment. If it and the additional items aren't paid for by the end of this month, I will be contacting my lawyer concerning matters we discussed earlier. BST"

Em gathered all the papers and made a beeline for her room. Where had she put her divorce papers? She could remember the exact place in the apartment, but during their move, she hadn't kept track of them. An hour later, she was still delving into boxes in the garage, when Doris came in to find her.

"What's going on, Em? Our room looks like a cyclone hit it and this…" She circled the open boxes with items strewn around the cement floor. "What are you looking for?"

"My divorce papers." Em pushed away from the spot where she had been kneeling and stood. She brushed back a strand of hair that had gotten loose from her ponytail and looked around her in dismay. "I can't find them. I don't know where all my legal papers are, and that worm has the gall to say I'm supposed to pay for his college expenses."

"That's absurd. You're divorced. How can he…?"

"I don't know, Ma!" Em shouted in frustration. "Maybe there's something in my papers that says I have to pay for them. I won't know until I find those damn documents."

Em pushed past her mother and went back to her room with one destination in mind—the drawer where she had seen her cigarettes. They were months older than the ones she had tossed near Skull Valley, but they would have to do. Em grabbed the soft pack and some matches, and stuffed them in her shorts pocket before her mother entered their room.

"I'll take care of this mess later," Em said

as she headed for the door. "Right now I need some space."

"Em…"

"Not now, Mom." She held her hand up to ward off any further conversation. "I really can't handle anything more right now."

CHAPTER FOURTEEN

"I'M NOT GOOD with this legal mumbo jumbo." Em held her cell phone to her ear and took another puff on her cigarette and exhaled. Stale. She'd have to invest in fresh cigarettes if she expected any satisfaction from her sometime habit. "Once I find my papers, I'll need someone to go over them with me."

"I'll ask Harve," Jodie replied in a no-nonsense voice.

"No. Don't bother him. You were a paralegal. If you could explain…"

"Of course. I've gone through hundreds of divorce papers. From what you've told me, that ex of yours needs to be run over by an SUV."

"I'd prefer an eighteen-wheeler."

Jodie chuckled. "Right. Go for maximum damage."

"Bradley gave me to the end of this month."

"Well, as soon as you find them, phone me."

Em caught a sob in her throat. "Jodie. I'm just so afraid he might take Sammy away from me."

After she hung up, Em drew another puff, inhaling deeply. The dry, dirty taste held no appeal whatsoever. She tossed the cigarette to the ground and mashed it into the sidewalk with her sandaled foot. Oh, how she'd love to do that to Bradley.

It was dark by the time she got home. She went directly into the garage and started in on the boxes again.

"You in here, Em?" her mother called.

"Yes. I'm still looking." A scorpion skittered near her foot when she moved one of the boxes. It startled her, and a chill ran down her spine. She hated the creatures, and although their sting wasn't lethal, it could cause great discomfort. She quickly stomped on the scorpion before it could find another hiding place.

"There's no air-conditioning in here." Doris wiped the sweat from her forehead and pushed her damp hair back.

"I know, Ma. You don't have to help. You should be getting ready for tomorrow's class. You need your sleep."

"Like I'd be able to sleep knowing you're out here banging around...."

"I found it!" Hugging the papers to her chest, Em closed her eyes and whispered, "Thank you."

She had started for the door, when Doris called out, "You just going to leave this mess?"

Em turned around. Several boxes sat on the hood of Roger's Mustang. She removed them and placed them on the floor. "The mess is not going anywhere. I can tidy it tomorrow. In the meantime, you have to get ready for bed, and I need to go over these papers. Come on," she insisted with an agitated wave of her hand when her mother refused to budge.

"By the way," Doris said, following her out, "the reason I came out here to begin with was that Roger called. He asked that you call him back."

"Oh, but it's so late." Darn that Bradley, Em thought. His rotten letter even destroyed her chance to talk with Roger.

"That's okay. He said whenever you came in no matter how late. I didn't mention why you were out smoking up a storm."

Em ground her teeth before answering. "I had good cause."

"That may be, but you'd better shower and throw your clothes in the washing machine if you don't want Sammy to catch on. He's the best smoke detector going."

"No better than you." Em picked up her shirt and took a whiff. Sure enough. The smell was in her clothes. Probably her hair, too. She'd better shower before taking a chance and leaving the odor around the house. She went into the bathroom she shared with her mother and began to strip.

"Don't forget," Doris said through the door. "You're getting the boys off to school tomorrow. I'll be home by the time they're back."

Em tossed her clothes into the sink. "Okay." She ran the water and squirted some hand soap over the clothes. While they soaked, she took her shower.

Once dressed in her night clothes, she slipped into her bedroom. "You asleep yet?"

"Yes."

Em went over and sat on the edge of her mother's bed. "I apologize for my behavior today. I was short with you and ran out, leaving you with the kids. You're a treasure for putting up with me."

Doris patted Em's bare leg. "You worry me sometimes. Whenever Bradley's in the picture you get in a state."

"You're right. He knows exactly what to do to rile me. But Jodie has agreed to go over the papers with me. If necessary, I'll hire Harve as my lawyer to protect my rights, as well as Sammy's. No way will I let him get his hands on my son." As she rose from the bed, Em added, "And I'll make supper tomorrow so you can relax after work."

Thank goodness she had someone to go over the legal papers, Em thought as she left their bedroom. That knowledge and the soothing shower helped wash away all the day's anxieties.

EM FOUND A lounge chair by the pool and dialed Roger's number. He sounded groggy, as though she had roused him from a deep sleep.

"I'm sorry about calling you so late, but Mom said you needed to speak to me."

"Yes. Yes. What time is it anyway? Are we still in the same time zone?"

"It's after eleven."

"Same here. Where were you? Your mother said you disappeared before supper."

Em hesitated. No way would she mention Bradley's letter, or the fear that had taken hold of her earlier. "An errand. Samantha decided what she wants for her party, and I needed to check out some details."

"So everything's settled?"

"The invitations are ready. She's distributing them tomorrow in school." Em lay back on the cushions and watched the dark clouds roll over the distant mountains. They might get rain again tonight. "The ones for the relatives went out in the mail."

"I really appreciate your taking over this chore. How many are coming?"

"If they all show up, twenty on Saturday and about the same on Sunday."

There was a long pause and Em wondered if he had hung up or gone back to sleep. "Em, can I say something without getting you upset?"

Em sat up. The question had come out of nowhere, and she wasn't too sure how to respond. "I don't know." She waited a moment, not sure what he might want to say.

"Listen. Don't hang up, okay? If I'm overstepping let me know. Just...don't hang up."

She lay back against the cushions. "Go ahead."

He sighed. "Every time I mention Karen, you shut down." He waited but Em didn't offer any comment. "I'm going to say this, this one time. I had a wonderful marriage with Karen. We loved each other very much, and it's been hard...accepting the fact that she's gone. Out of my life. Out of the children's lives."

He paused again but Em couldn't add anything. "You still there?"

"Yes."

"I like being with you. And when we're together, Karen is the furthest..." He stopped again. "My thoughts are about how you make me feel, how you make me laugh." Another pause. His voice dropped to a near whisper. "How I want to hold you and kiss you. You, Em, not..." He didn't bother to add Karen's name.

After another moment of silence, Roger added, "You can talk now. I'm through."

Em leaned back on the cushions and stretched, one hand grasping the top of the chair. "I don't know what to say." She closed her eyes and thought about what he had said, enjoying the warmth seeping through her that had nothing to do with the Arizona weather.

There was a long pause before he said, "Have sweet dreams tonight, Auntie Em. Goodnight."

After she hung up, Em lay on the lounge. She felt comfy, comforted by his voice. Maybe he was finally releasing his hold on Karen and all those memories. Maybe he'd allow Em to fill the void.

The breeze that always preceded a storm tantalized her skin, and she pretended the warm caresses were Roger's feathery touch. Lightning flashed, making the puffy clouds visible in the darkened sky as they descended on the valley. A few large rain drops broke her trance. She hurried to gather the cushions and toss them into the shed. By the time she finished, she was soaking wet and cold. The only heat that remained in her body was the warm glow of her heart.

IT WASN'T UNTIL Tuesday that Jodie could meet Em to review the divorce documents. Jodie sat in a quiet corner of the Subway restaurant examining the papers while Em purchased their sandwiches and drinks. By the time Em got through the line with their order, Jodie had finished reading and put the papers aside.

"Bradley is one conniving idiot. Nothing in there says you have to pay for anything. Where does he come off sending these to you?" Jodie picked up the receipts and dropped them back on the table.

Somewhat relieved, Em took a bite of her turkey sandwich. She chewed on it for a while before saying, "Then he can't take Sammy away if I don't pay his bills?"

"He's yanking your chain, Em. These papers say you have full custody, and he's supposed to pay child support. He's also supposed to provide medical insurance. Has he done any of that?"

"Not since he lost his job and his insurance was terminated. Nothing at all on the child support since I left California."

"And you've been divorced how long?" Jodie glanced down at the papers. "Over a year?"

Em nodded. "I can't get blood from a stone. He's not working now that he's gone back to college." She was about to take another bite, when Jodie grabbed her hand.

"And you trust what this guy says now, this lying cheat who hasn't been honest with you since the day you met?"

Em's appetite suddenly disappeared. "What do you mean?"

"How can he take Sammy away? If he's not working, he can't support a child."

"You're right," Em said as relief swept over her. How logical. Whenever Bradley entered the picture, she lost the ability to reason.

"For that matter," Jodie continued, "how can he even pay for college? Is he a veteran?"

Em shook her head.

"Is he so smart that he gets scholarships? What about government loans?"

Em shook her head again. "He gets gullible women like me. For all I know, another woman is supporting him."

"How do you know he's not working? For that matter, how do you know he went back to college? Just because he sends you copies of receipts doesn't mean he actually kept those books. He could have bought them and returned them after making these copies."

Em sat back in wonder as Bradley's possible deception became evident. "Why didn't I think of that?" She leaned forward and slammed a fist on the table. "That scorpion! Of course. He figures he can say anything because I have no way to check. He knows I can't afford to take off from work and track him down in California."

"Ah, but we can check. Harve has this detective who works for him sometimes and he can find out everything for us."

"Detectives cost money."

Jodi ignored Em's statement and went on. "You know Bradley's social security number? This guy can track almost anything through the internet. At the very least, he can find out if your ex-hubby went back to college."

Em reached over and grasped Jodie's hand, nearly knocking the water glass over. She didn't say anything. She didn't have to. The joy she felt had to reflect in her eyes.

"I HATE THEM. I want to move out."

Em looked up from her magazine to see Sammy's scowling face in front of her. "We can't move out. We've got no place to go."

"Well, I can move in with you and Grandma."

"There's no room for another bed."

Sammy pushed her magazine aside and climbed into her lap. "I can sleep with you."

"What's the problem with Chip and Chaz?" Em waited until her son stopped squirming before wrapping her arms around him.

He thought a moment before saying, "They're takin' my toys and won't let me have them."

"This happen a lot?" Em enjoyed the snuggling. There hadn't been much of it since they'd moved in. Up to now he'd been perfectly happy with his friends.

With a shake of his head, Sammy went on to say, "Samantha told me I'm not one of her brothers. She says I'm only here temparoyolly."

"Temporarily?"

"Yeah, that one. What does it mean?"

"It means we're only here for a short time, and she's right, you know. When Mr. Holden finds a new nanny for his family, we'll have to go." That subject hadn't been addressed and probably wouldn't be for a while. Roger was so busy with training new people and transferring the work to Seattle he'd had no time to look into the matter.

"I don't want to go. I like it here."

Em hid her smile as her son reversed his position. She hoped he wouldn't have to move. She enjoyed living here, too, being part of Roger's family. If only they could make the situation permanent.

Just one problem existed. Karen's presence still dominated the house, through her photos, her decorating and that frightful portrait Em had to avoid every time she went past the living room. Roger had removed it, but several days ago, about the same time Samantha began acting rebellious, the picture returned. Karen's mother also made her presence known, calling every day, asking questions and issuing orders. Had the picture's reappearance anything to do with her?

"Where will we live if we have to leave?" Sammy's small voice interrupted Em's thoughts.

"We'll buy a house." Not as grand as this, but one they could call their own. Doris had set up an account with her first pay from Roger, and Em added what she could each payday of hers. "It will have a backyard where you can play with your friends, and you'll have your own room and won't have to share with anyone."

"I like sharing," he said as he pushed off her lap.

Really, she thought, *then what was this big problem with the boys?* By the time he'd disappeared and headed back up the stairs, she realized his real problem. Samantha.

The girl had become combative as well as

rebellious since her father left, disagreeing with anything and everyone. And Em hadn't figured out why. If only she could discuss it with Roger. Maybe she'd have a chance when he returned.

ANOTHER LUNCHEON WITH Jodie a week later turned into an eye-opener. "That detective found all this on the internet?" Em checked over the printed sheet of information in wonder. The attached bill would eat up what she'd allotted this week for their house fund, but it was worth it.

"Bradley Samuel Turner, otherwise known as slug bug, has a job and has not enrolled in any college within 100 miles of his address. Nor has he enrolled in online classes that could be thousands of miles away."

"So what should I do?" Em asked, folding the sheet and slipping it back into its envelope. "Call him, confront him, take him to court and get every last cent he owes me?" That would include the hospital bill she'd had to charge in Prescott when Sammy had to be admitted. Em sat back and tapped the envelope on the Mexican-tiled restaurant table.

"Right now, I'd say nothing."

"Nothing?"

"From the little I've learned about this man

and the way he affects you—" Jodie leaned closer "—I'd say don't antagonize him."

Jodie's words effectively silenced Em.

"I've seen it before. He's an abuser."

Immediately, Em rushed to Bradley's defense. "He's never hit me. Never even raised his voice."

"No, maybe not that kind of abuse, but the man radiates a need to control you. And he obviously gets some kind of pleasure from it. Even though he has no rights, he knows you well enough to pull your strings. He's doing that now with these threats."

"But he has no basis, right? He can't take Sammy."

"No. But he can make your life miserable. I've seen it before—civil suits with no real legal grounding that get thrown out eventually but ruin your life and drag on for years."

Em was close to a panic attack. "But what can he do?"

"How much does he know about your present living conditions?"

"Nothing. I haven't told him I moved, and anything he sends me gets forwarded. I guess I should notify…"

"Don't."

"Why not?"

"He might use that to take you to court."

"What?" Em rose slightly before flopping back onto her seat. "What are you talking about?"

"If he finds out you're living in another man's house and sleeping with him..."

This time Em did jump up. "I'm not!" she shouted.

Jodie stood and grabbed Em's arm, forcing her back into her seat. "That's not what I heard."

Em glanced around at several patrons, who stared back. She gave them a weak smile before returning her attention to Jodie. Leaning across the table, Em whispered, "What did you hear, and where did you hear it?"

Jodie met her halfway so that their faces were only inches away. "Samantha."

With an angry rap to the table, Em sat back. "Where does she come off saying such a thing? Roger and I have done nothing to warrant that accusation. And I promised her when we went shopping that I'd never do that outside of marriage."

"It came up?"

"You'd be surprised what comes up with that girl." Em squirmed in her seat and looked around to see if they were still the center of attention. "We were getting along fine, then he left for Seattle and she's become impossible, and I can't figure out why."

"The behavior started after he left?"

"Yes. And he's been away for nearly two weeks. Exactly when could we have done anything?"

"So, she's never witnessed anything."

"Some dancing at Sophia's wedding."

"No kissing?"

"One time. And she wasn't even home. That's it." Em held her right hand up. "I swear."

"Maybe she's confused, you know, not sure how…"

With a sigh, Em tossed her head back, before looking Jodie straight in the eye. "That kid knows more than I knew on my wedding night."

"You're probably right. Either way, you don't want any of this to land in Bradley's lap. Even if he can't make anything stick, he could put doubt in a judge's mind about your fitness as a mother. I've seen it happen. People with determination can screw everything up and make it look worse than it is, and it could mean a long drawn-out problem until the matter is settled."

"I don't believe this," Em said as she closed her eyes, clenched her hands and shook them in frustration. "Why do these things happen to me?"

CHAPTER FIFTEEN

IT WAS ALREADY October, more than a month since Roger and Em had had their kiss. He was back in Seattle again, where he'd spent most of his time. None of his stopovers in Phoenix had included any chance for him and Em to be alone. It frustrated him every time he thought of it, usually on the long commutes.

Roger tossed his suitcase on the hotel bed and took out the double gold picture frame with its hinged spine. He'd packed it every time he traveled, updating the pictures whenever new ones became available.

He stared at the side containing his children. How big they'd grown in the year since this photo was taken. On the other side of the frame, Karen smiled back at him. Who knew that only a few months after posing for this picture she'd be gone? They'd had nearly twelve wonderful married years together. Roger sighed and gave each picture a kiss before placing the frame on the night stand next to the bed.

He reached into the suitcase pocket and removed a packet of pictures Jodie had taken at his nephew's party. He began flipping through them, then stopped at the one he wanted. Em grinned at the camera with her arms wrapped around Sammy's neck. It was impossible not to grin back. She made him smile, not only when he was with her but also during those long times when they were apart. Just thinking about Em...

Over the past month they hadn't had the opportunity to share even the slightest kiss. If the children didn't intercept every stolen moment, then Doris took over and watched their every move. He'd had more freedom as a teenager.

Roger picked up the phone and dialed his home number. Everyone should be in bed by now, including Doris, the Wicked Witch of the West. He grinned as he thought of how she now had his home running like a well-oiled machine. Everyone helped, and he hadn't found kitchen duty such a drudge, after all. At least it gave him a chance to spend a few minutes with Em, even if it usually included one or more children.

He let the phone ring once then hung up—their prearranged signal. He dialed again.

"Hello." Em's voice was soft and low, and he pictured her hunkered down on the couch in an effort to keep anyone else from hearing her.

"Hi. The kids in bed?"

"Finally. Mom's totally done in, as well. How's Seattle? Enjoying the rain?"

"Nope. Missing the sunshine." He choked back his desire to say, *You're the sun, radiating warmth and light. I miss you.*

"Well, we certainly have plenty of that to go around. It's still hitting 90 here."

Were they reduced to talking about the weather? Roger flopped onto the bed. "I've been thinking, we haven't had a moment to ourselves since you moved in. How about you and me going out on that date when I get back?"

"Oh, a date?"

Roger chuckled. He picked up the photo of her and Sammy and set it against the picture frame. "Yeah, a real honest-to-goodness date. We'll go dancing, too, if you want, or maybe to a play. What do you say?"

"I'd love to. When?"

"Saturday night. I'll be flying in Friday on the redeye."

"Saturday? Oh, no, we can't." Her voice rang with genuine disappointment.

Roger sat up and tossed his legs over the side of the bed. "Why not?"

"It's Samantha's birthday. She turns fourteen

and we're having this special party for her. Remember, that boy-girl thing you agreed to?"

Roger smacked his forehead with his palm. He had agreed to let Samantha have the kind of party she wanted during their trip to Tucson. It was this Saturday? Of course he'd put it out of his mind once Em took over all the preparations. Samantha had mentioned it during his short time at home, along with a not-so-subtle hint about getting her ears pierced.

"A few adults should be handy. Jodie's taking the boys to the movies and then keeping them overnight. It's up to you, me and Mom, unless you think we should ask someone else for additional help."

"No. We don't need overkill. But I thought we had another week."

"And don't forget Sunday we're having your family over."

Roger cradled his head in his hand and leaned an elbow on his knee. "Then Monday night I'm flying back here after checking in at the Phoenix office." He began to rub the spot above his eyes where a headache had clamped itself.

"Plan on Monday," he said, standing and reaching into his bag for some aspirin. "We'll have dinner before I take off, in that restaurant that spins around overlooking Phoenix. Sound okay?"

"Sounds great." He shook two pills from the bottle and was considering swallowing them without water, when Em whispered, "I've got to hang up. Somebody's coming down the stairs." A moment later the line went dead.

Damn. The phone call left him frustrated. His dreams would have to do, just as they had since Em became a part of his life. He popped the pills into his mouth and headed for the bathroom and some water to wash them down.

When he returned, he took Em's photo and studied it for a moment. It produced another smile. He slipped it in front of Karen's and ran a finger over the curve of Em's face.

Once he was back in Phoenix, he planned to ask Em to marry him. Metro had given him a firm offer to move him and his family to Seattle to run the customer-relations operations. At least he had a future now, something to offer Em along with his name. He hoped that would be enough for her to commit to his large, sometimes unruly family.

He reached into his bag again and removed a tiny blue box. Originally, he had gone into the jewelry store in search of a ring, something to present to Em when he popped the question. But all his confidence had slipped through his shoes the moment he'd searched the display. What did he know of her tastes, her desires? Nothing.

Had her first husband given her an engagement ring? Was it a diamond? He had no desire to duplicate anything that might remind her of Bradley Turner. Roger tried recalling what he'd bought for Karen, but that had been years after they were married, and she had picked it out herself.

He did know Em favored pierced ears for Samantha. So, instead of a ring, he checked out the earrings, searching for something for his daughter that wouldn't shatter his teeth every time he looked at her. He had settled on tiny diamond studs. Samantha would be thrilled to finally get what she'd been begging for, and he'd please Em, as well.

After Roger repacked the box, he stretched out on the bed, crossed his ankles and folded his hands under his head. If only his own wishes would come true. "She has to say yes," he said in a desperate whisper. He couldn't imagine living the rest of his life without Auntie Em. Tomorrow he'd give Doris a call to find out what kind of engagement ring Em had had, and then he'd go shopping for the biggest and best ring he could afford.

EM COULDN'T SLEEP. She went outside to sit in a lounge chair near the pool and gazed at the moon, enjoying the cool night breeze. Did the same moon shine over Roger now, or was it lost in perpetual rain clouds?

Now that October had arrived, the summer heat was gone, and she could appreciate why she had moved to Phoenix. The dry air had helped Sammy's asthma to such an extent that he rarely needed his medications, although he still carried them in his backpack in case of emergencies. A seasonal bout could always come on, and she didn't want him unprepared.

She had to stop calling him Sammy. That first day of school he had come home with a long face. "My teacher won't call me The Bus."

Thank goodness, Em thought, thoroughly annoyed with hearing that moniker. "So, what's she going to call you?"

"She says my name is Bradley, and I can go by that or Brad. What should I use?"

All these years she'd avoided calling him either one because they reminded her so much of his father and her devastating marriage. "Well, Brad is more like a nickname. And it has four letters like Chip and Chaz."

"Right," he said beaming. "I forgot about that."

She had so many happy memories like that

one to replace the bad. Em smiled and leaned back on the chaise lounge.

She hadn't heard from Bradley. Whether that was a good sign or not, she didn't know. She felt guilty not sending him her new address, but her phone number hadn't changed. They still had the one from the apartment and a whole year to get their mail forwarded. She wouldn't dwell on the issue.

If only Roger would hurry and come home. She missed him so much. He was flying in late tonight, too late for her to stay up and wait. Em got up and stretched. Might as well go to bed. The sooner she went to sleep, the sooner she could wake up and find Roger safely home.

EM AWOKE WITH panic gripping her heart. She stayed as still as possible in an attempt to determine what had awakened her. Doris snored softly in the next bed.

There it was again. Coughing? Was Sammy hacking away only hours after she had considered his health improved? She got up, threw on a robe and headed for his room.

A nightlight in the upstairs hall guided her through the darkened corridor. She tried to recall if he had dropped his backpack in his room or somewhere in the kitchen. Maybe she should go downstairs and get another inhaler from the supply she kept in her medicine chest.

Em stood indecisively by his door and waited for another bout of coughing. Nothing. Why disturb him if he had already gone back to sleep? She turned and had started for the staircase, when a beam of light flooded over her.

"What are you doing here?" Samantha asked.

Startled, Em backed away. "I didn't know you were up."

Samantha leaned against the doorjamb of her room and folded her arms across her chest. "So you're doing it with my dad after all. All those denials were a bunch of crap." The look of disgust she aimed at Em chilled Em to the bone. Samantha's chin began to wobble, and she turned abruptly, then slammed the door in Em's face.

Another light streamed into the darkened hall. "What's going…? Em, is that you?" Roger asked.

Em swiveled to see him silhouetted against the light. When had he come home? "Yes. I…I thought I heard someone coughing." She glanced back at Samantha's door. Did she hear crying? She would speak to the girl and set her straight after she spoke to Roger.

"That was me," he said as he approached. "I took a drink of water. Went down the wrong tube. Come here," he whispered and pulled her into his arms. All thoughts of Samantha disappeared as Roger warmed her within his embrace. Their lips touched in a real kiss, not the ones she'd been forced to recall in her dreams.

Em hummed in contentment as she placed her arms around his shoulders.

Samantha's door slammed open, sending a shaft of light over them. Roger and Em blinked and broke apart. Roger rubbed the back of his hand against his mouth while Samantha brushed tears from her cheeks.

"You gotta do it right by my door?" she shouted. "If I wanted to see porn I could surf the internet."

"Quiet, Samantha," Roger said in a tightly controlled voice, "You'll wake the rest of the house."

"Is that all you can say to me? 'Quiet, Samantha?'" she said, her voice hitting an hysterical high note. "You make me sick!" She backed away and slammed the door anew.

Roger reached for the doorknob and pushed his shoulder against the door, but it was already locked. Em grabbed his arm and kept him from driving a fist into it. "Don't. You'll wake everyone up. Give her a chance to calm down."

For several moments Roger stood in front of the door, taking deep breaths. Finally, he backed away and said, "I'll speak to her in the morning."

"I'll see you then, too."

"No, come with me," Roger said as he grasped her wrist and led her toward his bedroom. Em pulled back, her bare feet gripping the tiled floor. She wasn't about to add anything to Samantha's arsenal.

"No."

Roger stopped. "I just want to show you something."

Slipping her arm free, Em started for the stairs. "Then bring it downstairs." She scurried away before he had a chance to object.

Her heart was racing. She empathized with Samantha and wished she could minimize her pain, yet she also wanted to bask in Roger's arms. One part of her hoped Roger wouldn't follow her. She wasn't sure she could control this longing, this need to be with him.

When she reached the kitchen, Em opened the refrigerator and enjoyed the cool air it offered. For several moments she examine the contents, looking for something to calm her nerves. Milk. That always worked in the past. She took out the container of low-fat milk and poured herself a glass. When she heard the scuff of footsteps on the stairs, she sank onto a chair at the kitchen table and clutched the cold glass of milk in a viselike grip.

"You in here?" Roger asked and switched on the kitchen light. She placed her hand over her eyes to cut the glare. "Sorry." Immediately the lights dimmed to a soft glow. "Here," Roger said, placing a tiny, square, blue-velvet-covered box in front of her.

Em's hand convulsed, and she nearly tipped over her milk on the table. It couldn't be! It looked like an engagement-ring box with a small embossed gold diamond on the top. She tried catching her breath. They hadn't even had their first date. And this certainly didn't come off as the most romantic proposal.

"What is it?" she asked, afraid to let her thoughts continue down the road they were traveling.

Roger reached across the kitchen table and popped open the box. Two diamonds sent rainbows of color skittering across the wall and ceiling. "Samantha's earrings, although I'm not sure I want to give them to her at this point, after the way she acted tonight."

Em couldn't respond. She was too busy admonishing herself for being stupid, idiotic, and just plain crazy. How could she have had the audacity to imagine Roger might propose marriage?

"What do you think? Will she like them?" While Em stared, mesmerized by the diamonds' sparkle, he continued, "They're not too small are they?"

Em cleared her throat. "Um, ah, no. They're beautiful. She'll love them."

He reached for her hand, but she pulled away. "It's late. We'd better get to bed." Once on her feet, Em took off for her room.

You're the world's worst fool, she scolded herself. *Just because he's said he likes you doesn't mean he's interested in marriage.* Tears started the moment her head touched the pillow, and she spent most of the night muffling her sobs. She didn't get to sleep until the sun brightened the horizon.

IT WAS MORNING, close to eight o'clock when Roger came down for breakfast. All three boys greeted him with requests for his participation in some athletic sport. "Not now," Roger said as he seated himself at the table. He smiled at Em, who was busy buttering toast, and gave Doris a nod. She winked and pointed to her ring finger. He quickly looked away. The last thing he needed was someone noticing the conspiracy between them.

"Today's Samantha's birthday. Has she come down?"

"Old sour ball," Chaz said.

Chip came over and wrapped an arm around Roger's shoulder. "She doesn't get up in the morning when there's no school."

"Oh, why not?" Roger didn't direct the question at anyone in particular, but Doris answered him as she poured his coffee.

"The princess doesn't care to communicate with the local riffraff and stays pretty much in her room. On occasion, when she thinks we need instruction on how to live our lives, she'll grace us with her company."

Roger slammed his fork onto the table and looked at Em. "Since when?" She glanced up but turned her attention to the boys.

"If you're finished, take your bowls over to the sink, and go out and play."

"You going to give it to her, Dad?" Chip asked as he followed Em's instructions.

Chaz joined in with, "Samantha bosses us around and starts trouble."

Sammy didn't say anything, but his serious scowl and silent nod spoke volumes.

"Go on boys." Doris shooed them to the back door. "When I finish in here, we can play baseball." Reluctantly, they did as they were told.

"Is anyone going to enlighten me?"

"Her whole behavior changed right after you

left for Seattle the first time," Em said in her soft voice.

"That was over a month ago, and I'm just hearing about this now?"

Doris let out a prolonged sigh. "We thought we could handle it."

"You had so many worries and problems dealing with work," Em added, "and we didn't want to add…"

"Get this straight, you two." Roger picked up his fork and shook it at them both. "My family comes first no matter what other problems I may have. What's going on with Samantha?"

"She's been fighting with everyone—me, Em, the boys. So far no problems with school, but that can't be far behind."

"And you didn't think this was important enough to mention it to me?" Roger tossed his napkin on the table and started to stand. "I'm getting to the bottom of this."

Doris grabbed his arm and sat him back down. "There's more. Em, tell him."

Em sat with her elbows on the table, her chin pressed into her clasped hands. "She's been going into rages, similar to last night, accusing me of having sex with you."

Gripping the edge of the table, Roger sat back in astonishment. "What?"

"Nothing I say seems to calm her. And she's

told other people, as well. Jodie, for sure, and maybe her grandmother Millie. She talks with her almost every day."

Roger reached for Em's hand. "Did these calls from Millie begin right after I left?"

Em nodded. "I think so. Millie won't talk to Mom or me."

Doris piped up. "That's not true. She's lectured me a few times. Says I'm not fit to run this household. And told me she didn't like my accent. My accent! I've lived in Arizona all my life. What kind of accent could I have?" Doris squinted and stared at the ceiling. "Called me trash on one occasion. Probably was when I told her she could take her opinion and put it where the sun don't shine."

"Mother, you didn't."

"Wouldn't talk to me after that, but she's sure been giving Samantha an earful."

Roger pushed his chair away. Millie. So destructive. Not only would he get to the bottom of this, he'd keep that woman from ever interfering with his family again. Grandmother or not, he wouldn't allow her to create discord among the people he loved.

He sat back. "Your accent? You don't have an accent."

"That's what I said." Doris became concerned and leaned across the table. "She's confusing me with Sophia, isn't she?"

"That seems unlikely. She knows Sophia left more than a month ago." Roger scowled, and glanced at his watch. "Excuse me. I've got to make a call."

CHAPTER SIXTEEN

"SAMANTHA," ROGER SAID when he tapped on her door. He tried the doorknob. Locked. Putting more muscle behind his next knock, he raised his voice. "Samantha, open this door. Now!"

"Jus' a minute," a sleepy voice said.

Teenagers. One minute you have them all figured out, and then they pull a 180. Samantha had actually been human before, during and after their trip to Sophia's wedding. A person whose company he enjoyed, someone who treated everyone with respect. What had happened to create these problems?

He counted to thirteen before the lock clicked. Waited still longer until she opened the door. "Whatcha want?" Samantha said through a yawn. She adjusted a white robe over her light blue pajamas as he entered the room.

Roger fought to control his anger. He strode to a chair, dropped a pile of clothes to the floor and sat.

"It's your birthday. Thought I'd come up and

give you your present." He opened his hand and showed the little blue box that he'd been clutching. She responded with wide-open eyes and a mouth forming a round *O*. Good. Her desire for material goods had woken her.

"Thanks, Dad," she said reaching for the gift, her grin of pleasure softening the anger he had accumulated. Roger leaned over, elbows on his thighs, and grasped the box between his hands, keeping it out of her reach. "First take a seat," he said, staring at the box. "I have to talk to you."

When he looked up, Samantha had shuffled to her bed, arms crossed over her chest, a look of scalding distrust on her face. He waited until she sat down before he began.

What could he say that would make sense to Samantha? How did one discuss with a fourteen-year-old daughter the subject of sex? Since starting up those stairs to Samantha's room, he'd formulated several approaches. Now he felt tongue-tied.

"Soooo." Samantha raised her eyebrows. "What trick am I supposed to perform to get my gift?"

Hoping to stall longer, Roger cleared his throat.

"Well?"

"I understand you've been telling people

Em and I are…" He couldn't say the word and thought of several euphemisms before settling on "…fooling around."

Samantha pressed her lips together.

"Where did you get that idea?" he continued.

She looked away, suddenly fascinated with something in the corner of her room.

"Let me tell you here and now, we aren't and we haven't." She sat straighter, focusing on something closer to him. "Em made a promise to you, and we're abiding by it."

Samantha turned to face him. "You mean what she said about doing it only when she's married?"

Roger nodded.

"But you'd go ahead if she hadn't promised?"

Roger didn't like the tone of Samantha's voice. He felt heat rising in his neck. Why was being honest with his daughter so hard? "I'm attracted to her."

"Like you were to my mother?"

He swallowed. Could this possibly get harder? "Something like that."

Samantha guffawed, a forced laugh totally lacking any humor.

"We're not married, so we're not doing it." He expected his precise words and no-nonsense tone would finally put an end to the conversation.

"You weren't married to Mom."

Roger stood and scratched the back of his head. "That was different. Your mother and I were young and...naive." He could say stupid, but he never liked that word. "We didn't exercise any control."

Samantha's expression went from serious to puzzled in a matter of moments. "You're kissing all the time."

Certainly not all the time. Too few times, as far as he was concerned. "Is that what you're basing all this on, because kissing isn't..." His insides might be blushing, but he strained to keep his face muscles under control. Roger plopped back against the chair. "You know the difference, don't you?"

"Of course."

"Then why are you telling tales, making things up about Em and me? Do you have any idea how much these stories hurt?"

Samantha made a choking sound not much different from a sob.

"Has any of this come from your talks with Grandma Millie?"

"She talks to me all the time," Samantha said in a high-pitched voice that tore at his heart. "She says you and Em are living in sin. And it's worse than what you did to my mother, getting her pregnant with me. She says you're both going to burn in hellfire."

Roger flew to his daughter's side and cradled her in his arms before he even realized he had left his chair. "Oh, honey. I had no idea she was filling you with such nonsense."

Samantha continued to cry as though a dam had broken. Through halting sobs, she said, "I was a mistake. Nobody wanted me."

"That's not true. Your mother and I couldn't have been happier when we learned you were on the way. We always wanted to marry. Your arrival just made a wedding happen faster than we planned. And for that I'll always be grateful."

"But you should have waited till after you were married to have me."

"If we waited, we would have had another child and missed out on this special birthday." He handed the box to her, and she accepted it with shaking hands. "You going to look?"

She snapped open the lid. She fingered the sparkling diamonds a moment before saying, "My ears aren't pierced, Daddy."

"I thought I could do it." He pinched her earlobe, and she moved to get out of his reach. A smile slowly turned up the corners of her mouth as she wiped tears from her cheeks.

"Are they real?"

"Of course." He'd checked out the less expensive zircons, but Karen had always preferred the genuine article to a fake. She had waited until they could afford the real thing. He couldn't do any less for their daughter. Besides, now with a guaranteed job, he no longer had to worry about money.

"So you and Em have thought about doing it?"

Hadn't they finished with that subject? Roger got up and started for the door, still not comfortable having this discussion with his daughter. "No, it's not going to happen."

"It could if you got married." Samantha glanced his way before focusing on the diamonds again.

He gripped the doorknob. "Marriage? That wouldn't bother you?"

Samantha shrugged, but her mouth widened in a big grin.

"I'll give it some thought," he said as he closed the door behind him. At least she hadn't seen the widening grin on his face that he couldn't control. Knowing that Samantha approved felt good.

But his joy soon evaporated as he remembered who had caused all the anxiety in his home. How would he handle Millie? Roger had never realized how warped the woman had become. And to think she had wanted him to put his children in her care.

He walked down the stairs considering what he'd learned earlier that morning when he'd talked to Millie's older sister, Joanne. The two planned to attend the relatives' party on Sunday. According to Joanne, it might be the last time Millie would be able to visit them.

"I'M SORRY I acted so dumb last night," Samantha said to Em after breakfast when they were alone in the kitchen. "I heard the coughing, too, but I knew it wasn't Brad." Unlike Em, who still thought of her son as Sammy, everyone else in the family had adjusted to calling him by his new name.

"So, you talked to your father?"

"Yep." Samantha reached into the pocket of her cut-off jeans and pulled out the blue box. At least she no longer wore her father's baggy shirts, and today sported a striped jersey, instead. "See what he gave me for my birthday?" She snapped open the box and displayed the diamond earrings. "Can you take me to the mall today to get my ears pierced so I can wear the earrings to my party?"

"Sure."

Samantha moved the box around so that the diamonds would capture the light. The ear-

rings sent shafts of rainbows around the room.
"I want two holes in each ear, so I can use the
hoops Sophia gave me."

"Whoa, lady. Did your father agree to that?"

"Em," she wailed. "What good is one dinky
hole?"

"Maybe you should give the topic a rest for
a while," Em said as she placed the breakfast
dishes in the sink. Neither she nor her mother
liked using a dishwasher for small loads. "Your
father needs some peace. Let him get used to
the pierced look, then he'll be more likely to
consider more ."

"Okay. But I can only wait so long—" she
paused and gave Em an impish grin "—before
I get my tongue pierced."

"You little…!" Em shouted as she snapped
the dish towel in the girl's direction.

Samantha sashayed away, shaking with ri-
otous laughter. How good to hear that again.
Her talk with her father had worked miracles.
When the girl reached the hall, she waved and
blew Em a kiss. "See ya later, alligator."

"Happy Birthday, crocodile."

"What's all that noise?" Roger asked as he
entered the kitchen from the patio.

"We made up. Thanks. I don't know what
you said, but she's now a civilized human being
again."

"Did she like the earrings?" A smile lighted his face.

"Loved them. I'll take her to the mall later to get her ears pierced—unless you want to do it."

Roger grimaced. "No, I'll stay and help Doris with the party decorations. Who had the idea of stringing Christmas lights?"

"Samantha."

"I like it. The place will look festive. They can do for tomorrow as well when my parents come. Everything ready for today?"

"Pizzas and a giant sub are ordered and will be here around five. The cake's in the fridge and the drinks are sitting on ice in the cooler."

Roger came up behind Em and wrapped his arms around her waist. He kissed her ear and pulled her closer. Em dropped her hands into the soapy suds and melted against him. "I've been noticing how well you fit in with my family," he said in a husky voice.

"I've noticed that myself." Em closed her eyes and enjoyed the warmth spreading through her. She drew her hands out of the water and placed them over his.

"Oh, Em," he whispered before kissing her neck.

"You helping her with the dishes?" Doris asked.

Both Em and Roger stiffened. "Yes, Mom,

he is." Immediately, she plopped her hands back in the water.

"Well, see that you don't take long. I need some help outside." Doris opened the patio door and stepped out.

Em turned around as he headed for the patio. And for the second time that day, a person she loved blew her a kiss.

As FOUR O'CLOCK arrived, so did the guests. One by one the young adults entered the house in varying hair styles and hair colors, including fluorescent pink and neon blue. Most of them had pierced at least one body part. Roger stood by the door greeting his daughter's friends, several he remembered, but he'd never met the new ones she'd made in high school.

Several times he shuddered inwardly, but he pasted a smile on his face. Why would any girl want to put a hole in the side of her nose?

He must have voiced the question because the petite girl with pink hair popped the gold dot off. "Isn't it neat? It's glued on, and the hair color washes out," she said with a grin. "Samantha's so lucky you let her pierce her ears. My parents won't let me pierce anything."

A month ago, he had felt the same way. Roger glanced over at his daughter, now sporting her new gold studs supplied when she got her ears pierced. She'd have to wait at least a month while her ears healed before she could use the diamonds. Whatever his misgivings had been, he now decided pierced ears weren't so bad.

Em had been greeting the guests and so had Doris. Roger turned to greet the latest arrival.

His jaw almost dropped as a skinny young man several inches taller than he was reached for his hand. "I'm Jimmy Newhouser. Pleased to meet you, sir."

"You're a freshman?" Roger asked, trying to extract his hand from Jimmy's grasp.

"Nah. Junior." He looked past Roger and grinned. "Hey, Samantha." He waved and headed toward the birthday girl.

A junior? Jimmy what's-his-name looked more like a freshman in college. The fact that he was clean-cut, with no crazy hair coloring, tattoos or piercings, didn't relieve Roger's anxieties.

Other guests had brought brightly wrapped presents. Jimmy had his in a brown paper bag. Despite the boy's polite manners, Roger made a mental note to follow the progress of that bag.

The party guests proceeded through the house to the backyard, where lawn chairs and tables lined the patio. Several people stripped out of street clothes to reveal bathing suits. Others jumped directly in the pool wearing all their clothes, including their shoes. A few athletes went over to the volleyball net and began hitting the ball. The brown bag lay under a chair.

"How's it going?" Em asked him a while later, patting his arm.

"I counted 28. Didn't you say she invited 20?"

"Some might be gatecrashers, but no one's creating any problems."

"So far." He glanced toward the brown bag. It had disappeared and so had Jimmy. Roger looked around for his daughter. Sure enough, she had vanished, as well.

"Did you see where that tall kid went?"

With a frown, Em glanced at the house. "I saw him go inside."

After a quick surveillance of the area, Roger headed for the kitchen. He should have taken Em's advice and had a few more adults around to supervise. With Doris assigned to the house to make sure none of their possessions gained legs and walked out, he and Em had to cover the rest.

"You see Samantha come in with a tall kid?"

Doris moved away from the window and indicated with a quick nod the direction they had gone. "Said she needed to show him the bathroom. As though he couldn't find it himself." She took a sip of her drink before asking, "How's it going? You holding up?"

With a chuckle, Roger leaned against the counter. "Is it that obvious?"

"You have been a little stressed over this party."

"When did these kids grow up? The ones I know, I hardly recognize. And the hair styles. Do they usually look like this?"

"Halloween is just around the corner. I bet they just thought they'd start early."

A giggle came from the hallway. Roger tensed. "I'd better go see what they're up to."

Jimmy stood over Samantha with one hand braced against the wall above her head. His daughter laughed, and pushed him away. Was she enjoying Jimmy's attention or trying to escape?

About to reveal the contents of his brown bag, Jimmy stopped when Roger said, "Samantha, here you are. We're all waiting for you to open your presents." The two young adults separated just as the doorbell rang.

"The food's arrived," Roger shouted with an overabundance of enthusiasm. He opened the door to a young man with yellow hair that formed a dozen spikes across the top of his head. A gaily wrapped box peeked out from under his arm.

Samantha rushed to the door and grabbed Spike-head's hand. "Come on. You don't want to miss the party." Before Roger could speak, he and Jimmy were left alone in the hall.

"Maybe you'd like to give me that," Roger said, pointing to the brown bag Jimmy was placing behind his back.

"Ah, nah, I think not." In his attempt to avoid Roger, Jimmy smacked into the wall. A crash, then a leaking bag, confirmed Roger's assumption. Teenagers hadn't changed much from his day.

"I'll get you something to clean that up, and then you can call your parents for a ride home," Roger said as he headed for the kitchen.

"I got my own car."

Disbelieving, Roger stopped midstride. *How old is he?* Roger shuddered as he remembered how Em had fixated on him when he was so much older. He'd have to have a talk with this Jimmy and prevent any potential problems.

When he returned with a broom and damp mop, Jimmy had gone and only the wet bag and broken bottle of beer remained on the hall floor.

Although annoyed because of the time taken away from the party, Roger swept up the broken glass and then wiped down the floor with the damp mop. No sense in leaving the stench for someone else to take care of, especially since Doris had disappeared from the kitchen. Just after he returned the broom and mop to the utility closet, a phone rang.

Em's portable phone sat on the kitchen counter, its red light blinking. He considered letting the call go to her answering machine then decided to answer it. After all, it could be something important related to the party.

"Hello," he said, his thoughts distracted by the activity past the window. Samantha and Spike-head were laughing with a group of friends.

When no one answered his greeting, he returned his attention to the phone. "Hello," he said again, adding vigor to his voice. If this was another telemarketer, he'd hang up and get back outside.

"Is Emmy Lou there?" a male voice asked.

The question startled Roger. He'd never heard anyone call Em by her given name. A telemarketer for sure, reading her name off some list.

"Sorry, we're not interested in buying anything." But before Roger could hang up, the man's strident voice sounded clearly over the phone.

"Well, I'm not selling. Who the hell are you?"

Roger glared at the phone, held it several

inches from his face and hollered, "Who the hell are you?"

A click on the other end told Roger he could get back to the party. And not a moment too soon. Through the window, he could see several people hoist Samantha over their shoulders and toss her into the pool.

THE MOON GLOWED above trees strung with various colored Christmas lights. A goodly portion of food and debris lay scattered over the grass and sidewalks. Roger would pick everything up tomorrow, once his energy returned. Everyone had left, and Samantha had retired to her bedroom to go over her birthday booty. Amy had taken her iPod home. Still interested in extending the party, Doris brought out her CD player and put in a recording of Frank Sinatra, music that was more to the adults' liking.

"Who gave her that T-shirt?" Roger asked as he danced a slow dance with Em. Although he enjoyed the feel of her, her delicious smell, he could barely make his feet move in time to the music. Never had he spent a more harrowing day.

"Which one? She got several."

"The one that says 'I make good men go bad.' I want it burned before she has a chance to wear it."

Em laughed quietly near his ear. "You'll have to give her some leeway sometime."

"No way. Even when she turns fifty, she'll always be my little girl." He added a chuckle to Em's soft laughter. "Maybe I'll let her wear it then."

CHAPTER SEVENTEEN

"HAVE YOU TALKED to your son about the birds and the bees?" Roger asked Harve. They were sitting in lawn chairs under the shade of a paloverde tree while they drank their beers. The rest of the birthday party, close to twenty assorted relatives, was watching one of the boys swat at the piñata.

"You lost your marbles? The kid's only seven."

"Forget it. I've been dealing with some crazy topics. It got me thinking." Roger brushed away a few of the tree's tiny leaves that had fallen on his slacks. After a long pause, he added, "I'm going to ask Em to marry me."

"You're what?" Harve straightened in his chair and leaned closer.

"You heard me. I'm asking Em to marry me. I bought her a ring before I left Seattle."

"Are you crazy? What has it been—two, three months since you met?"

"I've known her since we were teenagers."

"Yeah, and as I recall, you considered her a pain back then."

"She grew up."

"You love her?"

Placing the empty bottle on the ground, Roger leaned forward, his arms resting on his thighs. "I don't know. It's different from Karen. It's comfortable. I don't feel pressured. Like this downsizing problem at work," he said, turning to Harve. "I can talk to Em in a way that helps me solve my problems. With Karen, we talked, but I had to solve the problems on my own."

"She's divorced, you know."

"Of course I know that."

"Have you worked out a prenup?"

With a short laugh, Roger sat back in his chair. "I haven't even found out yet if she'll consider marrying me."

"Think about it. For all you know, she's got an agenda of her own. You've got to protect yourself and the kids, just in case." Harve took a swig of his beer. "Doris is divorced, too, isn't she?"

Roger looked at his brother-in-law and scowled. "You're saying divorce runs in the family?"

"You want me to quote statistics?"

"I want you to tell me I'm doing the right thing."

Harve stood. "If you need my approval, marrying her is definitely wrong. But, since you're going to be a damn fool and do it anyway, I'll draw up the prenuptial agreement. Don't tie the knot till she signs it." He raised the bottle in a salute before heading for the picnic table piled high with food.

Lost in thought, Roger remained under the tree. Were some families more prone to divorce? Most everyone else in his family had problems, but they'd worked them out over time. He'd never contemplate marriage while maintaining an easy way out in the back of his mind. Was that what Em did when she married? Had her divorce arrangements been formulated ahead of time?

If she felt that way, maybe he should consider a prenup. He didn't want to jeopardize all that he'd worked for. More important, he didn't want to put his children in the position of potentially losing another mother.

EM WATCHED THE party from the safety of the kitchen window. Karen's mother was out there somewhere, and she didn't want to risk running into her again. Grandma Millie had a way of looking through Em as though she didn't exist.

On the other hand, Roger's parents welcomed her as one of the family. Em knew most of the cousins, too, from when she had lived with

Jodie. They all had families of their own, now, with children about the same age as Sammy.

Em closed her eyes and whacked her forehead. *I've got to stop calling him that.* "Brad," she said aloud. "Brad, Brad, Brad." Brad was enjoying himself, as well. To see him running around with all the children was wonderful. If only he'd continue to remain healthy.

Her attention turned to Roger. He appeared more rested today, now that the teenage party was over. A breeze played with his hair, and she longed to tame it with her fingers. Little chance of that with so many people around. She waited patiently while he discussed some topic with Harve. Once he left, Em decided to join Roger.

"Want another beer?" she asked as she approached. She handed him a bottle of Budweiser then sat in the chair Harve had vacated. "Nice party."

He smiled at her, twisted the cap off the bottle and took a swig. "Better than last night. At least now I can drink a beer."

"Oh, I'm sure you could have had one last night." She pressed her lips together to control a smile and gazed off at the horizon. She didn't miss his scowl.

"Sure. If I'd gotten into Jimmy What's-His-Name's stash." He sat up straighter, before leaning toward her. "What kind of idiot brings beer to a birthday party for a fourteen-year-old?"

"Only a sixteen-year-old trying to make an impression."

Roger sat back and took another sip. "Well, he's not going to darken our door again. I can tell you that."

Although she tried her best, Em couldn't contain a chuckle.

"What's so funny?"

"Dear, dear Roger." She patted his arm, forcing herself to keep things platonic. "You have to stop carving laws in stone and remember what you were like as a teenager." When he didn't interrupt, she continued, "Your rigid rules are like waving a red flag in front of a bull. Teenagers have to flout authority, even if they don't really want to."

"So you're saying if I don't allow Jimmy Whatever to come around anymore, Samantha will become that much more interested in him?"

"Possibly. Right now, though, I think she's more interested in the one with the yellow spiked hair."

"Auntie Em," Roger said in a choked voice. "That's what you had, yellow spiked hair."

"And didn't I turn out all right?"

They both started to laugh. How wonderful it was to see him relaxing, enjoying their time together.

He leaned closer. "You turned out just right." He placed his hand, cold and damp from the bottle, against her cheek and pushed a strand of hair back over her ear. His touch was warm.

"You know what I wish," he said in a low whisper, despite the fact that no one was near enough to hear. "I wish we could put some slow music on and dance like last night."

"As I recall," Em said, lowering her own voice, "you weren't too happy about those slow dances."

"Because Samantha was dancing with Spike-head. Seeing that spoiled my concentration."

"And what did you want to concentrate on?"

"Holding you in my arms. Moving as one with the music."

"Like they were doing?"

"Woman, what's with you?" he said sitting back. "Here I'm trying to draw you into a conversation, and you keep throwing those horrible images at me. Have you no romance?"

"How far do you plan to take this conversation?"

"Not far enough, I'm afraid." He gestured to the throng of people in the yard. "Whenever we start to talk about anything personal, someone always manages to interfere." With a sigh, he turned back to face her. "And I want very much to get personal." Leaning over, he murmured, "How about we chuck this whole party business and go somewhere else?"

Em fell back against her chair in laughter. "Try and control yourself until tomorrow. We have a date, remember?"

"Some date. A quick dinner and then I'm off to Seattle again." Suddenly, his expression became pensive as he looked beyond her.

"Here you are, Roger…and Emily," Grandma Millie said. Em didn't bother to remind Millie her formal name was Emmy Lou. She'd already corrected her twice, but the woman refused to remember it. "I'd like to talk to you privately, Roger, if your friend doesn't mind."

A chilling breeze wafted around them now that the sun was setting, but it had no effect on the woman's white curls. *No wonder,* Em thought, *she's carved in alabaster.* Em started to get up to leave, but Millie put her hand up, indicating she should stay put.

"Please, Roger. Could we go in the house? It's beginning to get cold out here," Millie said, glancing at Em as though she was the cause of the nocturnal chill. As Roger stood, the older version of Karen locked her arm in his, and they headed for the patio doors.

"Hello, Joanne. We haven't had a chance to

speak," Em said to the woman who had shadowed Millie. "Would you like to sit?" She pointed to the seat Roger had vacated, determined not to let Millie's putdowns irritate her.

Joanne collapsed onto the folding chair. "Yes, thank you."

"Are you Millie's younger sister?"

The woman leaned closer and tapped her arm. "Aren't you sweet. No, I'm five years older." She sighed. "I'd really appreciate it if she'd slow down. Physically, the woman is a dynamo." Joanne sighed again. "Unfortunately..." She turned and looked at her sister's retreating back before giving her full attention to Em.

"When I was talking to Betty, she said you and your mother are staying with Roger."

"Yes. It's a temporary thing. My mother is taking care of the children, and I'm helping out." She wasn't too sure how much information she should provide Joanne, what with all the problems her sister had created.

Joanne sighed and looked down at the ground a moment. "Millie is staying with me, now. She won't be calling anymore and disrupting things." Joanne gripped Millie's arm. "I realize she's put Roger's family through a lot. I'm hoping...the doctors said it's going to get worse. Dementia. It's quite heartbreaking to see the degeneration."

Em placed her hand over the other woman's. "I'm so sorry."

"You never knew her when she was in her prime." Joanne glanced over her shoulder again and stood. "I better go check on her. I haven't had any opportunity to talk to Roger since we spoke on the phone."

With a sigh, Em looked around the yard. What she needed was social contact to wash away the heartbreaking news about Grandma Millie, even though now the woman's actions made more sense. She walked away from the chairs and headed for the refreshment table, where her mother cleared the remaining food.

ROGER CONCENTRATED ON the scuff marks on his sneakers as tears streamed down his mother-in-law's face. He felt uncomfortable in her presence. Always had. Never more so than today when she had so openly slighted Em.

Millie had asked to see the portrait she had commissioned for Karen's thirtieth birthday. He took her into the living room expecting to remove it from behind the couch. When had someone put it back up? It certainly couldn't have been Doris or Em. Now, as he glanced at the painting, set regally on the living room wall, his discomfort increased. He had come to terms with his own grief, in large measure through his growing affection for Em. It no longer felt right having Karen dominate his life the way this portrait dominated the room.

"I suppose now that you're carrying on with that Emily, I won't get much chance to see her anymore," Millie said, pointing to the portrait.

Roger stiffened. "It's Em, Millie, and I'm not carrying on with her. And I'd appreciate if you'd stop insinuating such things to Samantha."

"Em," Millie said, swiping her nose with a lace hanky. "What a stupid name."

Since she totally ignored his reprimand, he let the issue go, determined instead to defend Em to the fullest. "Her name's rather endearing, actually." He paused before adding, "She's rather endearing."

Perplexed, Millie regarded him. "And who's this Samantha you keep mentioning? Another woman you're carrying on with?"

"Samantha's the birthday girl. Your granddaughter."

"Isn't this Karen's birthday?"

"Millie, Karen died several years ago."

Just then, Joanne, came into the room with Samantha. Roger reached for his daughter and placed an arm around her shoulders. "This is

Samantha, Millie." He glanced up at the portrait and saw similar features in Karen and Samantha. No wonder his mother-in-law had difficulty telling them apart. Especially after what Joanne had told him when he'd called her yesterday—that Millie was being treated for the first stages of Alzheimer's.

Millie walked over to Samantha. "Don't be silly. This is Karen." She tried brushing her hand through Samantha's hair and the girl backed away.

Stepping between them, Roger said, "Go back to your party, honey." He turned to Millie as Samantha made a quick exit, avoiding her grandmother. "I've been giving this a lot of thought, and I really feel you should have this painting."

"You and the children need her here. They can't be allowed to forget their mother."

Her confusion was playing havoc with his ability to cope. How could he reason with someone who was beyond reason? He'd never had to deal with anyone with dementia before. "The children and I can never forget her. Karen will always be the love of my life."

Em paused in the hall, a few feet from the living room. She'd heard voices and then Roger's declaration. What had come before or what would come after didn't matter. That one statement annihilated her dreams and reinforced her fears. She had no chance with Roger, never had.

For several moments, Em stood transfixed, not willing to be seen. This was absurd. Her mother had asked for a sweater from their room, and Em had to pass the living room in order to get it. She took a tentative step then doggedly continued. Maybe if she kept her head down and didn't make eye contact, she could traverse the hall unseen.

"Well, there she goes. Sneaking around like some cat burglar."

Em froze at the sound of Millie's contemptuous words. Gingerly, she pivoted to acknowledge the woman.

"Millie, that was uncalled for," Roger said as he stepped between them. "Em lives here. She doesn't have to sneak around."

"Well, she wouldn't be here at all if you had taken me up on my offer to care for the children. Paying that Spanish woman when you're losing your job. It's an outrageous waste of money."

So, she still thought Sophia worked here. Oh, well, it did no good to correct her. Roger considered telling Millie that he did have a job, but that would not only spoil his plans to surprise Em when he asked her to marry him, it would also make no impression on her. Instead, he said, "Em and her mother have been a wonderful influence on my children. I couldn't ask for more."

Em smiled at him appreciatively.

"She'll never replace Karen," Millie continued as though Em wasn't standing a few feet in front of her. "Hope she knows that." Millie returned her gaze to her daughter's portrait with a look of rapture. "Her spirit will always be in this house. Nothing can take that away." Millie turned her attention back to Em and scowled. "No matter how much you try to worm your way into this family."

Em heard the chastisement in Roger's voice as he spoke to his mother-in-law, but didn't stay around to listen to all the words. Millie was right. Hadn't Roger said as much moments before? What she needed, longed for, was undying love and commitment. Unfortunately, he'd never be able to give them to her. Not when they remained in the hands of a ghost.

Em rushed to her room, all thoughts of her mother's sweater washed from her mind. Any hope she may have fostered about Roger's interest in her was lost. He could never love her when he still cared for Karen.

But she longed so much to have Roger hold

her. She'd wanted memories of being in his arms, if not in his heart.

Em pulled open one drawer after another in search of her cigarette pack. Where had she put it? Where would she smoke once she found it? Disgusted with herself, she slammed the last drawer shut. Every time her life crumbled around her, she reached for a smoke. What a rotten crutch.

She noticed her answering machine blinking. With a resigned sigh, she pressed the button and sprawled on her back on her bed, her hands extended and her feet still touching the floor. This was her first chance to relax and let all her cares evaporate.

"You have two messages," a female voice said. "First message, Saturday, seven thirty-three p.m." That had to be yesterday when they were all outside singing "Happy Birthday" to Samantha.

"What's going on, Emmy Lou?"

Bradley's strident voice instantly brought Em to a sitting position.

"You're still not answering your phone? Isn't your little errand boy around to take your messages? So help me, if I find you're living with some guy..."

During the pause, Em sprang to her feet and stood by the machine, staring at it, her hands on either side of it. Had Bradley called before? Had Roger answered the phone? Why hadn't he mentioned it to her?

"You better not be if you want to keep our kid. Wait till the judge hears you turned into a little slut." His last remark was followed by a loud click.

The female voice came back with, "Second message, Saturday, seven forty-two p.m."

"Did you get my bills? Express mail a payment today, or so help me, Emmy Lou, I'm going to my lawyer." Click.

Blackmail. Is that what she had to look forward to? Pay Bradley blackmail to keep him from dragging her through the courts with unfounded suits?

"Em?"

Em spun around as her mother entered the room.

"I thought you were going to get me a sweater." Doris chuckled as she went to a drawer. "The party's about to really get started. Did you speak to Millie's sister? Joanne said Millie's being treated for Alzheimer's. And all this time I thought she was just crazy." Doris shook her head. "That's a real shame. Poor woman."

Doris pulled a blue sweater from the drawer and turned. "Why Em, what's the matter?" she asked, her voice full of concern. "You look positively awful. Are you feeling all right?"

Em shook her head. "No," she said in a strangled voice, clutching her throat. "I think I may be coming down with something."

"Well, take a hot shower, some aspirin and get into bed. I'll check on you later."

Once her mother was gone, Em collapsed onto her bed. The tears flowed freely, the dam that had held back all the pain of her past mistakes now broken. Number-one mistake being her ex-husband. How did she ever fall for anyone who could be so cruel?

"WHAT ARE YOU going to wear?" Samantha asked Em. It was late Monday afternoon, and Em felt as nervous as a teenager going on her first date. For that matter, it was her first date—with Roger. They'd have little chance to do more than eat in the revolving restaurant, since he had to make his plane for Seattle.

Good. Their time together would be short, followed by a week of time alone where she could sort out her life.

"So, what are you wearing?" Samantha asked, again intruding on Em's thoughts. Ever since Em had returned from work and taken her shower, Samantha had been stationed in Em's room, sitting on the bed and offering all types of advice, from what perfume to wear to maybe borrowing Samantha's new diamond earrings, still in the little blue box until she could wear them. "You should wear the black dress. It's perfect."

"I thought I was supposed to save that for you."

"You can get it cleaned. Besides, Dad's so much in the Dark Ages he won't let me wear it till I'm forty.

"Tonight's really special, isn't it?" Samantha continued. "I think he's going to ask you."

Em reached in the closet and fingered the rhinestone straps before slipping the dress over her head. *Ask me what?* Em thought. *He wanted to know more about her, he'd said. What exactly did that mean?* Em caught her breath as fear swirled through her. Maybe he'd discussed something with Bradley. Had Bradley made threats? Would Roger want her to move out? How on earth could she extricate herself from this family?

"Do you think?" Samantha asked.

Em manipulated the tight dress over her hips and adjusted the rhinestone straps on her shoulders, keeping her thoughts to herself as she answered, "Do I think what?"

Samantha bounded from the bed to help with the zipper. "That he'll ask you?"

Em glanced at the young girl to see what she might possibly be referring to. She seemed excited, happy, even. Obviously, she had no inkling what had gone through Em's thoughts.

"Ask me what?" Em ventured, assured that the girl had something else on her mind. Adjusting the thin straps, Em fussed with the top, worried that she might be showing too much cleavage.

"Marriage, silly!"

Marriage? Afraid she might topple over, Em placed her hands on the dresser and braced herself. "Where do you get your ideas? This is our first real date."

"Duh." Samantha rolled her eyes and acted like a bored teenager. "I know these things. I read romance novels. I watch TV."

Em clamped her lips. How could she end their conversation? "Should I wear my hair up or down?" she asked, more to change the subject than for an actual opinion. Roger liked her hair down, and she preferred it that way, too, now that the Phoenix heat had subsided.

"Up, definitely up, and I've got the perfect thing. Wait. Don't do anything until I get back."

Em sat down on the edge of the bed, her nerves shattered. So, she'd put her hair up and avoid further discussion. Taking it down once they were in the car would be an easy matter.

Oh, if only she could have a cigarette. What if Roger did ask her to marry him? What would she say? But would he? How could he? No, there was no way.

"Here," Samantha said as soon as she burst through the doorway. "It's a comb Sophia gave me that *señoritas* wear down in Mexico. Isn't it pretty? I'm letting my hair grow so I can use it."

Accepting the comb, Em looked at the shiny black surface with its inlay of mother-of-pearl. "It's beautiful." Em made a French twist and slipped the comb in where it would hold her hair in perfect order. "Are you sure you want me to use it?"

"Of course. I've got it wired so I can hear everything you say."

Em hesitated. Vivid pictures of the girl listening to their conversation increased her nicotine craving tenfold. "Just kidding," Samantha said, adding a giggle.

She used another comb to pull out a few blond tendrils around the back of Em's neck so that the effect wasn't so severe. Once done, Samantha plopped down on the bed then immediately jumped up to run to the door.

"Dad, you can't come in. Shoo." The door slammed before Em had a chance to see him.

Why was Roger here? Weren't they supposed to meet at the Hyatt after he finished work at the local office?

"He's getting anxious. So…" Samantha said, as she sauntered toward Em, arms held behind her back. "Are you going to say yes?"

"You're jumping to conclusions. This is nothing more than a simple dinner."

Samantha chuckled. "We have simple dinners all the time. He wants you alone. So, what are you going to say?"

Taking a deep breath didn't help Em one bit. What she needed was air infused with smoke. When Samantha looked as though she might block her exit, Em realized she'd have to provide some answer. "I don't know. I'm already a nervous wreck. I can't handle much more."

Samantha came over and gave her a hug, an unexpected show of affection that served as a balm to Em's spirits. "I just want you to know, it's fine with me." When she backed out of the embrace, Samantha brushed a tear from her eye. "I won't be able to call you Mom, though." Abruptly, she turned and ran into the hall.

"What was that all about?" Roger asked as he entered the room. "Samantha nearly knocked me down. She looks like she's crying?"

"She's okay. We just got a little emotional," Em replied, as she brushed some moisture from her lashes and checked her makeup in the mirror. She glanced at her hair and realized Samantha really had skills. Em had never thought of making the French twist so much softer. She'd have to compliment Samantha the next time they spoke.

When she turned to face Roger, she saw wonder in his eyes and something more. It made her feel wanted, secure and dizzy with expectation. With her free hand she reached up and brushed the hair off his forehead. "How come you're home? I thought I was supposed to meet you at the Hyatt."

"I forgot something." He patted his pocket.

"I could have picked it up for you." She grabbed a long crocheted shawl in shades of purple and placed it around her shoulders.

Roger pursed his lips before breaking into a grin. "I don't think so."

"Have our plans changed?"

"No," he said, before reaching over to take her hand. "You look sensational."

"So do you." He wore his usual business attire, a dark blue suit and pale blue shirt with a red print tie. It always made him appear ready to take on the world. What did he plan to take on tonight?

"I'll tell you more in the car," Roger whispered. He moved closer so that their hands were pressed between their bodies. "Right now, we better get out of here before your mother grounds me for entering your room."

CHAPTER EIGHTEEN

THE WINDOWS OF the rotating dining room displayed a scenic view of Phoenix lit by a setting sun. The view held no interest for Em. Even the attractively prepared food was tasteless. All because Roger fixated on a topic she preferred to forget.

Em never should have brought up Bradley's call. When she asked Roger if he'd answered her phone, he replied, "Sure, some rude telemarketer. Did he call back? I didn't think it important enough to mention it."

"It wasn't a telemarketer. It was Bradley."

"Your ex?" Roger asked. "He never gave his name." From then on, Bradley became the focus of Roger's conversation, something she had no desire to pursue.

"Divorce is hard. When did you and Bradley decide to break up?"

Em fidgeted with her fork, pushing some potato concoction to the side, and glanced at the waiter. He rushed to the table and refilled their water glasses. "When he got a job."

"What?" The slight guffaw that accompanied the word didn't help Em's state of mind.

Her remark sounded ridiculous without an explanation, but she had no desire to continue. "I'm not very comfortable with this subject," she said once the waiter retreated. Whenever she thought of her marriage, it reminded her what a blind fool she had been. She didn't like thinking of herself in those terms. "Can't we discuss something else?"

"Sure. It's just that I want to know as much about you as possible—the good, the bad and the ugly."

"Well, my life with Bradley was mostly…" She took a sip of her water, then put the glass aside before glancing up at Roger. "None of those." His warm brown eyes regarded her with a compassion she hadn't expected.

"I'd like to know more, but if you don't feel comfortable…."

Maybe she should delve into the bleary details. Why keep secrets? Pushing her skepticism aside, Em propped her face on one hand and pushed something green around her plate with the fork in her other hand.

"Before we were married, Bradley was attending college, going for a business degree. The goal was for him to get an education that would give him a step-up in the business world.

I was to continue working after the wedding while he completed school."

"And you didn't mind being the breadwinner?"

"I never thought of it that way. We were building a foundation for a good life. Once he had his degree, a fabulous job was guaranteed. I could stop work. We could start a family." She smiled at her naïveté. "Things didn't go as planned."

"The baby came?" Roger sighed and fiddled with his fork. "I know how an unexpected birth can throw a monkey wrench into plans."

"That's what happened with Samantha?" She sat up. Although she was familiar with the details, she appreciated the change of subject.

"Right. Fortunately, I only had a few months to go in college when we learned Karen was pregnant. We had planned on a big wedding once I graduated, but took a quick trip to Vegas, instead. It was tough the first few years with a new baby. That can put a strain on any marriage."

When Roger paused, Em continued her story. "That wasn't our problem. We were married a year before Sammy—I'm sorry, I'm still having a hard time calling him Brad."

"That's okay. What was the problem? Bradley couldn't find a good job after graduation?"

"Oh, he never graduated. He kept changing his major, dropping courses that weren't challenging enough."

"And you put up with this? I can't believe it. Not the Auntie Em I knew, who fought like a hellcat any time she didn't get her way."

"I was in love." Em stared at the table while the silence stretched out. Love. What did she know of the subject? "Then I lost my job."

"That first layoff?"

She looked up and nodded. "I couldn't find anything immediately, and Bradley was forced to find work. Even without a degree, he managed to get an excellent position."

"Problems solved. What could go wrong after that?"

"Try everything." Em pulled in a deep breath before continuing. "We owed everyone, and his job alone wouldn't pay the bills. Once I found another job, he put his money aside for a house for us. But the credit cards that were in my name continued to build. One day he moved out into an apartment of his own, taking any money he'd saved for a house and leaving me with a mountain of debts."

Roger reached over and clasped her hand. "That had to be devastating."

The contact felt warm and comforting. "I was in shock. But it was worth it."

"How can you say that?"

Em withdrew her hand and sat back. "I got my son."

Roger sat back as well, a look of distaste crossing his face. "Does Bradley have visiting rights? Has he even called before this?"

Em hesitated, not sure if she should divulge what had occurred in the past months. Or mention Bradley's last phone message. She decided not to. "He can visit, but he's never been interested in seeing his son. He told me if I took Sa...Brad out of California, I could kiss him and his insurance goodbye."

"Insurance?"

"He kept Brad on his medical plan at work. But once I left the state, it became my responsibility. As long as I didn't make any demands on him, he wouldn't contest my full parental rights." Em paused. "Unfortunately, the jobs I've held never covered Brad."

"I never realized asthma could be such a problem."

"But Brad's improving. He could outgrow it or eventually have it completely under control." Talking about her former husband was making her tense and ruining her appetite. Especially now that he'd started his blackmail scheme. The check she'd written out still remained in her checkbook. She'd have to send it out tomorrow, for sure, if she hoped to avoid any problems. Em pushed her plate of unfinished food aside.

With a heavy heart, she reached for the water glass again. This was supposed to be a night of untold wonders. Samantha thought her father would propose. Her disappointment couldn't possibly equal the letdown Em felt after her own expectations fizzled. Instead of leaving her with a high, the night would close with a grueling testimony of her failure as a wife. Her head began to throb, and she massaged her forehead. She couldn't wait to get home.

"Em," Roger said, leaning across the table and reaching for her hand again. "My marriage also ended in disaster. A different kind, to be sure, but it's made me leery of considering marriage for a second time." He squeezed her hand. She had no desire to hear all about Karen's death and his great passion for her. But he obviously needed to share, and Em wanted to offer any comfort she could, so she didn't interrupt.

"The first time around, you and I both married for love," Roger continued. He cleared his throat and gripped her hand tighter. "I propose something different—a business arrangement. We get along. Our children get along. We're attracted to each other. I think it could work."

Em sat motionless, afraid to move, speak, breathe. What was he saying? Was this a proposal of marriage? A loveless union between two people who got along well enough to consider such a thing? She tried pulling her hand free, but it wouldn't budge.

"What could work?"

"Marriage. I think we should get married."

Em closed her eyes and held her breath for a moment. This was what she'd always wanted, a chance to be Mrs. Roger Holden. Only one thing was missing. Where was the declaration of undying love she'd heard so often in her dreams? Before she could speak, Roger withdrew his hand and pulled out a blue box from his pocket.

Confused, Em wondered why he had brought Samantha's earrings. He flipped the lid and slid the box across the table. One large, single diamond sent its radiant rays twinkling toward her.

"Will you marry me, Auntie Em?"

She saw flashes of Karen, laughing, clinging to his side, and suddenly knew Karen would always be between them. How could Em tell him that she didn't want second best, no matter how much she wanted to be part of his family? Although her heart was breaking, Em reached over to the velvet box, snapped the lid shut and pushed it back to him. "I...I can't."

IMMEDIATELY, ROGER THOUGHT he recognized her reasons for saying no. He should have picked a more intimate place to present the engagement ring.

And, although they may have met fifteen years before, their real knowledge of each other was limited to the past three months. Under normal circumstances that might not be enough time to make a life-changing decision, but Roger didn't have the luxury of time. He needed an answer before he left for Seattle, and he wasn't about to accept "I can't." She could. She would. All he had to do was convince her.

Roger tossed his napkin on the table and pushed back his chair. "Come on. We can finish this conversation in the car."

They both stood. Roger dropped several bills, enough to cover the dinner and a tip, grabbed the blue box and followed Em to the hallway, leaving most of the meal behind.

Once in the elevator, Roger glanced at his watch. The trip to the airport would take all their time, and fighting traffic wouldn't add any romance to their discussion. Convincing Em that he needed her help in raising his children required time. And what about Brad?

Didn't he need a father? Roger had begun to feel her boy was his, as well. It would be as if he'd lost one of his own children if he couldn't keep them all together as a family.

"Let's go to a park, someplace where we can talk."

"But your plane?"

"I can take a later flight." A redeye again, that wouldn't allow him much sleep. But a park setting would be more romantic and might give him the leverage he needed. He certainly wouldn't get much sleep if he didn't try to convince Em. No way could he live with the knife-like pain that had stabbed his gut when she'd refused his offer.

EM'S TURBULENT EMOTIONS had her head spinning and her heart racing. If he still planned to pursue this marriage, she'd have to come up with some answer. *You don't love me* wouldn't work. If prompted, a declaration of love might fall easily from his lips, but she wanted it from his heart.

They drove in silence until they entered Encanto Park. Once out of the car, they walked arm in arm along the waterways. "Is this okay?" Roger asked and indicated a bench facing the water. Reflections of the park lights and the moon danced across the water's surface, and ducks floated contentedly in small groups near the shore.

"I know I stated it badly," Roger said, "but I really want to marry you."

"Why?" Em had to know. Obviously, it wasn't because he loved her. She pulled her wrap closer around her shoulders to protect herself from the chill. Now that summer had passed, the nighttime temperatures dropped dramatically once the sun went down.

Roger appeared taken aback, but after several moments, he said, "You're great with the kids, especially Samantha. They adore you."

What about you? Em thought. "And…"

"You're fun to be with. Great sense of humor. Competent in just about everything." He looked away. "Your mother's a better cook, though." He turned back and smiled.

"Did I miss anything?" His arm curled around the back of the bench and circled her shoulders.

Em tried to keep her mind focused on potential problems, but his nearness, his breath fanning her cheek, wreaked havoc with her concentration. She moved away.

Roger Holden's wife. She wanted that more than anything else, yet she had felt that way about Bradley, as well. How could she marry another person who didn't love her? Finally, she said, "I don't want to make another mistake."

"Mistake?"

"I told you what life with Bradley was like. He deserted me when I needed him most. He left me in financial ruin."

Roger removed his arm and leaned forward, resting his elbows on his thighs. "I wasn't going to mention it, but Harve suggested we draw up a prenuptial agreement. You can put everything in it you need to protect yourself."

"And you'd put in everything to protect yourself?"

"Of course." He sat up and turned to face her.

He expects the marriage to fail, Em thought. Why else would he need a prenuptial agreement? What could she expect? A year, maybe two? Would he stick it out until all the kids were out of high school?

Em contemplated the possibilities. Wasn't it better to have a short time with Roger than none at all? She hadn't gone into her first marriage expecting financial gain. At least in this one she wouldn't come out with financial ruin. She had to be practical for her son's sake.

Roger sat back but didn't look at her. "Some people believe prenups are a way to work out the terms of a divorce before the need arises, but I don't like the idea of divorce. I'd hope we could work on any problems that might come up and not take the easy way out."

"You think divorce is easy?" Hot flashes behind her eyes made Em tense. Up to this point, she had held her emotions in check, not willing to show how much their discussions had disturbed her. But this was too much. What did he know about divorce and the heartbreak it caused?

Before Roger could say anything more, her words tumbled out. "Divorce is the most miserable state a person can be in. You feel like an absolute failure. You go over every aspect of your life, trying to see where you went wrong. You worry day and night that it may bring catastrophic harm to your child." She drew a deep breath before spewing out her final words, "No one who's gone through it considers divorce easy."

"Em, I didn't mean… Your situation was different. Bradley was…"

"What? An opportunist? Out for whatever he could get? A free ride? And why not? He had such a dupe, ready to do anything he asked." Into it now, Em let her anger flare. "How do I know you aren't the same, out to get whatever you can?"

"You think I'm another Bradley?"

"Well, you are unemployed or will be. I can't

support you and four children on what I make."
Totally out of steam and unable to think of anything further, Em clasped and unclasped her hands in her lap.

Boy, could she use a cigarette. Not only would it give her hands something to do, it would go a long way toward relieving this tension. To her surprise and further annoyance, Roger started to laugh.

"No need to worry, Auntie Em. I've got a job offer. A very good one, in fact, and I can take care of the whole pack of your family and mine with no problem at all." He put his fingers beneath her chin and forced her to look at him. "My old boss at Metro offered me the same job I had before, only with an increase in pay. I don't need any financial support."

His tone softened. "And I want very much for us to be a family. I want you, your son and mother to join me and my children. We can make it work."

Em took in another deep breath, to fortify herself so she could go on. "Not if I have to compete with Karen all the time."

Roger gazed past her when he spoke. "I've already made arrangements for Karen's mother to have the painting. I can't erase Karen from my life." When he looked back into her eyes, he continued, "But I'll try not to have her come between us. Now, if you have no further objections," he said, a smile in his voice, "I'd like to get back to my proposal. Will you please be my wife?"

Em glanced away. Eye contact, when he looked at her with such affection, made concentrating so difficult. What more could she ask for? At least her feelings about Karen were out in the open, and he'd promised not to have her come between them. Maybe they *could* have a life together. Her life over the past month certainly had some wonderful perks.

"So, I'm not a very good cook?"

Roger rested his head against hers, his mouth next to her ear. "I'm not interested in your cooking, Em."

She leaned into the soft warmth of his lips moving along her ear. Closing her eyes, she relaxed against his shoulder. When his hand caressed her chin and eased her ever so slightly so that their lips touched, Em let all her suppressed feelings surface. She joined him in a kiss that expressed her love and all that she was willing to give. Maybe he didn't love her now, but in time...

Moments later, Roger asked, "Will you marry me, Em?" He kissed her again, preventing her from speaking. One arm held her firmly against him while he slipped the box into her hand.

When she finally came up for air, Em held the box for a moment before giving it back to him. His expression went blank. She hadn't meant to reject him again and quickly said, "Will you put it on my finger?"

"Then it's yes!" he exclaimed with such excitement that Em had to smile. After snapping the box open, Roger removed the ring and placed it on her finger.

He took her back into his arms. While his lips worked their magic, Em held him close to her heart. "Yes, I'll marry you," she whispered.

When he finally looked at her, Em knew she had made the right decision. He may not love her, but she could live with that. At least she'd have everything she wanted for as long as he'd have her. It felt natural, right to be cradled in his arms.

For several moments he caressed her cheek, then he leaned closer. When his lips were nearly touching hers, he whispered, "I'm really looking forward to you becoming Mrs. Holden as soon as possible." He slipped a stray strand of hair over her ear. "Agreed?"

With a quick nod, she showed she approved.

The sound of footfalls on the sidewalk slowed her racing heartbeat. They weren't alone. She opened her eyes and remained still as a man walked by with his dog.

Once the man had disappeared, Roger said, "We'd better head to the airport."

CHAPTER NINETEEN

AFTER THEIR EXTENDED kiss, they walked back to the car. "Samantha knew you were going to ask me. Did you talk to her about it?"

Roger opened the door and helped her into the Mustang. "No, of course not."

Once he settled in the driver's seat, Em said, "She must be psychic."

Roger chuckled. "Okay, I kind of let something slip when I gave her the earrings."

"Like what?"

He started the car. "As I was leaving her room, she mentioned marriage, and I asked her if it would bother her. I saw tears in her eyes when she left your room. She isn't against it, is she? Because I kind of got the impression she was for it."

"Actually, she wanted me to say yes. But she told me she couldn't call me Mom." Em paused. "I understand."

Roger patted Em's knee. "The boys won't be a problem. I've already trained Brad to call me Dad."

Em chuckled. "That you did. I'll bet back at that hospital you never expected to eventually have him for a son."

"Can I have him as my son? Will Bradley allow me to adopt Brad?"

For a moment, Em sat back in wonder. "I really can't say." Knowing that Roger wanted to legally call Brad his own warmed her, but how could she convince Bradley it was in his best interest? That thought began to churn inside her. She tried setting it aside by asking, "How interested are you in adding other children to your family?"

"Our family," he corrected, and she silently nodded. Roger pulled the car into the entrance to Sky Harbor. "I hadn't thought about it." He drove into the airport parking garage, then faced her. "Do you want more? Four's already a handful."

"Accidents happen."

"We will have no accidents. I'm all for having a dozen more, but not unless you want them."

"I'll think about it." Yes, a child by the man she loved. Definitely. "But you can forget the dozen." She started to chuckle. "I might consider one."

"I love it when you laugh." He helped her out of the car and grasped both her hands. "I've got

a new job and this beautiful creature who con-
sented to be my wife. I can't wait to get married, settle in a new place. Have you thought
about what kind of house you want?"

He dropped her hands and reached into the
back for his laptop and suitcase. After locking
the car and handing Em the keys, they headed
toward the elevators.

"What I'd want? For heaven's sake, I've had
no chance to think that far ahead."

"Sure you have. I know you and your mother
have been saving toward one. You must have
some idea."

Em could barely believe it. Roger had meant
what he said about removing Karen's importance and putting his new wife first.

A new house of her own would give Em
the chance to create something with her own
imprint. Better yet, an old house—maybe his
parents'?—would be too perfect. What more
could she want? A mature rose garden, plenty
of room for all their children with extra space
for any future additions. And then that delightful cottage for her mother. "You're including
my mother in this? You expect her to stay with
us on a permanent basis?"

"Absolutely." They entered the elevator
and Roger pushed the button to the floor they
needed. "We can have rooms attached to our

home or a separate house, close enough so we'll have a babysitter when we need one."

When they were out in the lobby, Em stopped him. "I'd love to live in your parents' home. Jodie told me they want to sell, and I'm sure they'd prefer to keep it in the family."

His forehead furrowed as he narrowed his gaze. "My parents' place?"

Em nodded.

"But, Em, it's in Phoenix."

"Right. It's a great location close to everything including the schools the children attend. They won't have to change anything." Em's voice rose as the excitement of the day began to take hold—marriage to the man she adored, a new home to call her own. About to burst from pure pleasure, Em doubted if she could handle much more.

She glanced at Roger and wondered why his puzzled expression hadn't changed. "What's the matter? Don't you like my idea?"

"I'm just trying to fit it in with our move to Seattle. I don't see how we can keep a house in both places."

"What are you talking about? Why would you need a house in Seattle?"

"That's where my job is. That's where I need to live."

"But you said you were getting your old job back."

"Yes. The one I transferred to Seattle."

A chill began to invade her. "When did you find this out?"

"My last trip. I'll be transferred the first of the year."

"Seattle? You're transferring to Seattle?" Slowly she pushed away from him.

"Yes. The boys will love it—fishing, boating…"

"We can't move up there," Em said, her voice rising on a note of panic.

"But…"

"Brad can't live in Seattle. He needs a dry climate for his asthma."

Roger said something under his breath, but Em was too concerned with her own thoughts to pay any attention. The world she had created only moments before, of marriage and a life with Roger, had just tumbled in ruins around her.

EM AND ROGER didn't talk on the short walk to security.

"I'll have to go in." He held out his arms, and she wrapped hers around him. In one wonderful moment she was warm, cuddled and wanted. When he squeezed her to him, her feet left the floor, and she clung to him with all her might out of desperation.

Please don't leave me, she thought. *Please don't go to Seattle.* But she remained silent, unable to put additional pressure on him. When he finally loosened his hold, she slipped down and stood next to the black tape designating the aisles to security.

She remained nestled in his embrace, as people pushed past them. Roger whispered close to her ear. "This job—it's what I do. It's what I know."

Em moved her head so that her mouth brushed his neck. She felt his pulse, his life blood pounding against her lips. Unable to speak, she kept her eyes tightly closed to control the flood of tears that threatened.

"I have to go there for the kids. I can't sacrifice their well-being."

She nodded, unwilling to risk using her voice.

"I'm not a gambler, Em. I know men with more education than I have who've gone years without finding any work in their profession. And as you said, it wouldn't be fair to you to support me while I look for work."

She wanted to take back those words, tell him she'd sacrifice everything to keep him, if he'd only stay in Phoenix. But unlike Bradley,

Roger was too proud to allow her to support him until he found what he needed.

Reluctantly, Em backed away. "I understand." She put her fingers over his lips so he couldn't offer any other reasons. She knew them all. Besides, his children were as important to him as her son was to her. How could she fault him for that?

Her throat was tight as she said, "You and the kids will do great there. And they can always come back for a visit." Em tried to smile. The tortured movement hurt so badly that she stopped and pressed her lips together. "You'd better get going," she said, as she pulled her shawl closely around her shoulders. "You wouldn't want to miss your plane."

He kissed her again, this time on the cheek. She slipped the ring off her finger and put it in his hand. Abruptly, she pivoted and headed toward the elevators without a backward glance.

Somehow she managed to retrace her steps and get back to the Mustang. She had no desire to stay at the airport. It reminded her of everything she had lost and was about to lose. Already she missed the ring she'd returned. It had felt so right, so perfect on her finger.

How would she survive without him?

CHAPTER TWENTY

EM TOSSED IN her bed, swirling in and out of dreams that left her exhausted. Roger was calling to her, his arms opened wide, motioning for her to come. Rain poured on him, while she stood in sunshine. Someone coughed behind her, but whenever she turned to see who it was, no one was there.

Several times during the night, Em woke, sat up and listened. Was Sammy coughing? When the house remained quiet, she lay back and relived the previous hours and Roger's proposal.

Despite his remark about their marriage being a business deal, he had to care for her a little. Then again, since they could never be together, maybe it was best he didn't love her. He didn't need the added torture she felt.

At the first sounds of her mother stirring, Em tossed her feet over the side of the bed. Tears she'd managed to hold back threatened to overflow. Afraid that she might wake her mother and have to provide an explanation, Em gathered her clothes and running shoes and left the room. Once she had a chance to absorb what had happened last night, she'd be able to face her mother and her inevitable interrogation.

"I'm not going to cry," she told herself as she slipped into her shorts in the powder room off the hall. Despite her resolve, she needed to swipe the towel across her eyes.

"You need a cigarette," she told her reflection. That should calm her and give her the composure she lacked. She found money in a jacket pocket in the hall closet and headed for the door. With any luck, she'd have half the pack smoked before she came home.

ROGER SAT UP and tried to rub the crick out of his neck. A day's growth of beard was itchy on his chin, and he scratched the stubble. If he had known his flight would be delayed this late, he could have spent the night sleeping in his own bed instead of on a seat in the terminal thinking about...

He had to stop thinking about last night and the time he'd spent with Em. Each remembered moment ended with that final blow of rejection, not of him, but of the life he could provide for his family in Seattle.

To keep his mind off last night's agony, Roger now kept busy making a list of all the chores he had to complete on this trip. Number one: find a real estate agent to start checking out homes for him and his children. He needed something close to a good school. Maybe a place on one of the islands, where they could spend quality time boating and fishing.

The man in the molded plastic seat next to him leaned over. "Any idea why we're delayed?"

"No, not a clue."

"Bet it's engine trouble. You hear about the plane that went down last week?" The man nodded sagely. "Engine trouble."

Roger returned to his list. Number two: find an agency to help him locate a housekeeper or nanny, someone to watch over the boys while he worked. If only Doris would leave her grandson behind. She was wonderful with the children, providing love with a good sense of discipline. How would they adjust to a new nanny?

"You take out extra insurance?"

Roger looked up. The man next to him was fidgeting in his seat. The last thing Roger wanted to discuss was the possibility of a plane crash right before he boarded.

"It's automatic when I purchase the ticket." He tried to return to his list, but the man continued.

"I've got a million on me. We go down," the

man said, aiming his thumb toward the floor, "and my wife's set for life."

"Yeah," another man across the aisle added. "She's probably the one who created the mechanical problem." His wife tittered and swatted his arm before slipping her hand in his. Roger smiled at the affectionate couple. Two people growing old together and still enjoying each other's company.

He crossed one knee over the other and focused on number three: find someone to help him with Samantha. She'd give him the most problems, getting in with the wrong crowd just to spite him. He visualized tattoos, pierced body parts. They'd fight, she'd run away and end up on the streets, lying in an alley somewhere without friends or family. The vision made him cringe.

He glanced down at his watch to check the time.

What was going on? If the delay continued, he'd miss his afternoon meeting with the president of the company to discuss his transfer. The man sitting next to him had gone to the desk. "Another half hour," he said as he returned to his seat. "I got appointments. What about you?"

"If it's only a half hour, I'm okay." The man looked as though he might start a conversation, so Roger took out his pad again, but he couldn't concentrate.

Maybe he and Em could consider a long-distance marriage, with her staying in Phoenix, raising Brad and Samantha, while he stayed in Seattle with the twins. It certainly would solve several problems. *Let's face it, I'd go broke or die from exhaustion commuting that distance on a regular basis.* Especially if he had to deal with these damn delays. He checked his watch again. Fifteen more minutes.

Finally, they were called to board the plane. The man and woman who had been sitting across from him came up behind him. "It's a shame you couldn't spend all this wasted time with your wife," she said, adding a smile. Roger smiled back, not willing to correct her.

"I saw you both when we entered the terminal. A lovely woman." She smiled again. "And the two of you, so much in love." Her words ended on a sigh, and she returned her attention to her husband.

Love? Was that what you called this knife sticking in his chest? Was he giving up on love?

As he waited in line, he thought of what he'd told Em—he wasn't a gambler. No, he certainly wasn't. All his life he'd taken the safe route, the one with the least amount of friction. Then why was he transferring to Seattle—disturbing his sons' lives, destroying his daughter's as well as his own? Oh, the move might provide a job, but it certainly offered little else. It didn't offer love.

"Your boarding pass," the flight attendant said.

So what if he had to start over, sell the house, use the money he'd put aside for his retirement and the kids' education? He was still young, still able to make his way in the business world. He could tackle anything with Em by his side. He turned to the couple behind him.

"You're right. My wife is a lovely woman, and I'd be a fool if I left her behind." The man looked stunned, but the woman beamed a smile at him and extended her hand. Roger gave it a firm shake before heading for the exit.

THE BRISK WALK to the corner store did little to help Em unwind. The thought of smoking the cigarettes did even less. A liability, that's what they were, and she refused to let them hobble her anymore. She needed all her strength to get on with her life, to care for her son and mother. Tossing the unopened pack into the trash, Em raced back to the house. Her job took on added significance now that Roger planned to move from Phoenix, and she had to prepare for work.

"Where did you take off to?" her mother asked when Em entered the kitchen.

"A walk." Em opened the refrigerator and pulled out the container of orange juice. Only a small amount remained, but out of habit, she poured it in a glass before swigging it down.

"So—did he ask you to marry him?"

Em placed the empty glass on the counter and wiped her mouth with the dish towel. "You been talking to Samantha?"

"As a matter of fact, I have. We thought he'd ask you last night. So…?"

"He asked me."

"Well, don't keep me in suspense. You two getting married or what?"

"No." Em paused, aware of how quickly her outward calm was fading. She drew a deep breath. "He suggested a business deal, a pooling of our two families for the greater good." She glanced at the clock. "I've got to get to work." Her voice cracked.

In an instant, Doris was by her side. "I'll call and tell them you'll be late."

"Mom, I…"

"You're not getting out of this house till you tell me what's going on. Might as well shower, too," Doris said, as she pushed Em toward the hall. "I'll have breakfast ready when you get out."

About fifteen minutes later, Em returned in her beige slacks and cream knit shirt, pulling her damp hair into a ponytail. "Smells good, Mom. By the way, Roger says you're the better cook."

"I should be. I've had a few years more practice." Doris sat down across from her daughter and propped her elbows on the table while she worked hand lotion into her fingers. "So tell me what's going on."

Em picked up some scrambled eggs on her fork, put them in her mouth, then paused a moment to chew and swallow before answering. The eggs tasted like paste, and Em wasn't sure she could keep them down. She pushed the plate away.

Doris finished massaging her hands and shoved the plate back in front of Em. "I can't believe you said no just because he didn't offer hearts and flowers all tied with a neat satin bow."

Em sat back and lifted her chin. "That would have been nice with a little love sprinkled in."

"Haven't you learned by now that love is just fairy dust Cupid throws to blind people?"

Em's chin was starting to wobble. If she didn't stop the conversation now, she'd end up bawling her eyes out and never get to work. She stood and carried her dish to the sink.

"But you'd have him. That's what you want, isn't it?"

"He wants to move to Seattle. His company offered him a job there. And Sammy—Brad can't live in a wet climate."

Doris opened her mouth, then closed it. After a long sigh, she said, "So what do we do now? Get another apartment? We haven't got enough put aside to buy a house."

Em felt as though the eggs she had eaten might suddenly reappear. She kept her mouth tightly shut and swallowed several times in an attempt to keep them down. "I don't know," she said, when she thought it was safe to speak. "I was hoping you could offer a suggestion."

Doris got up, walked over to Em and placed her hands on her shoulders. Grateful for the chance to make contact, Em clasped them. "I love him so much and want to be with him," she said. "But I can't go there."

"Sure you can. I can keep Sammy with me. You could…" Doris sighed as Em squeezed her hands. "It was only a suggestion."

"Thanks." Em pulled free of her mother. "I'd better get to work. Can't afford to lose this job."

Before she could go much farther, Doris pulled her into her arms and the two embraced. "I'm so sorry," Doris said, tears in her eyes. "I really thought you two could make it together."

The phone rang, and Doris went to pick it up as Em gathered her purse. "No, she's not here," Doris said in a strident voice.

Em motioned to herself. Was the call for her? Doris shook her head and moved away so that they no longer made eye contact.

"She'll call you when she's good and ready," Doris shouted.

Em came around her mother and removed the phone from her hand. "Who is it?" Em mouthed.

"Bradley."

The white plastic turned into a burning ember in her hand. For a moment, Em stood transfixed. How could she talk to him, this man she had grown to despise, the father of her child? The one person who could destroy her life.

Slowly she placed the receiver against her ear. "Yes, Bradley? What is it?"

"What's going on with you?" he said in that authoritative voice that always made her cringe. "You never return my calls, you haven't responded to my letters. You too busy fooling around with that guy you're living with? Or don't you care that I want my son living with me?"

Could her psyche possibly withstand more pain? For several seconds Em bit her tongue and stared at the window above the sink, not seeing anything beyond the glass pane. Hadn't she had enough? At what point could she get this slimeball off her back? No time like the present. She'd already gotten rid of one bad habit; why not try for two?

"I had a detective check up on you, Bradley." Em drew a fortifying breath and continued. "Seems you aren't going to college, and you still have a job. Did you figure I'd never bother to verify all those bills you sent me?"

"What the hell you do that for?"

"Because I can't trust you. Never could." She felt her momentum increase, like a locomotive picking up speed when it starts to move. She could be an intimidating force, too, once she put her mind to it. "I've got a new lawyer. One who has me and my son's interest at heart."

"Say, listen, Emmy Lou, I…"

"You owe six months' child support, Bradley. Get it in the mail today or you'll hear from my lawyer by the end of the week."

She pressed the disconnect button and returned the phone to the counter. Motion caught her attention, and she glanced at her mother. Doris gave her a thumbs-up and a grin that lit her features. Em duplicated the motion before grabbing her purse and heading out the door.

The locomotive was still going strong inside

her as she entered her van. She'd contact Harve and have him go after the money Bradley owed her. That might help the family get back on their feet. She concentrated on that thought in an effort to keep all the other problems at bay.

EM STAYED LATE at work to make up the time she'd missed that morning. The sun was on the horizon when she pulled into the drive and saw the sign. She slammed on the brakes.

Boy, Roger sure didn't waste any time. Em got out of the van and walked across the desert landscape, the tiny stones crunching beneath her feet. With hands on hips, she examined the printed sign—House For Sale by Owner—with Roger's phone number scrawled underneath. She controlled a wicked desire to knock it over.

When had Roger placed the sign there? She hadn't seen it this morning, but then she hadn't been firing on all cylinders for the past twenty-four hours.

Brad chose that moment to run out the door, propel himself into her arms and wrap his legs around her waist, almost toppling them into a barrel cactus. He was tangible, something she could cling to, something to help her keep her tentative hold on sanity.

"You're almost too big for this," she said,

returning his stranglehold. "I bet you weigh a hundred pounds."

He pushed away so she could see his face. He grinned, showing off the space where he'd lost a tooth. "Dad's here," he said. Immediately, his smile disappeared and he covered his mouth. He squirmed and jumped down. Before she could ask questions, he scooted into the house.

Bradley was here? Oh, no! Dread gripped her stomach. Every dealing with Bradley Turner brought havoc and ruin. Why had she ever said the things she had? Of all the stupid… Her one attempt to frighten him had backfired and brought him after her. He'd prove she wasn't a fit mother.

How had he found her? Em wondered as she proceeded slowly toward the front door. She'd never sent him a change of address after they'd moved from her mother's apartment. Why would he follow her to Phoenix unless it had something to do with his son? Maybe he really did want the boy back. With mounting trepidation, Em entered the house.

Slowly, she walked the hall past the staircase and living room into the kitchen. Several dishes remained on the table, but otherwise, the room was empty. Em followed the noise to the family room, her tension rising with each step.

She made a quick appraisal, looking for her

former husband. When Roger turned around and smiled, she felt disoriented. Where was Bradley? How come Roger was here? Then she realized Brad had referred to Roger as Dad—again. No wonder her son had worn a guilty expression and refused to look at her. Thank goodness. She'd repeat the lecture later but right now relief swept over her. At least she didn't have to deal with her ex-husband.

"What's this? A party?" she asked the assembled group. Everyone in the household was present, and they were all smiling as though posing for a picture, as if she were the camera. She scowled at the surreal image they presented and turned to Roger. "Why aren't you in Seattle?"

When Roger didn't answer, the boys went into a giggle fit. Roger raised an eyebrow and pointed toward the hallway. "Isn't it about time you guys were headed for bed?"

"No," they said between chortles.

He turned to Doris. "Mrs. Masters. Will you do the honors?"

Doris herded them into the hall. "Say goodnight."

"Goodnight," they said in unison, followed by more laughter.

"What on earth is so funny?" Em stood by the doorway and watched the procession march through the hall and up the stairs. Since Roger remained close-lipped with his hands behind his back, she hoped Samantha would offer an explanation. Instead, the girl yawned, a drawn-out, Academy Award-worthy dramatization of utter exhaustion.

"I think I'll go to bed, too." She reached up and gave her father a peck on the cheek. Roger waved his hand in dismissal, and Samantha took off after the boys.

"You look like a woman with a lot of questions," Roger said as he slowly approached Em.

"I am. And so far I haven't had any satisfactory answers."

He stopped in front of her, still holding his hands behind his back. "Ask away."

"How come you're home?" she asked again. "And…" The answer came to her in a flash as she started to ask the next question. It made her quiver with excitement. Had Roger found a way for them to be together? "…and why is Brad calling you Dad?"

"I'm home because my plane was delayed."

Disappointment dampened her spirits immediately. "Oh," was all she could think to say.

"It gave me a chance to think, and I came to some very important decisions. Mainly, I want to grow old with you." He brought his hands around to the front. "For you," he said, offering a single red rose. "It's a little worse for wear. I've been holding it for the past two hours, waiting for you to come home."

"I had to make up time at work." Em took the rose and held the bloom to her nose. She closed her eyes and breathed in the sweet smell. The roller-coaster ride was beginning again. Would this ascent to happiness be followed by another plunge to despair? She opened her eyes and looked at Roger. What more could she expect?

He reached into his pocket and pulled out a blue box. "This is for you, too. It's the same one you returned earlier."

She kept her hand fisted. "I still can't accept it, Roger." After a slight pause, she added, "Unless something's changed."

"Everything's changed." He removed the ring from its velvet lining, opened her hand and placed it on her finger. "Your mother said you never had an engagement ring. Let this be the beginning of many firsts."

Em looked at the rainbows of light emanating from the ring, which blurred as her eyes misted over. "But...you're selling the house. Moving to Seattle. I can't..."

"I'm selling the house because I'm not moving to Seattle."

"But why? If you're not...?"

"We need a place of our own. One that doesn't come loaded with memories."

One without Karen, Em thought as she smiled back at Roger.

"And don't get too attached to that ring. We may need it for collateral if I'm not able to find work in Phoenix." He grinned.

Em covered the ring protectively with her other hand. "Never. I'll work a second job if I have to just to keep it."

Roger clasped her arms. "Would you?" He pulled her into an embrace and nuzzled her neck. "Oh, Em. If that plane had taken off on time, I'd have been on the next one heading back just to be with you. I couldn't leave you behind. I love you so much."

Em let the warmth of his embrace flow through her. Roger loved her. What more could she possibly want?

EPILOGUE

"WILL WE BE able to dive in it, Dad?" Chip asked

"No," Roger said as he laid out the poles that supported the above-ground pool.

"What good is it, then?" Chaz tapped his foot on the large section of plastic. "I liked our other pool better."

Brad placed an arm around Chaz's shoulders. "Yeah. That was a real pool," Brad said. Roger glanced at his newest son. Bradley had finally come through with the signed papers that had allowed Roger to adopt the boy.

"So is this one, and it will keep you just as cool when summer arrives."

Doris ambled across the grass and set a tray of glasses and a pitcher of iced tea on the lawn table. "Haven't you noticed? Summer is already here." She was right. It wasn't even June yet, and the temperatures were heading toward triple digits. After Doris poured the tea, Roger took a sip and wiped his brow, running his hand through his hair.

He turned to Em and grinned. "Want some? I'll bring it over."

"I can get it," Em said from her seat under the trellis. "I'm not an invalid, you know."

"Stay there. I could use a rest in the shade." Roger scooted through the rose garden, avoiding several thorny branches that threatened to grab him.

"I'll have to trim those." He sat down next to her and placed an arm on the back of the bench.

"Wait until tomorrow," Em said after taking a refreshing sip. "José and Sophia are driving in for lunch, and he can show you the proper way to do it."

"Don't you trust me?"

"Not in my garden."

Roger leaned closer and pressed a kiss against her cheek. "And just when did this become your garden?"

"On our wedding day." Em shifted into a comfortable spot against his chest as his arm enfolded her. He hadn't bothered to shave, and the bristles gently massaged her skin as he moved his hot, damp cheek against hers. After several hours of working in the sun, any lingering scents of soap and aftershave had left.

"You need a shower."

"You going to help?" he whispered in her ear.

Em grabbed a handful of his damp athletic shirt and pulled him closer. "How did you ever manage without me?"

With eyes closed, Roger pressed his lips against her hair. *How did he ever?*

He thought back to that sunny day the beginning of November when Em said "I do" under this same trellis. Close relatives and friends had attended the small wedding in the garden and the reception in his parents' house. Only, now it was their house, his and Em's home, to share with three sons, a daughter and another one on the way. Thanks to the ultrasound at the doctor's office, they knew they were having a little girl.

At six months, Em had begun to show. Roger patted her small round belly. "Kay kicking a lot?"

"Yes." Extracting herself from his embrace, Em straightened and stood, holding her hand against her back. "She has told me in no uncertain terms that she doesn't like my sitting on a hard wood bench. I'll go make lunch."

Roger grasped her hand, refusing to let Em go. "Have your mother do it. I need to clean up before we eat."

With a laugh that still warmed his insides every time he heard it, Em headed for the house. He watched her, wondering all the while how he could be so lucky.

Em continued at her job, which provided for her own daily expenses and the medical insurance she'd need for the baby. Headhunters had found several jobs outside the area that paid well, but Em had insisted she wanted to stay in her new home. Those same headhunters were working for him, now, looking for jobs in the Phoenix area. They'd lined up several interviews in the coming week, so he expected to find employment before his severance ran out. At times his unemployment weighed on him, since he knew that Em had supported a previous husband. And now Kay was coming—yet another mouth to feed. But he was optimistic about the future.

When they'd searched for names for the new baby, the boys had suggested Karen after their mother. Roger knew that wouldn't go over well with Em, so he'd dampened their suggestion. But Em had come through with a suggestion of her own.

Why not name her Kay for Karen? she had said.

Right, Samantha had agreed. *Like Em is for Emmy Lou.*

It was a name they could all agree on. Just another sign of Em's generous nature.

How on earth did he deserve someone as wonderful as Auntie Em?

* * * * *

REQUEST YOUR FREE BOOKS!
2 FREE WHOLESOME ROMANCE NOVELS IN LARGER PRINT
PLUS 2 FREE MYSTERY GIFTS

✻✻✻✻✻✻✻✻✻✻✻✻✻✻✻✻✻✻✻✻✻✻✻✻

HEARTWARMING™

✻✻✻✻✻✻✻✻✻✻✻✻✻✻✻✻✻✻✻✻✻✻✻✻

Wholesome, tender romances

YES! Please send me 2 FREE Harlequin® Heartwarming Larger-Print novels and my 2 FREE mystery gifts (gifts worth about $10). After receiving them, if I don't wish to receive any more books, I can return the shipping statement marked "cancel." If I don't cancel, I will receive 4 brand-new larger-print novels every month and be billed just $4.99 per book in the U.S. or $5.74 per book in Canada. That's a savings of at least 23% off the cover price. It's quite a bargain! Shipping and handling is just 50¢ per book in the U.S. and 75¢ per book in Canada.* I understand that accepting the 2 free books and gifts places me under no obligation to buy anything. I can always return a shipment and cancel at any time. Even if I never buy another book, the two free books and gifts are mine to keep forever.

161/361 IDN F47N

Name _____ (PLEASE PRINT) _____

Address _____ Apt. # _____

City _____ State/Prov. _____ Zip/Postal Code _____

Signature (if under 18, a parent or guardian must sign)

Mail to the **Harlequin® Reader Service:**
IN U.S.A.: P.O. Box 1867, Buffalo, NY 14240-1867
IN CANADA: P.O. Box 609, Fort Erie, Ontario L2A 5X3

* Terms and prices subject to change without notice. Prices do not include applicable taxes. Sales tax applicable in N.Y. Canadian residents will be charged applicable taxes. Offer not valid in Quebec. This offer is limited to one order per household. Not valid for current subscribers to Harlequin Heartwarming larger-print books. All orders subject to credit approval. Credit or debit balances in a customer's account(s) may be offset by any other outstanding balance owed by or to the customer. Please allow 4 to 6 weeks for delivery. Offer available while quantities last.

Your Privacy—The Harlequin® Reader Service is committed to protecting your privacy. Our Privacy Policy is available online at www.ReaderService.com or upon request from the Harlequin Reader Service.

We make a portion of our mailing list available to reputable third parties that offer products we believe may interest you. If you prefer that we not exchange your name with third parties, or if you wish to clarify or modify your communication preferences, please visit us at www.ReaderService.com/consumerchoice or write to us at Harlequin Reader Service Preference Service, P.O. Box 9062, Buffalo, NY 14269. Include your complete name and address.

HWDIR13R

LARGER-PRINT BOOKS!

GET 2 FREE
LARGER-PRINT NOVELS
PLUS 2 FREE
MYSTERY GIFTS

Love Inspired®

Larger-print novels are now available...

REQUEST YOUR FREE BOOKS!

2 FREE CHRISTIAN NOVELS
PLUS 2
FREE
MYSTERY GIFTS

HEARTSONG

PRESENTS